LUCKY KING

Books by Bruce Griffin Henderson

Waiting

Bruce Griffin Henderson

Copyright ©2020 by Bruce Griffin Henderson

All rights reserved.

Library of Congress Cataloging-in-Publication Data

Henderson, Bruce Griffin

Lucky King/Bruce Griffin Henderson

Print ISBN: 978-1-09833-481-9

ebook ISBN: 978-1-09833-482-6

Front cover design by Francesca Restrepo

For Meghan

LUCKY KING

A NOVEL
BY
BRUCE GRIFFIN HENDERSON

PROLOGUE

I am Lucky King. Fortune rests on my fingertips and rides out into the world on metal wheels and rubber tires. My skin is as thick as fatback, lined and weathered; they say I look old as Methuselah, but I know better. He was young once, he lived, he died. I am.

I live on Henry Street, in the shadow of the Manhattan Bridge. The bridge is old and rusted, but still carries tremendous weight; the weight of cars, the weight of trucks, the weight of trains filled with people crossing the river to pass their time in all the various ways that people will. Day and night I hear the rumble, the grind and growl, the echoes of these journeys. The regularity is comforting, like the movement of the tides.

There are a good number of birds living under the bridge. Pigeons. City birds. A relative of the dove, I am told. The majority of these birds are mottled grey, but some are white in color. They seem happy with their lot: chatty, full of bustle and industry. Glad, I suppose, to have a home out of the rain. At unpredictable intervals they take wing to fly wide circles in the sky overhead, then swoop down to the ground, alone or as a flock, to peck away at the sidewalk. A pizza crust, a wonton, a chicken leg with bits of dry meat at the knuckle—it's all the same to my feathery neighbors.

When a strong wind blows from the east in the morning, I can smell the ocean on the street where I live. On those occasions I am reminded of the many voyages I have made by sea. My last such passage brought me across the Pacific, that ocean of contrasting moods. By turns light hearted, warm and breezy, then cold, dark and menacing. Which reflects its true nature? The sum, I suppose. Living at the door of the Atlantic it strikes me that all waters are thus, and so do they give life even as they take it away.

My neighborhood is crowded with smells that bring memories washing over me. The sweet, meaty aroma of roasting duck reminds me of a village where I once attended a wedding between a man and a bride he had been promised. The acrid smell of evaporating urine, rising from the concrete on a hot summer day, walks me down long-forgotten alleyways in cities perhaps best forgotten. Fresh fish carries me back to markets, good and bad, here and there, that I have known. The sidewalks are lined with fish in this neighborhood—bluefish, tuna, salmon and flounder, their gills rising and falling against the unfamiliar air. These fish are propped atop melting ice in waxed cardboard boxes and sold with much hue and cry. Most are carried away by sundown; by ancient, stooped Chinese women, by Italian widows dressed all in black, by the young, the old, the propitious and the forsaken. But at the end of each day a few of these fish always remain, and late at night the unmistakable odor of decay appears unbidden. This too brings memories.

I have a full, active life. I am not like some of the older people you see, those sentinels of death, forever boxed in window frames. My curiosity pulls me outside, down three flights of worn marble stairs, onto the sidewalks and into the crowds—to see, to hear, to know. And while it may be true that all that is now known has always been known, wouldn't you agree that it is still incumbent upon each of us to discover the central truths for ourselves? To experience life and ponder its meaning?

I have known for some time that my landlady lets herself in to my apartment while I am gone. Perhaps she is looking for meaning. Or just trying to fill some empty time in what may be an empty life. The neighbors across the hall tell me that they once discovered her in their living room when they returned home from shopping with their young daughter. This wealthy woman in a thick, white fur coat, her hair a pile of straightened thread resting on its luxurious collar. She was turning the page of a family photo album with the manicured nail of her index finger when they opened the door. If she was startled it didn't show, they said. Surprised to see her standing before them, they asked what she was doing. "I thought I smelled something on fire," she answered. This woman owns many of the buildings around here.

In the basement of the building next door there is a dormitory of sorts. Eight rooms built from plywood and pine boards. Each room has four beds, set like two sets of shelves into the wall. There is a single toilet at the end of a makeshift hallway that runs down the center of the room, a windowless place illuminated only by the harsh light of a lone, bare bulb. The air in the basement is close and reeks with the smell of sweat and excrement. A man who lives there told me he rents a bunk by the hour, and when he opens his eyes there is always someone waiting for his berth. It's no better, he said, than things were in Beijing.

Almost all of the men who sleep in those beds are restaurant workers. They deliver food on second-hand bicycles with plastic bags that cover the seats. Or they work on the line in the kitchen, bent over steaming woks, cooking noodles and rice, vegetables, beef, pork and chicken. They work for tips or for a few dollars an hour. They work to send money home or to pay off their passage to this new country. All because they were told there is much opportunity here. And, of course, that is true for some.

I, too, work in the food business. But due to my age and the breadth of my experience, my work is more specialized. I write fortunes in a wholesale fortune cookie shop. The business is called Lucky King. It is a small operation with just four employees; in a good week our combined efforts produce no more than a few thousand cookies. But these confections are made with great care, and we are blessed with loyal customers.

My colleagues call me Lucky King. Of course that is not my given name. But out of habit or choice, it is the one I answer to. They are not the first people I have worked with, nor do I expect they will be the last. They come and one day they are gone. Gone back home, gone to other restaurants, gone to other towns. My co-workers come and go, but I remain. For now, and many other nows, I suppose.

This world is ever changing. And sadly, jobs like mine have been—to a great extent—mechanized. Most fortune cookies in this city come from one of two factories, both of which are miles away from here. This, I believe, is a shame. Who would want such a product? A stale cookie, wrapped in stiff, noisy cellophane, with a fortune that bears no relation to its subject. Alas, businesses economize where they can. It has always been so. In the end I am happy to have something to do. Work is good; not only for the income it provides, but also for the idleness of mind it displaces. Because so much discontent is bred by boredom and empty time.

I see the effects of the lack of productive work on the streets of this city. Young people, out of school and without jobs, adrift. They shout at each other about nothing of consequence, produce children with no intention of providing for them, and sometimes assault strangers, family members and one another. In short, they are lost.

It is my belief that spare time is largely overrated.

As such, I try to keep a good number of my hours occupied with industry. And that is why most days find me in my small corner of the kitchen, doing the job that I have come to consider my vocation.

I live a simple life, but it is a life of clear purpose. The bulk of my time is spent thinking, the rest writing. The latter is performed with the aid of a fine instrument: a Williams No. 4 typewriter. Built, I am told, sometime around the year 1903 in a place called Derby. I suppose this machine is crude by today's standards, but it suits my needs well. By selecting a key one can print a letter on paper. And that, after all, is the essence of my work—letters on paper.

ONE

"Hello America, and good evening. You're listening to Jack DuVal, and I'll be your host tonight and every night here on the American Radio Syndicate. Our topic this evening is Affirmative Action. We're here to discuss whether Affirmative Action has helped or hurt our great nation, and if it is bringing us together as a people or tearing us apart. We'll be opening the phone lines up later so you can tell us exactly what you think, but first I'd like to introduce our guest for this program. He marched through the South for civil rights with Dr. Martin Luther King in the early 1960's and he has been a frequent third-party candidate for the Presidency of the United States. I'm pleased to welcome the Reverend James Williams to the show. Good evening Reverend Williams."

"Good evening Mr. DuVal."

"Please, call me Jack. Now, I think my audience may already know where I stand on this issue, but for your benefit and the benefit of anyone who may be listening for the first time, I'm going to articulate my position. I don't like Affirmative Action. I don't like it one bit, and I'll tell you why. I'm a forty-seven year-old white man—and I don't need to tell you how popular that makes me in this day and age—who came from nothing and made himself a success with a load of hard work and ambition. That's the long and short of it. Nobody was there to help me make it because of the color of my skin or my gender or anything else. And if you want to know, I'm proud of what I've managed to achieve. And I'll tell you another thing: I'm not sure what I would hate worse, if I had lost an opportunity along the way to some quota-filling person of color, or if I were the guy or the gal who got a job because of the color of my skin and I had to spend the rest of my life wondering if I really had what it takes to make it. What do you think about that, Reverend?"

DuVal lit a cigarette and leaned back in his chair, setting a solid-gold engraved lighter down beside a pack of Marlboro red. He stretched his lean frame to the fullest length possible while still remaining seated in his black mesh Aeron chair, took a deep breath through his nose, and leaned his head from side to side, drawing a satisfying crack. DuVal wondered if the smoking or his movements bothered his guest. In truth, he didn't much care. He was there to ask questions and get responses. His ratings were through the roof and, in the end this guy—and everybody else—could shove it if they didn't like it. Go sell your shit on somebody else's show. Whatever it is you're selling. And it's always something. He looked across the desk at his guest. What a bozo, DuVal thought. Reverend Bozo. If this guy ever gets elected to public office I'm leaving the country. Or shorting every stock I own. The guy probably spends more getting his hair done every year than most of his followers earn. And that medal he wears around his neck—give me a fucking break. Tells anyone who'll listen that Martin Luther King gave it to him, but it looks like he won it on a carnival midway.

"Well, Mr. DuVal, I think that you are over-simplifying a very complex situation for which there are no easy answers. The original intent of what we call Affirmative Action was twofold: to redress the wrongs of the past—specifically to compensate African Americans in some fashion for their enslavement by the so-called white man and, secondly, to level the playing field, or create equality of opportunity for women and people of color, all of whom have suffered immeasurably at the hands of the so-called white men who have run this country since they first began slaughtering its indigenous population over two hundred years ago. I will concede that Affirmative Action is not perfect—in my opinion it does not go far enough. By any standard of measure women and people of color do not enjoy the same opportunities or reap the same rewards that white men do in this country. What we should be talking about where African Americans are concerned are reparations. But that's another topic."

The Reverend unfastened the top button of his shirt, and wiped a single bead of sweat away from his temple. He wondered if he had gained a few pounds. His new shirts seemed tight at the neck. Maybe the tailor was trying to save a few pennies on fabric—he was always bitching about the price of sea-island cotton. At two hundred per he could cut them right. He'd give him the benefit of the doubt and get re-measured next time.

Reverend Williams watched DuVal take a long drag from his cigarette and exhale an almost endless plume of smoke into the still air of the studio as he prepared to speak. Stupid cracker, he thought, smoking cigarettes with all we know about it.

"But, Reverend Williams, there are some people—and I include myself in this group—who would argue that we have the Civil Rights Act, we have anti-discrimination legislation in place, and any failure to achieve equality in income and power is due to a self-destructive culture and an aversion to hard work. I mean, after all, it's easier to sit around bellyaching about what you don't have than to go out and get it. And what explains the Asian Americans? They've been victims of terrible discrimination in the past—hell, we rounded up the Japanese and put them in camps in World War Two—and yet they score higher on standardized tests than any other group. And they seem to have no problem getting out there and earning a buck, for that matter. Maybe Charles Murray was right in *The Bell Curve*. Maybe there's something genetic at work. I don't know, what do you think? On that note we'll take a break to hear from our sponsors. When we come back we'll give the Reverend a chance to respond and take some calls from the folks who are listening in tonight."

DuVal took his headphones off, ran the fingers of one hand back through his hair, and tamped the glowing nub of his cigarette out. A trace of soreness was lingering in his throat. He was recovering from a cold that had recently ravaged the station. The women and their fucking children; disease vectors, he thought. But at least his voice was getting back to normal, with most of the rasp of the previous week gone.

DuVal's voice was a powerful instrument. A strong, rich baritone, with only the slightest touch of his native Oklahoma accent remaining. His listeners, caught in traffic on the way home from work, tuning in from the second shift or a late day at the office, found its warm tone reassuring. Even his critics praised the quality of his voice, although their praise was most often delivered as a preface to some sort of invective or name calling: 'velvet-voiced extremist Jack DuVal,' for instance, or 'the sonorous hate-monger Jack Duval.' For the most part he paid his critics no mind—unless he could use their words for show fodder—secure in the knowledge that his audience neither read nor heard their words, and that his income dwarfed their own.

DuVal reached for the lighter that lay next to his cigarettes, pausing for a moment to savor its heft and read the small inscription that adorned its side: *A voice is a nice thing, Jack, but you'll never earn your living with it.* The words, carefully etched into the gold surface, served as a lasting reminder of a discouraging pronouncement his father had often shouted through a closed bathroom door. Within, sometimes for an hour or more after school or on weekends, Jack's voice would reverberate against the walls as he breathlessly introduced "Kind of a Drag," the hot new single by The Buckinghams, or read—with measured seriousness—interesting AP news items he found in *The Daily Oklahoman.* For even as a child, DuVal knew what he wanted to do with his life. Radio was his passion, his calling, and his connection to the larger world that lay beyond the wheat fields, beyond the lazy shallows of the Cimarron River, and beyond the pastures where cattle herds idly grazed in the fields that he saw from the windows of his family's house at the edge of town. There, he would lie awake at night, moonlight streaming through his bedroom window, a small transistor radio pressed to his ear, listening to WKY in Oklahoma City, or WLS out of Chicago. AM powerhouses, their crisp signals passing high and clear over the flat, fecund plains of America's heartland.

DuVal's father had wanted him to go into the family business: hardware.

"This store can be yours, Jack. It's a good, honest living," he had said.

"I told you, dad, I want to be a DJ."

"That's not a real job, son."

"Well, I'm not gonna stick around here selling hammers and nails to rednecks."

When DuVal made it to New York he went to a jeweler and had two of the lighters made at twenty-five hundred dollars apiece. He sent one to his father and put the other in his pocket, carrying it with him wherever he went.

The show followed a predictable arc. DuVal carefully goaded the Reverend into saying he sounded like a racist, and then responded to the epithet with a calculated mixture of hurt and anger.

"I resent that. And I'm a little disappointed that you'd resort to such a tactic."

"What kind of tactic are you referring to, Mr. DuVal?" the Reverend had asked.

"You know what I'm talking about. All any African American has to do to end a debate is utter the word 'racist.'"

"Well, if the shoe fits—"

DuVal waited for a rhyme, and was almost disappointed when one didn't materialize.

"I just think it's a cop out," DuVal said, "Playing the race card any time anyone says something you happen to disagree with renders the term meaningless."

The listeners loved it. They called in from every corner of the country to voice their agreement with, and support for, DuVal. Of course there was the obligatory prankster from Staten Island who called in, said "Howard Stern," on the air, giggled, and hung up. And that was fine too, because in the end, he was listening to DuVal, and not Stern. In radio, DuVal would often say, there are only three things that matter: ratings, ratings, and ratings. And his were high and climbing.

Jack DuVal preached to the converted. His audience supported him unconditionally. He was the voice of their anger, their righteous indignation, and their disenfranchisement. It was immaterial that (like most Americans) DuVal's audience lived lives that were full of more material comfort and political privilege than those of 95% of the people on the planet. They were pissed. Pissed about taxes, pissed about gay marriage, pissed about abortion. Pissed about the Kennedys. Pissed about the liberal bias of the media. Pissed about their 'Congress critters.' Pissed about the guy in the next cube, the neighbor next door, and the welfare mothers in New York City who couldn't stop having kids. Whatever "it" was, it was standing in the way of them living a satisfying life, and it pissed them off.

Fortunately, DuVal knew how to nurture this anger. Stoke the embers. Keep it burning like the Zoroastrian eternal flame. But DuVal, unlike the Zoroastrians, was far from resolute in his beliefs. In fact, he had few hard and fast opinions—he could argue either side of an issue and even switch in mid-stream if he thought it would suit his purposes. He was a pragmatist. And it was this pragmatism that had led to the creation (or evolution, more accurately) of his reductive, dogmatic on-air persona. He had discovered, over the years, that a certain segment—and quite a large segment—of the American population really didn't want to have to think for themselves. The world around them was too bewildering. They wanted someone with answers. Simple, understandable answers to the bedeviling complexities of modern life. Lost your job? Blame NAFTA. Or H1-B visas. Can't pay your taxes? Blame the liberals. It had to be somebody's fault. It really didn't matter whose, as long as it was someone else's. And if it turned out that what DuVal proclaimed in a broadcast was somehow misguided, or even patently wrong, who cared? People have short attention spans. They forget. Tomorrow is another issue, and another show. DuVal had come to this valuable realization—and started the long transition from drive-time jock to the host of his own syndicated radio program—during the hard-fought presidential campaign leading up to the 1980 election. On his way to becoming the 40th President of the United States, candidate

Ronald Reagan had achieved something truly monumental. He had effectively changed the character of political discourse in the country from meaningful conversation to meaningless sound bites with a single phrase: *There you go again*. Reagan had used that short phrase like a cudgel to pummel President Jimmy Carter in a debate, and it had played on the lips of middle America for months afterward. It was pure theater, and good entertainment. DuVal took note. In the end, Ronald Reagan had taught him two things: the lasting value of a clever sound bite and, more important, that if you state something emphatically and repeat it enough times— the benefits of supply side economics, that trees cause more pollution than automobiles do—people will believe it forever despite any and all contrary evidence that may emerge.

Jack DuVal's career had started at a small FM outlet in Stillwater, Oklahoma, in the mid 1970's. He didn't have the patience for higher education, so as an alternative to working in his father's store he wheedled himself a job as a gofer at one of the local radio stations. For a joke one Sunday night the jocks let him read the news and the weather. One night became a hundred, and he had a reel. A few decades later the road that had taken him to Wichita, Memphis, Seattle, Cleveland, and Los Angeles had finally delivered him to the big time: syndication. He had signed on with the American Radio Syndicate for two years at a couple of million per year. In less than a month that contract would be up. There were several offers on the table, and the money was ridiculous. He would be making an eight-figure annual salary—more money than he had ever dreamed possible. Overnight, he would be very wealthy.

DuVal lit another cigarette and pressed the talkback mic to speak with his producer, Diane Healy, who was sitting behind a glass partition next to the engineer.

"Is the car downstairs?" he asked.

"I thought Jeffrey just told you it was," she answered.

"Lighten up—I'm just asking."

"And I'm just answering that your assistant already told you it was."

"Fine, fine. Has the Reverend left the building?"

"He has. Along with his entourage."

What is it with these guys anyway, DuVal wondered? The more money they put together, the more people they drag along with them. Bodyguard. Stylist. Personal assistant. It's like clowns coming out of a car at the circus.

The coast clear, DuVal finished his smoke, grabbed his briefcase, and headed for the studio door. Diane was waiting in the hallway for him, and smiled as he appeared.

"Fooled 'em again," she said.

"It wasn't half bad," DuVal replied.

Diane had been working with DuVal for ten years, following him through four jobs in three cities. She'd started as a production assistant at twenty-five, and was now, arguably, the backbone of his show. She had an intrinsic understanding of what worked for his audience, and played the central role in selecting his guests. Both she and DuVal were gifted with keen memories for minutiae, and they could spend hours after a broadcast—especially if they felt it hadn't gone as planned, or as well as expected—dissecting every exchange. Or, as in this case, they could sum up a show with a kind of nuanced verbal shorthand. It wasn't half bad, in DuVal's parlance, meaning the show had been extremely successful from his vantage point.

"No, not too bad," Diane said, adding "the callers really shelled him."

"He loved it. Makes him feel like he's fighting for justice."

"We're headed into the election cycle, maybe we should book him now for next year."

"Is he running?"

"Does it matter?"

"Book him for June. July at the latest."

"I'll call his office in the morning."

"Good."

DuVal considered asking his producer if she wanted to have some dinner, then thought better of it. A quiet night at home on the couch sounds good, he thought. He wondered if she had other plans, anyway. It was hard to tell with Diane. She always looked put together; stylish, without being precious about it. If she had a date, he wouldn't find out until next day, if at all. Despite their close relationship, Diane had a tendency to be discrete about certain matters. She was thirty-five and single, but to all appearances—or at least to DuVal—she seemed to be more married to work than to the idea of marriage, or finding someone to marry.

For his part, DuVal had been married, divorced and, for the time being, was happy to leave it at that. He was certainly happier alone than he had been for the last few years of his marriage. He had met his former wife Hillary in Seattle in the late 80s, when he was doing a drive-time show on KISW. She was a local girl, working as a waitress at a restaurant where he frequently ate alone after his show. One thing led to another and they were standing in front of a Justice of the Peace. But the move to Cleveland had caused tension. It was a bigger job for him, but she was away from her family and friends, and with DuVal almost always working, she was often alone and lonely. They had fought. By the time he took a job in Los Angeles, it was over. Hillary moved back to Seattle, and DuVal took an apartment in Santa Monica with a view of the ocean. The best thing about his marriage, DuVal thought, was that it had ended before the money got really good. He sent her a couple of grand a month and never gave it a thought. And the ability to focus exclusively on work had done wonders for his career.

Diane handed him a thick book and a bulging manila envelope. Homework.

"Tomorrow night we have Joy McCorkle, author of, get this, *Better Sex For Born Again Christians*. Very entertaining stuff. Evidently she discovered that she can do more on her knees than pray."

"Bless her heart."

DuVal put the materials in his briefcase. Feeling the weight of the book, he was fairly certain he wouldn't be reading much of it. Instead, he'd spend an hour or so poring over the synopsis, her bio, and any good quotes the researchers had managed to pull for his convenience. He put a cigarette in his mouth and reached in his pocket for the lighter. As he pressed his thumb to the wheel that would spark the flint and ignite the flame, Diane reached out and grabbed his arm.

"Jack, I thought we agreed that you'd only smoke in the studio and your office. I can't take the complaints anymore."

"Duly noted," he said, lighting the cigarette and signaling his intention to leave with a wave of his arm that bisected a small trail of smoke climbing lazily toward the ceiling.

DuVal's car was waiting at the curb. An unfamiliar woman in a dark suit, the jacket worn over a white shirt and black tie, opened the rear door for him.

"Where's Ronnie?" DuVal asked.

"Vacation."

"Since this morning?"

"Yes, sir."

"Where'd he go?"

"Vegas, I think."

Poor bastard, DuVal thought. He'll piss his money away and buy himself another six months behind the wheel.

"You know where we're going?" he asked.

"Yes, sir. Duane Street, downtown."

"Bingo."

DuVal stepped through the rear door of the S-Class Mercedes. He settled into the soft leather seat, pushed the button to make the tinted rear window slide down a few inches, and opened the folder Diane had given him.

Joy McCorkle was pretty much what he had expected. Something akin to the bastard child of Tammy Faye Baker and Dr. Ruth. She believed that God was present in the church and the bedroom and could be honored in both places. DuVal read the book synopsis closely, jumping back and forth to her bio from time to time, taking notes and formulating questions as he did so. He thought he might ask her what kind of sex life she thought Jim Baker and Tammy Faye had back in the day. He figured Baker got laid more in prison. Looking up from his work, DuVal discovered that they were on Mott Street. Chinatown. Clusterfuck. He leaned forward.

"What's your name?"

"Brooke."

"Pull over, Brooke."

She pulled the car into an empty space in front of a fire hydrant, and looked up at the rear-view mirror to see the reflection of DuVal's piercing gaze.

"Can I ask you a question?"

"Of course, Mr. DuVal."

"What the hell are we doing on Mott?"

"The west side was jammed, sir."

"Okay. Well, for future reference, I hate Chinatown. Do not bring me here again."

"Sorry," the driver said, and shifted the car back into drive.

"Wait," DuVal said, peering through the windshield at a backlit plastic sign that read: WO HOP CHINESE RESTAURANT. "You can make it up to me."

DuVal pulled a fifty from his bankroll and passed it over the driver's seat back. He directed her to go into the restaurant and get him some steamed vegetable dumplings, an order of sautéed broccoli with garlic sauce and a Diet Dr. Pepper. A few minutes later she returned.

"They don't have the Dr. Pepper, do you want a Diet Coke instead?" she asked.

"No," he said, spewing a cloud of smoke out of the rear window of the car, "Get me a Mountain Dew."

She returned with a bag full of food, handing it, along with change from the fifty, through the open window to DuVal.

"Here you go," she said.

"Thanks," he mumbled in return, opening the bag and releasing a sweet, savory aroma into the confines of the car.

As the car pulled away from the curb, DuVal reached into the bag and located a glassine envelope. The envelope contained three items: a rectangular-shaped plastic container of soy sauce, a similar container of hot mustard, and a fortune cookie. He removed the fortune cookie and cracked it open. A small slip of paper fell out. He took the paper between his fingers and read the message: YOU WILL LOSE WHAT YOU TREASURE MOST. Unconsciously, DuVal patted his left trouser pocket for his lighter. Still there. He pulled the lighter out, holding it in the beam of his reading light. He read the inscription, and then lit the flame. He shook his head, and dropped the fortune into the breast pocket of his jacket.

They arrived in front of DuVal's building after another stop, this time DuVal directing the driver to run into the neighborhood Food Emporium to buy him a cold 12-pack of Bud Light. As DuVal struggled to get out of the car with the beer, the Chinese food and his homework, another resident of his building—a 50-ish man dressed head-to-toe in black with an obvious eye lift—walked out the front door and shot him a disapproving glance.

"Need a little help there, Mr. DuVal?" a uniformed doorman said, taking the 12-pack out of his hands.

"Thanks, Mike," DuVal answered, "grab a couple for yourself."

"I wish I could."

"Should I wait?" Brooke asked from the curbside.

"I'm in for the night," DuVal replied, "go ahead and take off."

The black car pulled away, turning north on Hudson as Mike the doorman helped DuVal through the lobby and into the elevator.

The elevator opened directly onto DuVal's floor, and into a loft that had far more space than he could ever use. It was 3000 square feet of mostly-open floorplan, with sturdy columns that supported the ceiling and provided a clear visual link to its provenance: a turn-of-the-century sweatshop. The co-op conversion had happened during the go-go 80s, when the artists who had pioneered the neighborhood were flushed out to make room for people with money (investment bankers and trust-fund brats, mostly) who wanted to live where the artists were.

The previous owner had been a dentist who divided his time between thriving practices in Manhattan and Saddle River, New Jersey. He was a grotesque figure who fancied leather pants, cocaine and young women— much to his wife's displeasure. The loft had sat furnished and unoccupied for over a decade while the couple waged an epic divorce battle. When first shown to DuVal, it looked like a museum of the 80s: metal restaurant shelving was everywhere from the kitchen to the open areas to the bedroom, and paintings by Mark Kostabi adorned the exposed brick walls. Stepping into one of the walk-in closets in the master bedroom, DuVal saw a row of Norma Kamali jumpsuits with padded shoulders hanging from a curtain rod and thought he had accidentally walked into the costume trailer for a science fiction movie. He paid $2.5 million for the place and didn't go back until all vestiges of the former tenants had been exorcised. To that end, he hired a highly-recommended decorator, who for weeks called him at work several times a day asking if he had received the swatches or the photos he'd e-mailed.

"Small lamps!" he would exclaim, "It's all about small lamps!" Or, "What do you think about sand!?!?"

Unsure, when confronted with this type of question, if the decorator was talking about the physical stuff found on the world's beaches, or using the word as a description of a color or a mood, DuVal had finally asked him use his best judgment, and to please refrain from calling again him until it was time to move in.

After eating several mouthfuls of the broccoli from its waxen paper box, DuVal removed two cans from the 12-pack, and placed the remainder on a lonely shelf in the double wide, stainless-steel refrigerator of his chef's kitchen. He walked the expanse of his living area, slid a glass door to the side and stepped out onto the terrace. The terrace was DuVal's favorite thing about the loft. It was twenty feet deep and spanned the width of his building, offering unobstructed views to the south and west. Where the southern and western walls met was a custom-built spa, which (he had been told) could hold up to eight people comfortably, and overlooked the tip of the island and the harbor beyond. DuVal paid a gardener to visit twice a month to care for the flowering plants, small trees, and shrubs that had been placed around the terrace in accordance with a very expensive landscape architect's plans.

Setting the two beer cans on the edge of the spa, DuVal disrobed. He then lit a cigarette and, while expertly holding it in his mouth as he took a long drag, simultaneously picked up and opened one of the beers. He stepped into the warm, swirling water, careful to hold his beer and cigarette aloft as he settled the bare skin of his ass onto the hand-painted Italian tile that comprised the interior of the spa. He looked out to the Statue of Liberty, tiny on the horizon, and thought about the twin towers of the World Trade Center, which only ten months ago had loomed so large in the foreground.

"What a fucking thing," he said into the cool, night air.

TWO

It was a far-away noise, which came closer and closer until its insistence roused Diane from a profound, dreamless slumber. The telephone. In the darkness she felt for the offending object on the bedside table.

"What time is it?" were the first words she managed to urge across her dry tongue and into the receiver.

"One A.M.," answered DuVal, "maybe a little after." "Feel like some company?"

"Sure," Diane heard herself saying, "come on over."

As she hung up the telephone and turned on the light, Diane wondered why she had said yes. Was sleeping with DuVal the right thing to do? What was right, anyway? Diane imagined herself to be, for the most part, a moral relativist. Were she not, it would have been intolerable working for DuVal. She had no trouble, for instance, reconciling her support for abortion rights with her opposition to the death penalty. One seemed okay to her, and the other didn't. Sleeping with DuVal had seemed okay to her, for a while, anyway. But was it now? Or was it simply a matter of convenience? She was too sleepy to think about it with any degree of seriousness.

As she stood in the shower Diane reflected on the origin of this aspect of their association. It was a drunken night, a few years before, after the announcement earlier in the day of a significant increase in ratings for the show. Was it in Cleveland? L.A.? She summoned the memory from her repository of less-important thoughts. DuVal, she recalled, was in the final stages of his divorce and was carrying with him the wounded look of a scolded child. That vulnerability to which some women seem to have no natural immunity. They were celebrating. DuVal, after several drinks, and several more after that, was in no condition to drive; Diane, ever aware of the producer's obligation to look after the talent, had offered him a lift home. At the curb outside his building (with the Pacific waves crashing in the distance, Diane remembered, it was L.A.) there had been that pause, that lingering moment between two people when the decision is made to indulge the natural curiosity about the previously unseen physical characteristics and hitherto only imagined sexual proclivities of the other party. It was enthusiastic and slapdash. Heady. Infused with the titillation that comes with doing something that is marginally verboten.

Diane wondered what she would feel over the coming hours.

The intercom sounded as she squeezed a lump of toothpaste onto her toothbrush. She ran, naked and damp, across the hardwood floors of her apartment, then lifted the receiver beside the door.

"Hello?"

"A mister DuVal to see you," the doorman replied.

"Send him up."

As she waited for DuVal's knock at the door, Diane's thoughts traveled from her doorman's perception of this kind of late night visitation to her recent desire to move out of the neighborhood. Greenwich Village was fun, and her place was fairly nice (it's so *intimate*, the broker had cooed, as if small was something someone would actually want), but with her job's Midtown location and Christopher Street being the heart of boystown, the Upper West Side was looking more and more attractive. If she ever wanted to actually meet a suitable man, anyway.

Most of Diane's New York friends lived on the Upper West Side, with the exception of the few who had children. The ones with children had all moved to Park Slope, Brooklyn, which had become a sea of expensive baby strollers that carried pampered little Joshes, Jakes, Zoes and Maxes.

When Diane signed her lease, she had asked for a single-year term; her tenure with DuVal had taught her that there was no such thing as a permanent address. So she unpacked, but decorated halfheartedly. Now, for reasons she didn't fully understand, she was beginning to long for a home as much as a man.

DuVal knocked. Diane's jaw locked around her fancy toothbrush, flattening the Italian bristles and freeing her hands to unlock the deadbolt. She opened the door.

"Hey," said DuVal, his breath redolent with the twin odors of cigarette and beer. "How are you?"

Diane closed her eyes as he reached his arms around her, squeezing a little too hard.

"DuVal," she said, unintelligibly, "let me spit."

"Suit yourself," he replied, and headed into the bedroom.

The act itself was on the short side. Perfunctory. A few score of strokes and a grunt. Not a disgrace, Diane thought, but not that good either. Probably what married sex feels like. There was a certain comfort in the familiarity of it all; comfort that came with the fact that DuVal truly cared about her, and not just because she was a great producer and arguably the architect of the show's success. But because he loved her. But there was a difference between love and *love*. And this, Diane realized, as she did each and every time she paused to reflect after sex with DuVal, wasn't *love*.

DuVal lit a cigarette.

"Have you ever used an Internet dating service?" he asked, breaking the opaque silence that hung like an 800 thread-count sheet between them.

"What?" Diane asked.

"Have you ever used Match.com or any of those things?"

"Why?" Diane replied, suspiciously.

"No reason," said DuVal, "just wondering."

"A few times," Diane answered, internally compiling a list of DuVal's possible motives—jealously, curiosity, some previously unexercised need to make conversation that wasn't somehow work-related after sex.

"How'd it work out?" DuVal enquired.

"Okay," Diane answered, as she recalled the e-mail exchanges, the forced conversation over coffee, the laborious sifting through mountains of dirt to find a single gleam of hope that looked like a diamond but, on closer examination, turned out to be only a shard of broken glass; all of the things that she associated with her Match.com experiences.

"I mean, did you meet anybody? DuVal prodded.

"Look, Jack, I'm don't really want to talk about this. It makes me feel—I just feel awkward discussing this with you."

"Well, don't. Feel awkward, I mean. I'm just curious. I've been reading about it all over the place."

"Well if you're curious about it, why don't you try it?"

"Me?!?!" DuVal scoffed, spewing forth a roiling ball of smoke that for a moment before dissipating threatened to collapse back onto his face like a miniature mushroom cloud.

"Why not you?" Diane asked, propping herself up on an elbow to look him more directly in the eye.

"Well, for one thing, how would it look?"

"You mean because you're so famous?" Diane asked, trying, somewhat unsuccessfully, to prevent scorn from inflecting her speech.

"Well, that's one thing," DuVal answered, impervious to any form of mockery. "And for another, I don't really want to have to correspond with a lot of people."

"I salute your optimism."

"You know what I mean," DuVal replied.

"Of course," Diane replied, "you have a love/hate relationship with the human race. They love you, you hate them."

"Forget it."

"Look, Jack. Give it a try. Use a fake name. Use a fake picture. Nobody looks like their picture anyway."

"I don't want to."

"Fine," Diane said.

"Okay, fine."

Silence again overtook them. They lay side by side for several minutes, until DuVal's breathing fell into a gentle, regular rhythm. A rhythm that comes only with sleep.

"I hope you don't mind," he said, waking with a start, "but I really can't spend the night." He sat up. "My trainer's coming first thing in the morning, and it'll be easier if I wake up there."

"I understand," Diane said, glad she would have her bed to herself. Glad, rather, that she would not be sharing it all night with DuVal.

"Yeah, I know, I just thought you might be expecting me to stay," DuVal said, pulling his pants on, carefully tucking his penis and testicles (and the material of his boxer shorts along with them) into his left pant leg.

What a thing, thought Diane, to have a dick; and, she laughed to herself, to have it run your life. She lay back on the bed and closed her eyes.

"You'll forgive me if I don't show you out, Jack. The door locks itself."

DuVal finished dressing and said goodnight, bending to give Diane a peck on the forehead. She heard him fumble for the doorknob in the dark, heard the door squeak as it opened, heard the lock click as it closed. In the late-night quiet she could hear the elevator doors open and close, and she knew he was gone. She rolled over on her side and opened her eyes. The moon was full, and its gentle light cast a radiant glow in the nighttime sky. It streamed through her window and across her face, illuminating the bedside table in its path. And there it was, shining ever so slightly in the moonlight—DuVal's lighter. He'll shit, she thought. She picked up the telephone receiver and tapped out his number, its pattern burned indelibly into her memory. He wasn't home yet. After the beep (the beep always lasts too long, she thought) Diane left a message on DuVal's voice mail.

"I've got your lighter, I'll bring it to the office with me tomorrow."

Please don't call me back, Diane thought, I need some sleep.

THREE

DuVal awoke in pain to the increasing volume of his alarm clock's rhythmic beep.

He was hung over to the degree that the joints of his knees and elbows ached as much as the outskirts of his swollen brain, which seemed to be forcefully pressing against the confining bone of his skull. The smell of metabolized alcohol coming from his skin, combined with the odor of smoke that emanated from his hair as he ran his hands through its matted disarray, created an atmosphere in his bowels that could best be described as imminently volcanic. It was the type of thing one was ill-advised to ignore. He didn't think he had drunk enough to deserve what he was feeling: the inexplicable-yet-overwhelming sense of dread that was beginning to gnaw at him as he tried to piece the events of the previous evening back together.

It had started simply enough; a bag of Chinese food, a few beers, a dip in the spa, a few more beers, with perhaps a short glass of whiskey to help matters along. Nothing out of the ordinary. He remembered going to Diane's and having sex, during which things began to get a little fuzzy. Booze was like that, he knew from bitter experience; sometimes it took a little while to catch up on you. You have a few drinks, and when you aren't particularly paying attention it comes down on you like a bag of heavy, wet sand. It was like age in that respect.

He had stopped for another six-pack on the way home, it turned out, and there was whiskey in the house already. You can get in less trouble at home, by a degree, but trouble has a way of leaving no avenue unexplored. After all, there's always the telephone. Drink and dial. And then it bloomed in his mind like a red tide, choking out any optimism he may have possessed for the coming day. He had, indeed, made a few phone calls the previous night.

There was an ugly bit of business about his lighter. While attempting to enkindle a cigarette he had noticed that it was missing. More accurately, its absence had finally registered in his drunken, muddled mind. In the moments following that panicked revelation, DuVal had combed the vast expanse of the loft twice in a reeling search for his 24-carat good-luck charm. The dragnet had turned up little. The cigarette had been lit (at a dear price: the better part of an eyebrow) from a ring of fire on the stove. The smell of singed hair had stuck with him even after he drew in, and exhaled, a long blast of hot, acrid smoke.

Ultimately, DuVal had noticed the blinking red light on his answering machine. He'd listened to the message, and ascertained that his lighter was in fact in Diane's possession. It was at this point that reason had taken a back seat to drunken suspicion. He had dialed her number.

"Jesus Christ," he remembered Diane answering, "what time is it?"

"You took my lighter," he'd accused her, as certainly slurring then as he was wincing now at the memory.

"What are you talking about?"

"You don't go and take a guy's lighter because you're pissed he won't stay the night."

"Jack, you're drunk," she said, adding, "I called you to tell you that you'd left your lighter here."

"So?" he had countered.

"So do you think I would've called you if I'd taken your lighter? Think about it before you answer."

"Maybe."

"Jack. Get some sleep. I'll bring your lighter to the office in the morning."

"I don't love you."

"I know," Diane said, and hung up.

Jesus. Had he really told her that he didn't love her? If so, why? What was the fucking point? His memory of the conversation was spotty. Some of the details were lost. Diane's transcript of the phone call was undoubtedly more complete than his, but it was likely that he would only hear her version when it suited her needs, and by that time the dialogue would have been sharpened to a razor's edge. What to do? Ignore the situation? Pretend it hadn't happened? No, that wouldn't work. Not because it was the cowardly way out, but because the knowledge of the conversation—and the knowledge that she possessed the knowledge of the conversation—would gnaw at him until he cleaned things up. It would linger in his mind like an unwelcome houseguest. He would do the right thing, and offer a pre-emptive apology to Diane when he arrived at the office.

That decision made, and with other unsavory details beginning to surface in his consciousness, DuVal moved through the chronology of his brownout. He had trouble remembering a clear rationale for his second phone call. Or, rather, what he had hoped to accomplish by making it. This much he knew: he had realized at around 4 A.M. that it was three hours earlier on the West Coast. And really, 1 A.M. is not that late. In fact, DuVal had reasoned, it was probably an ideal time to call his ex-wife Hillary, because in all likelihood she would be at home. Under the auspices of making sure that the monthly check had been sent, he had carefully tapped his old number into the phone.

"Hello?" a male voice had answered.

"Who're you?" DuVal had replied.

"Who are *you*?" the voice had answered.

"I'm the guy who pays the mortgage on the house you're in. Put Hillary on, assclown."

"Christ, Hillary, I think it's your ex," he'd heard the man's voice say.

Seconds later, when he heard his ex-wife's voice, it too, betrayed more than a little annoyance.

"What do you want, Jack?"

"Who was that?" DuVal had queried.

She had replied that, unless she was to marry the fellow, his identity was, and would remain, none of his fucking business. DuVal had offered a half-hearted apology and added that he had only called because he was concerned about her, and by the way, didn't we have some good times way back when?

"You're drunk, Jack."

"Not really," he had said, in his own defense.

"If you want to talk, call me in the daytime. Sober. I'm hanging up now." And she did.

Ruminating on the conversation saddened DuVal. Yes he was a little embarrassed that he had called his ex-wife. But still. He had married her in good faith, given her some of the best years of his life, and now would pay her for what looked like would be the remainder of it. She could've been a little more understanding.

Suddenly, DuVal's phone rang. The sound triggered a new salvo of pain in his head. 8 A.M. He ran the length of the loft, his testicles sending tendrils of suffering upward into his already-distressed abdomen as they slapped against a thigh, or were slapped in turn by his flaccid penis. Uncomfortable as that was, he sprinted forth, praying he would not hear the ringing sound again.

Approaching DuVal's building on the street below was LeAnn LaFavre, cell phone in her hand, impatiently glancing at the face of her Cartier watch. Her body had been toned to an almost solid state, the tiny molecules pressed closer and closer together until they formed a structure that was practically indistinguishable from marble. A pair of microscopic black shorts clung tightly to her lower trunk and their matching top was stretched across her surgically enhanced bust line, providing ample display space for the *swoosh!* of the Nike logo. The top was covered by a Nike warm-up jacket, its logo emblazoned on the back, and its front strategically unzipped to reveal the aforementioned bust line and Nike logo. She was such a hot trainer that she had an endorsement. Everything and everyone is always either being bought or sold, DuVal had thought, when she'd told him of the sponsorship. He caught the phone in mid-ring.

"Please go away," he said, by way of a greeting.

"I'll call your assistant later to rebook," she answered.

"Fine. Go."

She flipped her cell phone shut and stepped wordlessly to the curb to hail a cab, wondering where to spend the two hundred dollars she had just earned stopping by DuVal's building.

The combination of fatigue and chain-smoking the night before had taken a heavy toll on DuVal's voice. He was hoarse. He made the mature decision to go back to bed for a few more hours. But there was twinge of soreness in his throat that he thought he should first address. He made his way to the kitchen and ran the hot water until steam rose from the sink. He poured two tablespoons of salt into the bottom of a glass and filled it the rest of the way with hot water, stirring the mixture briefly with a spoon. He gargled the milky solution, mouthful by brackish mouthful, until it was gone. It seemed to help. He swallowed three Advil and fifteen milligrams of Ambien, and retired to the comfort of his bed. Nobody understands how hard it is to be me, DuVal thought, as the Ambien worked its special magic and sleep began to soundlessly wash over him like gentle waves on the shore of a powder-white stretch of beach.

FOUR

It was a somber DuVal, chastened by folly, who appeared at the studio later that day. His head hung slightly forward from his neck as if lead weights had somehow become embedded in the frontal lobes of his brain. DuVal's mind was heavy with thought, remorse, and the leftover effects of the sleeping pills he had taken only a few hours before.

"Hello, Mr. DuVal," the receptionist said, as he came out of the elevator and onto the floor.

"Hello, uh, good afternoon..." he replied, unsuccessfully searching the hazy labyrinth of his mind for the woman's name.

He offered similar perfunctory greetings to several of the other nameless functionaries that he passed in the hallways as he made his way toward the sanctuary of his office. One foot in front of the other, he thought, steady as she goes.

Seated behind a desk at his post outside DuVal's office was Jeffrey, his assistant. Jeffrey had been with DuVal for only a few months, but had managed to make himself quite comfortable in that time. At the moment DuVal approached, he was speaking into the microphone component of a telephone headset while admiring his forehead in a desktop mirror. The desktop mirror had arrived in a box of personal effects Jeffrey had brought with him on his second day in the office.

"What are you looking at?" DuVal asked, hoping to catch the thin, well-coiffed, twenty-something man off guard.

"My eyebrows," Jeffrey replied, carefully covering the small hole that might transmit his words to the party on the other end of his telephone conversation, "I had them waxed last night. What do you think?"

"Sad," DuVal said.

"I'll write down the number of the salon," Jeffrey replied, "You might want to give them a call."

"Funny," DuVal said, shaking his head as he opened the door to his office.

The office was a source of some satisfaction for DuVal; it was thirty stories above the streets of Manhattan with floor-to-ceiling windows facing north and west. He relished telling people that he could almost see Canada from his desk. And while that was not quite true, he could see well past the tip of Manhattan to the north, past the point where the cliffs of the Palisades revealed the Tappan Zee bridge on a clear day, and a fair distance west out into the once-lush meadowlands of New Jersey. On any day, if he craned his neck toward the south, he could watch smoke rise from the petrochemical wastelands of Bayonne. It was a good place to prepare, hang out, make telephone calls, and store all the swag that came his way from guests and various other seekers of his favor. For DuVal, it was also like a spoil of war: a hard-earned piece of property that was symbolic of his status at the Syndicate.

Facing his desk was what DuVal liked to call the wall of shame: photographs of himself with various political figures and celebrities, most of whom looked strangely air brushed in real life. Especially prominent was a picture of him glad-handing the President in the White House at a special dinner for the elite of the news media. As DuVal stared at the picture he remembered when it was taken; throughout the reception and the meal he had marveled that he was actually there. Of course, it was no special honor. It was simply a routine effort to curry favor with the press. Business as usual in Washington. He remembered that when he shook hands with the President he had been struck by softness of the man's hand. And when the Chief of State told him, in his comforting southern drawl, that he was a big fan of the show, the smiling DuVal had wondered how someone could be so absolutely sincere in his insincerity. It was a skill that the President had honed to an art form. And one that DuVal, in his heart of hearts, knew he also possessed.

It was just after three, a few hours before show time. DuVal lit a cigarette with the Bic lighter he had bought in the deli downstairs. He had half-expected to come in and find his lighter on the desk but, to his considerable disappointment, it wasn't there. Diane must really be pissed, he thought.

Heralded by what seemed to DuVal to be an unnaturally loud electronic chirping sound, the voice of his assistant Jeffery suddenly came over the intercom on his telephone.

"Dave Miller on line one, do you want to take it?"

"Yeah."

DuVal pushed the speakerphone button and leaned back in his chair. Agents and lawyers, as a group, were perhaps DuVal's least favorite life forms. They always gave the impression, in his opinion—no matter how much money you made—that you were somehow working for them. And, of course, the business had been set up so you couldn't wipe your ass without first calling, and then paying, at least one of each. Dave Miller, DuVal's agent, was a noteworthy case in point. There had been times, during the recent (and delicate) contract negotiation phase, when Miller had not taken his calls. Or, had been curiously missing for hours at a time. DuVal was in possession of the knowledge that he was far-and-away Miller's most lucrative client, and had put him on notice that he was no longer willing to take short shrift. Especially—although he had omitted this part from that discussion—from a little shit from the Five Towns whose father in-law owned the agency where he was employed. Thus, the speakerphone. In the ulterior language of the business, being put on speaker when only one person was on the other end of the line indicated that the caller was of lesser importance. It said, in effect, that one was not significant enough for the other party to lift the receiver of the phone and devote their undivided attention to you or what you had to say.

"Hello, Dave," DuVal said, "what can I pay you for today?"

"Very funny, Jack. I was just calling to confirm that I'll be in your office at 5:30 for our meeting."

"Today's bad, Dave. Any way we can do it tomorrow?" DuVal opened the top drawer of his desk and sorted through a jumbled mess of pens, half-empty packages of cigarettes, letters, CDs and the odd cassette tape in search of a bottle of Advil.

"I really think we should do it this evening, Jack. We're very close on this deal. Besides, I'm in my car on the way uptown."

In truth, Dave Miller had worked from home for most of the day, and was only just heading into the long spiral roadway that fed an endless river of traffic on 495 into the Lincoln Tunnel. He could see the majestic skyline of Manhattan across the Hudson River, glowing in the late afternoon sun.

"I'll see you at five-thirty," he told DuVal, and disconnected.

Dave watched the traffic light that registered payment of his toll by the EZ Pass system turn from red to green. He then used his index finger to gently pull the button that made the window of his Mercedes slide noise-lessly up in preparation for entering the carbon monoxide-choked cylin-drical tube that extended under the sludgy bottom of the Hudson River. As he jockeyed for position to merge into the single lane of traffic that would carry him from New Jersey across to the New York side, Dave began to feel the familiar nervous excitement welling in his chest. The feeling built and expanded as he drove through the tunnel; it crept up his spine to the base of his skull and down his abdomen into his groin. Coming into Manhattan his breathing became shallower by a degree, the air entering and leaving his lungs in short increments. Dave turned left and made his way around to Tenth Avenue, which took him uptown. He looked at his watch: it was almost five. He turned left on Forty-Fifth Street.

Though beginning its descent, the sun was still up, so the selection was poor; only two girls were working the stroll. He drove past a heavyset black woman in a tight leopard print dress. He thought she looked famil-iar—had he picked her up before? He couldn't remember. On the right at mid-block he saw his quarry. She was in her late teens or early twenties; it was hard to tell. She wore a white mini-skirt that was visibly soiled at the seat, as if she had spent some time sitting on the curb, or one of many tenement stoops that lined the blocks of Hell's Kitchen. A black tee shirt bearing a Guns N'Roses logo had been cut off to expose her stomach from the lower part of the ribcage to a few inches below the navel, which had been pierced with some sort of golden hoop. On her feet she wore a scuffed pair of platform shoes, which appeared to be a half size too large. There were bruises and tattoos of various sizes and colors on her arms and legs; her face, framed by fried yellow hair in a growing-out home perm, wore a vacant, bored expression. Dave pulled the car over to the curb and let the passenger side window down.

"Wanna party?" asked the whore, and then extended a pierced tongue, yellowed from nicotine and dehydration.

"How much?" asked Dave.

"Forty," she said.

"I'll give you twenty," Dave replied, ever the negotiator.

As she got in the car Dave thought about time. In rush hour traffic it would take a good twenty minutes to get halfway across (and a few blocks up) town. But DuVal wasn't going anywhere. He had a show to do. Still, it would have to be quick. They drove together to a nearby parking garage where the streetwalkers had an arrangement with the attendants. Ten bucks and they looked the other way. As he pulled in to an empty space on the second floor, Dave could feel himself getting hard. He gave his passenger a twenty and watched her head descend into his lap, her hands expertly unzipping his fly. As he leaned back in his leather seat he tried for a moment to remember what she had said her name was. Tiffany? Jewel? They all had names like that. He tried to block the thought from his head and surrender to the warm, wet sensation.

FIVE

DuVal reclined in his office chair, rubbing, then opening, his eyes. Diane stood before the desk, studying his face. He looked bad. His eyes were bloodshot, and seemed to be sunken deep into the recesses of their sockets. Dark half-circles sat underneath each orb, heightening the effect. He had evidently forgotten to shave, which was no big deal in radio, but it didn't help make him look less hung over. There was also a drawn look to his face that she hadn't noticed before. Had he lost weight? Granted, DuVal never ate much, but all that beer must have some nutritional value. Or at least some calories, she thought. She tried not to worry about him. After all, he was a grown man and could take care of himself—at least on some basic level.

"Jack," Diane ventured, "I forgot your lighter."

"What?" he replied, as if woken from a slumber.

"I forgot your lighter. It's back at my apartment—I'll bring it tomorrow."

"Don't worry about it," DuVal said in a conciliatory tone, "I've managed to locate some fire." He held up a recently purchased Bic lighter, hoping that the butane-filled plastic vessel might ward off discussion of the previous evening's events. "Anyhow, I probably shouldn't smoke so much today—my voice is a little tired."

"Yeah, you don't sound so good."

DuVal shrugged. "I didn't sleep too well."

"I gathered," Diane replied.

DuVal, sensing a door to a deeper conversation opening, abruptly changed the subject.

"So…Joy McCorkle," he offered.

"Right," Diane said, "I spoke with her publicist. She's in her hotel, and she'll be on time."

"Good."

"Oh, and as it turns out, she's been married three times."

"I didn't read that in her bio."

"It wasn't in there."

"Interesting," DuVal said.

"I thought you might think so," Diane said, as she set a folder of materials on Dr. Julie Davenport, the following night's guest, atop DuVal's desk.

Though she was put out with DuVal (and had intended to tell him as much), Diane, at that moment, was relieved to discover that he had actually taken the time to look at the materials she'd given him the night before. It wasn't something she could always depend on. His nonchalant attitude toward research was a source of recurring tension between them. If DuVal didn't do his homework, it made Diane look bad. And she had told him so often. Given that he had done so this time, she decided to table the discussion about the previous night. For the moment.

DuVal thanked Diane for her diligence. They agreed to speak again before show time—as was their custom—and Diane turned to leave. As Diane shut the door behind her, DuVal lit a cigarette with the cheap plastic lighter and drew the hot smoke deep into his lungs.

"He woke up on the wrong side of the bed this morning," Jeffrey whispered, in a conspiratorial tone that made Diane wonder if he was dishing or fishing.

"He says he's tired," Diane said, her response carefully crafted to deflect either attack.

"He is that," Jeffrey agreed, turning his attention to his computer screen, and typing a salvo of keystrokes.

Jeff77: DuVal and Diane. Fucking?

As she walked away from Jeffrey's desk, Diane heard the telltale sounds of an IM chat. Do assistants ever do any work, she wondered? Around the corner and down the hallway, she ran into Dave Miller. They shook hands cordially, and he bent to kiss her cheek. As he came close to her face Dave whispered in her ear.

"What are you doing later?"

"Call me," she said.

SIX

Diane lay back against a brace of pillows and paged listlessly through a copy of *Glamour*. She had been compelled to purchase the magazine at the newsstand by the bold letters on the cover asking "Are You Drawn To The Wrong Men?" The article was a turgid piece of fluff, but one that described Diane's situation all too well. For her sanity, she had tried to frame the facts in a better light. True, she was sleeping with her boss. Also, at that very moment there was a married man (with whom she was conducting what could only be described as a clandestine affair) on his way over to her apartment. For Claire, a 32-year-old advertising executive, and Alexis, a 27-year-old sales representative, these types of romances had ended poorly. But, Diane tried to reassure herself, those articles were—for the most part—fiction. Her friend Sarah was a freelancer for a several of the most popular women's titles and swore that she, and most of the writers she knew, just made all that stuff up. Plus, Diane felt, her situation was unique. She had no illusions. She was sleeping with DuVal because it was easy and devoid of attachment and entanglement, and Dave was a guilty pleasure, pure and simple.

In yet another case of you-can't-judge-a-book-by-its-cover, Dave Miller had turned out to be a really, really good fuck. He took his time, and he'd get hard if you snapped your fingers. Which was a very good thing, indeed. Except, apparently, if you were his wife. Because to hear Dave tell it, the sexual era of his marriage was long over. As was the affectionate era, the friendly era, and Diane could only imagine, the trusting era. In fact, Diane had gathered, the only thing that kept them together was his job. Regrettably, it seemed, his wife's father owned the agency where Dave was employed. It made sense from Dave's end, but she wondered what his wife got out of the deal.

But what did Diane really know about marriage? Other than that—as much as she and her friends talked about what assholes most men were and how they were better off without them—love, or at least a relationship, was still arguably preferable to solitude. It followed that, daunting as it seemed, she should start looking for a suitable partner. Not a Dave, or a DuVal, but someone who she could settle down with. Someone kind and interesting. With a good job. Sexy, but trustworthy. Someone, in a word, perfect. And that was the problem, Diane knew. She, and her friends (and most of the single people in Manhattan, and the rest of the country for all she knew) had wildly unrealistic expectations. Everyone was looking for perfection; using the slightest flaw as an excuse to walk away from something that might be lasting. And what if she, or someone like her, did find someone who actually was perfect? Wouldn't that perfect person be disappointed with their end of the bargain? It was a puzzle. And a great topic for a show. Not for DuVal, Diane knew. It was more up Dr. Phil's alley. Or Oprah's. Maybe, Diane thought, Oprah was suffering from the same thing. Steadman, if not a beard to cover the often-rumored lesbian relationship with Gayle, seemed like he had it all. But he certainly couldn't measure up in the income department. Who could? Oprah, at last report, made several hundred million dollars a year. And it's not like Bill Gates would be leaving his wife to take up with her. She had priced herself out of the market. Diane tried to put the complicating thoughts out of her mind and concentrate on the matter at hand. Company was coming and she needed to get ready.

To accommodate her sex life—or at least 50% of it—Diane had filled the top three drawers of her dresser with lingerie. She had received help. Dave was an aficionado of bed wear and had gifted her with substantial amounts of the stuff. She was no longer in the position of having to worry about wearing clean underwear in the event of an accident; rather, what had begun to concern her was the possibility of a fire or a burglary and the mistaken impression that any uninvited guests might be given: that she was running a bordello, or simply trying ensure the economic health of an entire industry.

Having set her magazine aside to begin her preparations, Diane slid a pair of white stockings up over her left, then right leg, fastening each in turn to a white garter belt. There was trouble with the hooks on the matching bustier but, in the end, triumph was hers. Next, she applied a fuller face of makeup than she would wear on any other occasion, the final touch of which was a dark matte lipstick she had recently purchased at MAC. She stepped into a pair of white platforms and adjourned to the bathroom to study the effect. She saw, in the full-length mirror, an image that she knew Dave would find titillating. Whorish, yet virginal.

As she admired herself in the mirror, Diane wondered: what am I doing? Sometimes she could compartmentalize better than others; sometimes it was okay to have sex for the sake of sex and not think about feelings or consequences, and other times she felt, well, bad. Not bad like she was beyond redemption, but bad like she was adrift. How could she be so in control at work, and so out of control personally? And with the same people involved in both places?

The buzzer sounded, abruptly shaking Diane from her downward spiral of thought. She made her way to the intercom slowly, careful to avoid a misstep in the unfamiliar height of her heels, and instructed the doorman to send her guest up.

When Dave Miller came through the doorway he was preceded by a white plastic bag, the contents of which Diane determined to be Chinese food. Ah, romance, she thought. He set the bag down on the kitchen counter.

"Hi," he said, then stopped in mid-sentence, allowing his eyes to fall slowly from Diane's face to her feet. She stepped forward and placed one of her hands at his crotch while the other settled at the back of his head. She pulled his face to hers.

After, they lay together naked on the bed. Minutes passed without either uttering a word. One of the advantages of Diane and Dave's arrangement was the comfort with which they could retreat to their own worlds after their trysts. There were no expectations of loving words, and no recriminations over unfulfilled needs. The atmosphere was more akin to what a marathon runner must feel after a solitary, satisfying training session. A warm, endorphin-fueled glow, that—for a string of blissful minutes—banished all worry and care from the mind. As a bonus, Diane's ass and inner thighs felt like she had just spent an hour on the Stairmaster.

Finally, Dave spoke.

"The Arbitrons are up again."

Diane took a deep breath, then replied.

"Do me a favor, Dave," Diane answered, "don't talk about ratings in my bed."

"I was just saying…"

"I know. But can we please leave that stuff at the office?"

"Sure, sure," he replied, rolling himself off the edge of the bed and walking out of the bedroom.

Diane lay alone in the soft light, thinking back to her magazine article. She heard the sound of Dave lifting the toilet seat, followed by a rush of water that tailed off into a few short spurts, which gave way to a few lonely straggling drops. She then listened to the sound of Dave lowering the seat after he had flushed the toilet. Married men, she thought.

Dave visited the kitchen, returning to the bedroom carrying the bag of Chinese food in one hand and a glass of water in the other. He set the glass on the bedside table, then sat on the bed's edge and reached into the bag, pulling a plastic fork and a small cardboard container with thin wire handles from within.

"Pork Chow Fun," he said, as the fork traveled from the container to his mouth. He ate the flat oily noodles quickly and enthusiastically.

"You don't have any Trappey's Red Devil, do you?"

"I don't think so."

"I didn't see any in the fridge, but I thought you might have some in a cabinet somewhere."

"Nope." Diane asked.

Dave stuffed another forkful into his mouth.

"Want some?" he asked, extending the container toward Diane.

"No, thank you."

"Suit yourself."

When he had finished eating, Dave set the empty container on the floor and reached back into the bag.

"Let's see what the future holds," he said, removing a small envelope. He took one of the two fortune cookies out of the envelope and broke it open.

"Don't let passion overcome reason," he read, adding, "it's a little late for that, wouldn't you say?"

Diane shook her head slowly in the affirmative, suddenly lost in thought.

Dave dropped the fortune to the floor beside the remnants of his meal, stood up, and walked toward the bathroom.

"Do you have a towel for me?" he asked.

"In the closet across from the toilet," Diane absentmindedly replied.

Diane took the remaining fortune cookie and set it on the table next to DuVal's lighter. Shit, she thought, I've got to remember to take that to the office tomorrow. She began to tidy up the bedroom, first collecting and consolidating the garbage that Dave had left on the floor. As she picked up the small slip of paper that contained Dave's fortune, she silently read the words. DON'T LET PASSION OVERCOME REASON. Good advice, she thought, I would do well to heed it.

Diane could hear the sound of the shower running in the background like a steady rain. She pictured Dave scrubbing his neck, his arms, his cock and his balls, replacing her scents with that of the soap. What did he tell his wife, she wondered? How late do agents reasonably work? The new deal for DuVal was probably a good smokescreen; there was a lot at stake. Still, his wife must know something is going on. Or at least suspect as much.

SEVEN

"Bastard," Jodi Miller said, aloud, although there was no one else in the kitchen—or the rest of the rambling house for that matter. "Fucking bastard."

She opened the door of the freezer and pulled out a frosted bottle of Belvedere vodka. With an expertly practiced movement, she held the bottle by the neck and unscrewed the metal cap with her thumb and forefinger, pouring three inches of the clear liquid into a highball glass. She liked the way that vodka became more viscous in the freezer, how it poured a bit more slowly and syrupy, and crept down the sides of the bottle in sheets.

She glanced at her wristwatch. The tiny hands of the Cartier tank indicated that it was well past one. She took a long drink from the glass and felt the cold sensation that filled her mouth turn magically warm as it traveled over her tongue, down her throat and into her stomach. As she tilted her head forward, twin beams of light streamed through the kitchen window and across her face.

Dave slid the transmission to P and flipped the driver's side sun visor down as the garage door slid quietly closed behind the Mercedes. He looked in the lighted mirror for traces of lipstick he might have missed while showering. Clean. He turned his head left, then right, sniffing the lapels of his jacket for the lingering odor of perfume. There seemed to be no detectable scent. He flipped the visor back up and turned the ignition key to the off position. He climbed out of the automobile, and listened to the satisfying, expensive "thwump" sound the heavy car door made as it shut behind him. It's good to have money, Dave thought. But his feeling of satisfaction was short-lived. Reaching for the doorknob to let himself in to the house, he watched as it pulled quickly away from his hand. In the doorway stood an angry wife.

"Do you have aaaany idea what time it is?" Jodi Miller asked, her enunciation a bit compromised by the effects of the alcohol.

"Not offhand," Dave answered, knowing fully well it was nearly one-thirty.

She's even more unbearable when she drinks, he thought.

"It's one-thirty in the fucking morning!" she said, "You can't even call?"

"I was working," Dave replied, as he pushed past his wife.

"Working? Working for my father, you mean? My father never worked until 1:30 in the morning," Jodi said, as she followed Dave into the kitchen, a little too closely on his heels. "And he built that agency from a single client into a company with over 900 employees. What are you doing that's so important that you can't call home to tell me you'll be out past midnight?"

Dave reached into the freezer and pulled out the bottle of Belvedere. He held it up in the kitchen light. The bottle was nearly empty. "Well, we've made a little progress on this," he said, largely to himself. He located a high-ball glass and poured himself a healthy drink. At last, he turned to face his wife.

"I told you, this DuVal deal is very tricky. Until we nail it down, there could be some late nights."

"Bullshit."

Dave decided to take a different tack. To go on the offensive, as it were.

"Bullshit? Let me tell you something—the world is a different place than when your father was out there doing deals, it's very complicated."

"Who are you fucking, Dave? Just have the decency to tell me."

"Jodi, come on," Dave said, averting his eyes from his wife's. He found it hard to lie directly to someone's face; and in his business, that inability was a giant, glowing Achilles' heel.

Jodi reached for her husband's crotch, catching Dave off guard. She began unzipping his fly. Dave flinched.

"What?" Jodi asked.

"Nothing," Dave replied, "just a little surprised, that's all."

He wondered if he could possibly get it up. I am so completely un-at-tracted to this woman, Dave thought, and began searching back through his memory for a mental image that might send a trickle of blood down toward his penis. He remembered his parking-lot blowjob from the Hell's Kitchen hooker. While the element of danger that type of assignation con-ferred was erotic in the moment, if offered little sustenance for the task at hand. He jogged his memory forward to the last few hours he had spent with Diane. There we go, he thought—much more fertile ground. As Jodi pulled his penis through the fly of his slacks he felt the beginnings of an erection starting to take hold. It wasn't the firmest foundation, but it would have to do. Dave leaned his head back as his wife lowered herself to her knees. If I can just keep my mind focused, Dave thought, everything could be okay. Suddenly, Jodi was on her feet again.

"What was that all about? Dave asked.

"I just wanted to smell your cock," said his wife, as she turned and walked away, heading toward their bedroom to prepare for what would, for him, almost certainly be a sleepless night.

"Nice." Dave said, pouring the remainder of the vodka into his glass.

EIGHT

The autumn morning sun, magnified as it passed through the window, felt like the head of a match pressed against Diane's skin. She opened an eye and leaned to the side to glance at the clock on the bedside table. 8:45. She had overslept. The gym would have to wait another day. It would get along quite well without her, she reasoned; it usually did. Diane inhaled deeply through her nose. A pungent, sweet-and-sour aroma hung in the still air of the apartment. Chinese food. So very like a one-night stand, Diane thought. It looks good when the lights are low, and loses the bulk of its appeal in the morning. She shifted her weight to roll out of bed. The first of her feet to venture forth found a used condom between itself and the hardwood floor. Shit, she thought, I must've missed that when I was picking up. She elected to deal with it after her shower.

The shower brought back memories of the previous night's activity. Despite his insistence to the contrary, she had a nagging belief that Dave still fucked his wife. This thought popped into her head often when she thought about sex with Dave. Why? What did in matter, under the circumstances? And anyway, it was equally likely, if not more likely, he didn't. Which made her wonder: do all married couples just stop fucking? If so—and many of her married friends had told her that was pretty much the case in their marriages—what were the upsides of that state-sanctioned union? Security? Companionship? What security was there in an institution with a fifty-percent failure rate? And your friends can provide companionship. Assuming you have any, and have the time to see them. Maybe that was the real upside: having a live-in friend who is around when you need them. Without the weird stigma of having an adult roommate.

Dave approached sex with a rare fervor, and a genuine, palpable hunger. A reasonable assumption was that this reflected sexual deprivation. Diane felt that it was largely inappropriate to ask Dave about his marital life, but she was curious. What was proper? She didn't know.

What she did know was that her attraction to unavailable men was a topic to which she had been devoting a considerable amount of thought to in recent months. It was without question a subject that was of great interest to her therapist, Dr. Sammuels, as it had been raised and dissected in many of their weekly meetings.

"Why do you think you continue this pattern?" Dr. Sammuels had asked in their most recent session.

"Low self-esteem. Isn't that what you'd say? That I believe—or feel—that I don't deserve better?" Diane had responded.

"I didn't ask you what I would say, I want to know what you think," the therapist had replied.

"Maybe that's what I think, too," Diane had added.

"Is that what you really think?"

"I don't know," Diane had replied, although what she really thought (and feared) was that she was a walking cliché. One of those women who was irreparably broken in a pedestrian, turn-of-the-millennium, shows-up-in-all-the-women's-magazines kind of way. And that thought made her think that perhaps it might be better to simply accept things at face value. An unexamined life may not be worth living, but too much introspection, in Diane's opinion, was probably not one of the hallmarks of a truly productive person. After all, she was a producer, both in name and in fact. And anything that reduced her productivity was a problem. She decided it would be best to table the internal discussion for the moment, and for many moments after that.

Leaving her apartment, Diane bought copies of the *New York Times* and the *New York Post* at the corner newsstand and then headed to Davo's, her local diner. In the *Times* Diane would find in-depth analysis of the world's events and a challenging crossword puzzle. Unfortunately, those things were virtually useless in her line of work. The *Post*, with its tireless exploitation of human foibles and its jingoistic editorial policy, would give her tangible ideas for highly-rated radio shows. It was also a hell of a lot more fun to read. She decided she would read the *Post* first.

Diane surveyed the room, her eyes quickly scanning a sparse mix of elderly neighborhood denizens and tourists. The morning rush having come and gone, she was free to occupy a larger table. One large enough, at least, to spread out a tabloid, if not a broadsheet. A cylindrical-shaped woman with an impressive up-do who stood behind a cash register on the counter urged her forth.

"Sitwhereveryoulike," she said, with a magnanimous wave of a pen-holding hand.

A sad by-product of the progression of time was that the authentic Greek diner was rapidly fading into the gaping maw of New York's past. It was getting harder and harder to find a regulation diner with its ugly fake-marble formica counters, worn vinyl banquettes, and display case full of cakes that stood seven inches tall and weighed almost nothing. Every corner was now home to a Starbucks, or worse, some new old-looking French bistro where the music was too loud, the service was too affected, and the crowd was too young. Davo's was holding the line, and at least one radio producer was holding it with them.

Diane looked up to the comforting sight of an approaching waiter with a substantial gut and a chest-full of hair so black and thick that you could see it through the cotton/poly blend of his short-sleeved shirt. He set a cup of coffee in front of her in lieu of a greeting. The coffee was thin, and a tablespoon of the brownish liquid had sloshed over the rim of the cup and into the saucer. She looked down at the saucer full of coffee, looked up at the shrugging waiter, and ordered an egg on a roll and home fries.

Diane laid the *Post* on the table, front page up. **ABORT FOES RAP RU-486,** the headline screamed. You could probably get away with an abortion show every three months, Diane reasoned. It was a great topic: extremely divisive, and guaranteed to fill DuVal's core audience with the kind of righteous moral indignation that would light up the phone lines. In a way it was too easy. The challenge was to come up with new material all the time—keep things fresh. And that wasn't too hard either, as far as Diane was concerned. As long as politicians kept fucking things up and lying about it, she figured she would be okay. She did miss the Clinton administration, however. It had offered mountains of easily-packaged material, delivered on a dependable, near-daily basis.

On balance, Diane felt that William Jefferson Clinton had been a good President. Of course, so much of that was circumstance, the luck of the draw. The planets had lined up on the economic side, he swung to the middle, and he'd gone for a nice, smooth ride. Except for the blow job/cigar/intern revelation and the impeachment, arguably.

She occasionally wondered if she actually had any steadfast opinions, other than whether or not specific events or issues would make for good radio fodder. Over time she had come to the conclusion that it was best to disassociate any personal beliefs from what she was helping to spew out across the country over the airwaves. Then, it seemed, she had stopped having personal beliefs. Or she had repressed them so deeply that they were impossible to identify or care about. Did that make her a bad person? She thought about it for a moment but lost the mental thread as a hairy forearm set a worn plate on top of her newspaper. She looked at his name tag. Stavros. Stavros at Davo's. It rolled off the mental tongue.

"Could I have some ketchup, Stavros?" she asked.

"Coming up," he said, with an upward jerk of his chin, turning on his heel to go fetch the condiment.

Where does a guy like that live, Diane wondered? Probably way out in Queens, she reckoned. And what was Queens like anyway? He had probably come from some beautiful Greek fishing village and spent a large part of every day wondering why he ever left. Who knows, maybe he has a great life. And who am I to judge anyway, she thought? I work twelve hours a day and I'm fucking my boss and some married guy. Diane rubbed her forehead.

"Ketchup," Stavros said, and placed the bottle on the table, "anything else?"

"Not right now," Diane replied.

The waiter added up Diane's check and placed it on the table under the edge of her as-yet-untouched plate. Not a sentimental fellow, Diane thought. She twisted the cap on the ketchup bottle and heard a satisfying pop, followed by a short burst of compressed air. Nothing like fresh ketchup, Diane mused, as she turned the bottle upside down and began shaking it furiously to get the first bit flowing.

It was nearly 10:45 when Diane finished her breakfast and her first perusal of the two newspapers. Not much was happening in the world, from her perspective. It wasn't that time was standing still, or that events were not taking place; it was that the same types of things just kept happening over and over. It seemed like war with Iraq was a virtual certainty, for instance, but that had happened just a scant decade before. Whether the coming war was or was not a repeat of the war that had happened in the 90s—or if it did, in fact, happen at all—was immaterial: as far as the show was concerned, it would play well for the foreseeable future.

Diane placed the newspapers in her bag and rose from the table.

"Thankyouverymuchhaveaniceday," her waiter said, in a single, staccato, Greek-inflected burst from behind the counter.

"I will Stavros, and you have a nice day too," Diane said, and then thought to add, "by the way, my name is Diane."

"Okay, honey," Stavros said, and gave Diane a wink that made her want to go home and take another shower.

It just doesn't pay to be nice, Diane thought, as she walked out the front door of the restaurant and thrust her arm into the air to hail a cab speeding uptown on the opposite side of the avenue. The cab swerved across two lanes of traffic and lurched to a halt in front of her. Diane opened the rear door and climbed in, then leaned forward through the partition to tell the driver the cross streets of her destination.

NINE

Cheryl Nevins climbed the steps of the Christopher Street subway station, eager to reach street level. The 2 train from Brooklyn had made several unscheduled stops in the tunnels as it winded its way toward Manhattan, pausing sometimes for a few minutes at a stretch before inching along to the next station. These pauses had been punctuated by various passers-through of the train cars, hawking goods or tales of woe with various degrees of believability, all looking for money. A Chinese man with a cardboard box-load of cheap electronic toys, gum and batteries:

"DURACEL! SIX FOR DOLLA!"

An apparently homeless man with suspiciously new sneakers rattling a change-filled tin cup:

"I am homeless and hungry. My family was burned out of our apartment. I am hungry. I do not rob. I do not steal. Please help me please. A dollar or a dime. Anything you can give. I am homeless and hungry. My family was burned out of our apartment..."

When she transferred to the 1 at Chambers the rate of progress had not been much improved. Cheryl had gotten a late start anyway, and now she was falling even further behind schedule. It had been her hope to clean the lady's apartment and get back home before the kids got out of school. Now, with 11 A.M. approaching, her plan was in jeopardy. She didn't want to ask her neighbor Shaniqua to sit the kids after school, because she was afraid that Shaniqua would think she was getting high again. If that happened, she might get reported to Children's Services and wind up in a fight to keep her kids. Cheryl had been out of Phoenix House for three months, and she hadn't touched the pipe yet. It hadn't been easy, either. Everybody she knew from back in the day was still in the projects. It seemed like nobody ever left. Alive, anyway. Where would they go?

An acquaintance from her building had hooked Cheryl up with a few apartments to clean for cash. It helped her get by. The state paid the rent, and she also got food stamps, but the kids needed new clothes. They wanted video games and everything else that the other kids had too, but most of it they would have to do without.

Cheryl owed people money. She had no idea how much money she had borrowed or stolen from her mother, her friends, and from strangers over the years when she was getting high, but she knew she could never pay them back in full. And not just the money either: she knew it would take a lifetime to repay the kindness that had been extended to her and the kids. Cheryl's mother had taken her three children while she was away. If she hadn't stepped in they would have gone to foster homes.

"I ain't doing it for you," her mother had said, "I don't want my grandchildren living with strangers."

Cheryl had broken her mother's heart. It wasn't the lying, the stealing, or even the drugs so much as it was the notion that she had put herself before her children. It was something her mother—and many of the other women her mother's age in the projects—would never understand. It was shameful. You always took care of your babies, because your family is all you have. A month after Cheryl had come back home, her mother had a stroke and died. It was as if she was waiting to make sure her grandchildren were okay.

Before the rehab, Cheryl had gotten to a place where she didn't care about anything but the rock. She would stay out all night, walking the streets to buy more, and then spend her days in crack houses smoking, dreaming, and sleeping when she could. Once she didn't come home for two weeks. Her kids cried all the time when she did come home and—with her haggard features and flat, lifeless eyes—she barely recognized herself in the mirror.

It was hard to even remember what it felt like to be high. It must have felt good. She knew that it had felt good to her to not care about anything, but those times had been rare. Even when she had been in a cool, dark room, with a rock in the pipe and a few waiting to be smoked, it had been hard to forget that she had children at home.

She wished she hadn't gotten pregnant so young. She loved her children, but she had given up her own childhood too soon. And with no man around it was hard to shoulder the weight.

Cheryl walked through Sheridan Square and down Christopher Street to the front door of the lady's building. The doorman nodded a curt hello as she walked by and passed through the doorway and into the quiet, expansive lobby. There, she would get the keys from another uniformed man sitting behind a counter that stood as a barrier between the lobby and the inner sanctum of the doormen's world: a smallish room that contained a pegboard of numbered apartment keys, a chair, a telephone switchboard, and closed-circuit television screens to monitor the goings-on in the corridors, elevators and the outer perimeter of the building.

"I come to clean 9A," Cheryl said.

"9A?" the man asked, opening a cabinet behind him to reveal the pegboard keys.

"Uh-huh."

"What time do you think you'll be done today?" he asked, holding the keys aloft for a demeaning second before dropping them into her outstretched hand.

"I hope I'm done by three," Cheryl answered, "I'm gonna have to hurry."

"Just remember to drop the keys off when you're done," the doorman said.

What does he think, Cheryl thought, I'm gonna move in and send for my kids?

As Cheryl let herself in to the apartment she smelled Chinese food. It smelled good. She had skipped breakfast and hunger was beginning to take hold of her. She decided to help herself to some cereal; a quick, easy snack that she could eat before starting to work. If there is any cereal to eat in the first place, she thought. She didn't understand women like this one; making all kinds of money and not a bit of food in the house. If I had the money, Cheryl thought, I'd keep the cupboards and the refrigerator full.

In the kitchen Cheryl found a box of Raisin Bran. She checked the refrigerator for milk before she poured herself a bowl. Skim. Who has skim milk on cereal? She filled the bowl with cereal and milk and ate quickly. The skim milk tasted watery. Still, it was better than going hungry. Cheryl finished eating, rinsed the bowl and spoon and began to gather the cleaning supplies. She felt better now. The cereal had taken the edge off. She'd clean the place as fast as she could and get back out to Brooklyn in time to meet the kids as they came home from school. Everything would be okay; she was confident. One day at a time, she thought, one day at a time. All she had to do was the next right thing.

In a little over three hours the apartment was almost done. All that remained was to sweep and mop the bedroom floor; then she could head home. The floors in the rest of the apartment had been swept and mopped and were quickly drying. Cheryl began to sweep the bedroom floor, working her way from one side of the room to the other. As she came around the bed she caught sight of a used condom on the floor. Damn, I hate to touch those things, she thought. She tried to dislodge it with the bristles of the broom, but had no luck; it wouldn't budge. Stuck to the wood, she thought. That shit's like glue when it dries. She went to the bathroom and got some toilet paper, balled the toilet paper in her hand, then snatched the condom from the floor, using the ball of toilet paper to shield the skin of her fingers from the condom and its contents. She stepped quickly back into the bathroom and flushed the ball of tissue and rubber down the toilet. Her man should've done that in the first place, Cheryl thought. But at least she's getting some. And she ain't gonna have a baby.

As the bedroom floor was drying, Cheryl decided to take a break and smoke a cigarette. She opened the bedroom window and pulled the pack of Newports from her purse. Damn, cigarettes are expensive, she thought. Good thing the Koreans in the deli will let you buy them with food stamps. If I had a car I'd take a run up to the reservation. Make a business of it. Cheryl dug to the bottom of her purse in search of a pack of matches. None. She went to the kitchen. Electric stove. Cheryl opened every drawer, but came up empty-handed. Shit, she thought, not a match in the house. Returning to the bedroom, she decided she would gather her purse and head down to the street. As she reached for her purse on the bed, a glint of sunlight—reflected off of a shiny object on the bedside table—caught Cheryl's attention. A rectangular cigarette lighter, next to an un-opened fortune cookie. Did I see those things when I was cleaning the table, Cheryl wondered? Must have been daydreaming. She threw the fortune cookie in a small wastebasket beside the bed, and decided to have a smoke before she got on her way.

At the open bedroom window, Cheryl lit a Newport, inhaled deeply and studied the curious cigarette lighter. It was a heavy, gold lighter with an inscription that read: *A voice is a nice thing, Jack, but you'll never earn a living with it.* She loved the way a lighter smelled after you lit it. It was kind of a tangy, metallic smell, and one that conjured a bittersweet mixture of memories in Cheryl's mind: childhood, her long-dead father, getting high. Cheryl stared out the window and thought about what life might have been like if her father hadn't died, if she hadn't gotten pregnant so young, if she hadn't grown up in the projects, and if she had never tried crack. Lost in thought, she absent-mindedly slipped the lighter into the pocket of her jeans.

TEN

Diane slid out of the elevator and down the hall toward her office, hoping against hope that no one would see her. Why? She didn't have to answer to anyone about her schedule or anything else. Except, of course, ratings. If DuVal was the boss, she was the other boss. And DuVal certainly didn't give a shit about when she rolled in to work. Plus, she had, in fact, been working for the last hour and a half in the diner—combing the newspapers for show ideas—the same thing she would have been doing had she been sitting at her desk. What am I? A 22-year-old P.A., Diane wondered? She didn't understand why she took her job so seriously. Or let it give her so much stress. At this point she could pretty much do the work in her sleep. And it wasn't as if they were saving lives; they were making entertainment. If the show went off the air tomorrow, people would miss it for a week or two, and then something else would come along to fill the early-evening hours of their lives. Some reality show, or a video game, or Internet porn. What did it matter, in the end?

Diane slowed her pace and held her head up high. As she moved further down the hallway, the men's room door opened and DuVal emerged. He was smoking a cigarette. Jesus, Diane thought, the fucking guy smokes in the shitter. DuVal looked up at Diane. "Good afternoon, Diane."

Fuuuuuck you, Diane thought.

"Good morning, Jack. How are you?"

"Find my lighter?"

"Oh, God, Jack, I'm sorry. I forgot to look," she said, truthfully.

"Jesus, Diane. I ask you to do one simple thing," Jack said, shaking his head. He turned and walked away.

"Jack," she called after him, "I'll look for it tonight, I swear. I send myself a reminder e-mail."

Christ almighty, Diane thought, that fucking lighter. She continued down the hall, wondering at how the need to produce fire held such powerful sway over DuVal's mood and psyche. Onward, she urged herself.

Approaching her office, Diane witnessed her assistant Kerri in full glory. She was seated at her desk, situated just outside the door of Diane's office, talking into her headset while typing furiously. The headset was attached to a telephone that was theoretically for business use, but how much of its traffic was devoted to business, or more accurately, its intended business, was anyone's guess. From the side of the conversation Diane could hear, she assumed this was a personal call. More accurately, she hoped it was a personal call.

"Oh my god."

"Oh my god."

"And I was all, 'As if!'"

"Totally."

But the telephone accounted for only one of Kerri's means of communication with the outside world. Diane knew from past observation that, likely as not, Kerri was also currently engaged in several ongoing e-mail exchanges and IM chats. What amazed Diane was not the notion that anyone would want to carry on ten conversations at once (she found this baffling), or how they were able to do so (not well, she suspected), but rather that a person who had absolutely nothing meaningful to say could find ten people to say it to. It boggled the mind.

But finding an assistant was a challenge. It was a delicate balance. Diane had suffered for hiring assistants who were too motivated. In those instances, the assistants had worked a few months and then become bored and inordinately covetous of her Rolodex, or Filofax, as it were. They thought they had paid their dues and wanted to be producers themselves. While their pluck was admirable, in practice this drive was of little use to Diane. Because technically, the producer's job was already occupied. By her.

Near the other end of the spectrum were those like Kerri. Kerri needed a job for the income, but work was also an important cog in the machine of her social life. It gave her an extra phone line, and something else to talk about besides the usual topics of clothing, hair and makeup, shoes, who said what to whom, and which of her friends had hooked up with which guy. Of course there were tangential topics as well: sample sales, television and movies (and the subset of clothing and shoes worn by actresses in those movies), as well as whether the guys they hooked up with were from within or without their circle of acquaintance.

Kerri had been with Diane for almost nine months. She had her faults, but she also had a good memory and was polite to almost everyone who called. On the letter scale, she was a solid C. Average. And average, these days and with this generation, was way above average.

"Good morning, Kerri," Diane offered, as she approached.

"Are you feeling okay, Diane?" Kerri asked, looking up from her computer screen and over the top of her designer-framed glasses.

"Yes, fine, why?"

"You're late, that's all," Kerri added, looking back at her computer screen and typing in a staccato salvo of keystrokes.

"Late?"

"I mean, for you."

"Yes, well, I'm fine. Thank you for your concern," Diane said, walking past her assistant and in to her office.

"I printed out your messages and left them on your desk, but a few more have come in since then. I'll print those out now," said Kerri's disembodied voice from outside the door. This was followed by another burst of typing.

Diane sometimes wondered what became of girls like Kerri. To Diane, Kerri's life seemed like a big wad of cotton candy: sweet, and not much substance. A couple of bites in and you're tired of it and left with a cloying aftertaste that you can't get rid of. On the other hand, Diane thought, who am I to judge? Is my life so great? Maybe being wrapped up

in a web of gossip, one-night stands and popular culture was deeply satisfying on a level she just couldn't comprehend. To each her own, as they say.

Diane slid in to the Aeron chair behind her desk and stared at her
list of messages. Fifty-three messages, not counting the ones Kerri had yet
to print out. Not too bad. She could probably get through her calls in an
hour and a half, maybe two, assuming not too many new calls came in the
interim, and she had no other interruptions. She scanned the list for calls
from Dave. Nothing. For a moment, her heartbeat quickened. Was that
anger she was feeling? Jealousy? She knew that either emotion was utterly
unjustified, but she had to acknowledge that she felt something. Queer.
What the hell, she thought. Why do I ball myself up over these situations
that I know can never work out? It's pathetic. She started to cry. It started
as a lone tear streaming down her cheek and erupted into uncontrolla-
ble sobs.

"Are you okay?" Kerri asked, peeking her head through the open door.

"I'm fine," Diane replied, "I saw something sad on the way to work."

"Oh. I'm sorry."

Kerri backed out of the doorway and gently closed the door behind
her. She settled back into the chair behind her desk and clicked into one of
the three IM windows that were open on her computer desktop, attacking
the keyboard with a blur of manicured fingers.

KerriRules: OMG. MY BOSS IS TOTALLY CRYING.

ELEVEN

Cheryl transferred from the local to the express at Chambers street. The Brooklyn-bound 2 train was crowded for mid-afternoon. The trains were almost always crowded now. Rudy Giuliani had cleaned up the city, and people were no longer afraid of the subway. It was a mixed blessing: unless you boarded at the end of a line, you were unlikely to get a seat. On the other hand, your fellow passengers were much less likely to rob or assault you. She supposed it was a fair trade.

Cheryl was carrying a white plastic bag containing beef with broccoli, chicken with garlic sauce and five egg rolls. On the occasions that she could afford take-out the kids always wanted McDonalds. But they would tolerate Chinese. Cheryl was too tired to cook, and she figured she would avoid an argument by bringing food to the apartment. Beggars can't be choosers, Cheryl's mother used to tell her. The kids could eat as much as they wanted when they got home from school, and have the rest later.

The smell of the Chinese food filled the subway car, and the other passengers cast glances her way, eying the bag as the train tunneled its way under the East River on its way to Fort Greene. A man entered the car rattling coins collected in a tin can and voicing a familiar lament.

"I am homeless and hungry. My family was burned out of our apartment. I am hungry. I do not rob. I do not steal. Please help me please. A dollar or a dime. Anything you can give. I am homeless and hungry. My family was burned out of our apartment…"

At the Nevins Street stop, Cheryl got off the train and scaled the stairs to Flatbush Avenue. When she was younger, Cheryl had often wondered at the relationship between her last name and the street name. She didn't know how long the street had been there, but her mother had told her that her great-grandparents had moved to New York from Kansas City in the 1920s. Had they named the street after them? Did her great-grandparents live in the projects? Had the projects even existed then? Who knew?

The smell of the food had triggered Cheryl's hunger. At her earliest opportunity, she rested the fragrant cargo on the flat top of a street-side newspaper vending machine, pulled the top of the bag open and looked in. There were several small packages piled on top of the entrees below, each containing a fortune cookie, a bag of tea and some condiments. Cheryl opened one of the packages and extracted a fortune cookie. She broke the cookie in half, slipped the paper fortune out of one of the halves and began to eat the other. As she chewed the crunchy cookie, she stretched the fortune between the thumb and index finger of each hand. Reading the small capital letters on the slip of paper, Cheryl's lips soundlessly shaped the words. AN HONORABLE LIFE IS THE ONLY LIFE WORTH LIVING. She folded the fortune in half and put it in her back pocket.

TWELVE

Jodi Miller raised the volume on the CD player in her BMW X-5. As she pulled out of the driveway, "Hotel California" by the Eagles was playing. She loved the song, and the waves of memories it was apt to bring washing over her. Among other things, it reminded her of the times she would accompany her parents on trips to Los Angeles when she was a kid in the late 70s. Before the divorce. They would stay at the Beverly Hills Hotel, and while her father spent the day meeting with clients and making sure the L.A. office was running smoothly, she and her mother would shop at Fred Segal or lay in the sun, ordering sandwiches to be delivered poolside, and feeling glamorous and important.

Turning the corner into traffic, the metallic chime of the cellphone ringer shook Jodi from her nostalgic reverie. She quickly lowered the volume of the music and answered the call.

"Hello?"

"Yes, Jodi?"

"Dr. Sammuels?"

"We were scheduled to meet at 1 today."

"I know."

"Well, it's 1:15 now."

"I know."

"Okay. How soon do you think you can get here?"

"I just left the house."

"I see."

"Can we do it by phone?"

"We could."

"Okay."

"But I think this is something we should look at."

"What?"

"Well, you've told me you're committed to doing this work, but you've been having an increasingly difficult time making it to my office on time, or at all."

"I know," Jodi said, "but I don't want to talk about that right now. I think Dave's cheating on me again."

"Why?"

"He came home at 1:30 last night."

"Where did he say he was?"

"Working."

"Maybe he was."

"*He represents radio talent*," Jodi said, emphatically, as a horn honked, and glancing to the side, she realized that she was perilously close to running into the car next to her. She swerved, honked back, and shot the driver—a fifty-ish man in a Honda Accord—the finger.

"FUCK YOU!" she yelled with exaggerated mouth movements, to better communicate through the glass window of her car door.

"What was that?" Dr. Sammuels asked.

"Some asshole almost hit me."

"Perhaps you should pull over."

Jodi pulled into the driveway of a random house and parked behind a Cadillac Escalade.

"Okay, I pulled over."

"Good. I realize that Dave represents radio talent. Why would that preclude him from working until 1:30?"

"Because it's the ass end of the business, and nobody cares about it."

"Well, it's clear that you feel that way. But perhaps it's important to Dave. And it's certainly important to his clients."

Jodi rolled her eyes. She thought about when she and Dave had first met in college. He was a poor kid from the Five Towns who promoted concerts on campus, and she was a rich kid from Manhattan who barely got accepted (even with a considerable endowment from her father's company) after having been booted from one private school to the next for truancy and generally disruptive behavior. Back then, he booked bands like Television, and XTC; acts that agencies like her father's would never touch. She thought he was cool.

"Jodi?"

"Yeah," she said, as a woman in a Juicy Couture tracksuit emerged from the front door of the house before her.

"Are you still there?"

"Yeah," she replied, was she watched the woman quickly cross the front lawn and square around just on the other side of her car door. Jodi pushed a button and the driver's side window slid noiselessly down.

"Can I help you?" the woman said.

"I don't think so," Jodi replied, adding, "I'm talking to my shrink."

"Jodi?" Dr. Sammuels asked.

"Yeah?"

"What's going on?"

"A woman is offering to help me."

"What woman?"

"The woman whose driveway I parked in."

"I'm expecting company. Do you think you could continue your conversation somewhere else?" the woman asked.

"I suppose so," Jodi said curtly, turning the key in the ignition and abruptly shifting the transmission from P to R. She goosed the accelerator, causing the tires to chirp against the pavement.

"Perhaps we should continue this session later," Dr. Sammuels offered, "what's the rest of your day look like?"

"I'm headed downtown to do some work," Jodi said, backing around into traffic, then shifting to D and punching the accelerator, again causing the tires to chirp.

"Call me after 8 if you want to. I'd like to continue this conversation. If I'm not in the office it will forward to my cell."

"Okay," she said, "I will."

Jodi pressed the End button on her phone, then pressed Talk and 3 in rapid succession to speed dial Pablo Morales.

"Pablo," she barked into the phone after his voicemail picked up, "I'm coming in. Meet me at 265 Henry in 30 minutes."

Bored, Jodi had set out—some years before—to find something to do with her time. She had settled on real estate. Specifically, buying and selling rental buildings in the city. She'd bought her first building in Chinatown in the mid 90s. Now she had several in that area, and several others spread out around the borough. They were all tenement buildings: solid monthly income, and growth on the equity side as well. Especially in the past five years or so. A management company took care of collecting rents, hiring and firing staff, and ensuring that the buildings were maintained. But a couple of times a week she made it her business to drive in to the city, meet with the supers—Pablo Morales being one—and take a walk through the buildings. It was her way of keeping the management company honest. These trips were also opportunities to look at other properties that she might be interested in acquiring, and go shopping in SoHo or on Madison Avenue if she thought she could avoid running in to her mother.

As it turned out, Jodi had a knack for the real estate business. In fact, she figured she probably made more money than most the dickheads she went to high school with; the ones who killed themselves to get good grades so they could go to Princeton and Harvard. But still, she wanted more. She was starting to think about leveraging her tenements to buy bigger buildings. Commercial buildings.

Jodi power-merged into the EZ-Pass lane cutting off a porcine middle-aged man with exceptionally bad hair plugs in a canary-yellow Corvette.

"Fucking loser," she whispered under her breath.

Traffic slowed to a crawl. In the lane next to her was a 15-passenger van carrying 17 passengers, all adults. Jodi stared at the occupants. She was glad to be ensconced in the soft leather upholstery of her fine German automobile. What was it like to have your whole life suck? To be stuck in some 15-passenger van heading into the city to sit in a cube all day? Then she thought of Dave. She was certain he was having an affair. Again. The thought filled her with rage and sadness. She wasn't sure why she stayed with him anymore, other than out of habit. That, and she was scared of being totally alone. She'd lost touch with many of her old friends since they had moved to New Jersey. And her old friends were boring anyway. Most had children, for one thing, and it seemed like that was all they could talk about. Jodi wondered what her life would have been like if she had children. Not that she particularly cared for children. But people had told her that you feel differently about them if they're your own. She wondered if children would have made her relationship with Dave better, or stronger. There was just no way of knowing, she supposed.

Jodi emerged into the daylight on the New York side of the tunnel. Turning south onto Ninth Avenue, she headed downtown. She dialed Dave's number on her cell. Voicemail. Jodi left her husband a message.

"I'm in town today, working. Why don't we have dinner? Call me."

THIRTEEN

Diane sat behind the closed door of her office, wiping the tears from her eyes. Her sobs gradually gave way to a few odd chest heaves, and she stopped crying. She took a deep breath and looked out over the Manhattan skyline.

"I am the producer of one of the most popular radio shows in America," she whispered.

Leaning forward, she took a tissue from the box on her desk and blew her nose.

"What's wrong with me?"

She straightened up in her chair and began the tedious process of returning calls to the people on the list of phone messages that Kerri had printed out for her. Most of the calls were from publicists, agents, and managers pitching ideas for shows. Many of the ideas were unsuitable for radio, or DuVal's show in particular; others were untimely, and a third group—which combined aspects of the former two—just sucked altogether. Conjoined-twin seven-year-olds, she read, recently and successfully separated, who walk, eat and sleep with their heads together as if still joined by flesh and bone. Interesting, Diane thought, but it wouldn't play for more than thirty minutes on radio. Perhaps DuVal could spin it into a political joke/metaphor about the Democratic and Republican parties. She made a note on her notepad.

Diane had instructed Kerri to get enough information about the pitches to enable her to make spot decisions. This allowed Diane to return calls left by B- and C-list publicists with a short word to their assistants. A-list publicists, those with heavy client lists, Diane would speak with directly.

The publicists, both male and female, were very much like those sad, almost-popular girls in high school. The ones whose desperation was masked beneath a shimmering veneer of enthusiasm. In a lifetime of wearing the right clothes, going the right places and doing the right things, these creatures would never realize their only ambition: to be the person everyone was looking at and talking about. They were precious little flowers whose only sunlight would forever be of the reflected kind. Each conversation and every inflection worked to bolster or chip away at the fragile egos of these perpetually adolescent souls. And although Diane loathed the task, she knew that flattering the publicists was the only way to ensure landing clients when they were hot. It was a never-ending dance.

By early afternoon Diane had managed to make her way through the entire list of messages Kerri had provided, all while juggling incoming calls and researching story ideas that had come to her while reading the morning papers. Thank god for the Internet, Diane often thought. An entire world of pulp at your fingertips, delivered at nearly the speed of light. Or faster than paper could be printed and shipped, anyway. Googling "abortion" for instance, would return millions of results, which ran the gamut from hard news stories to court cases to scholarly and scientific reports to quasi-religious manifesto sites coded, apparently, by the home-schooled children of separatist militia members in the upper reaches of Idaho. It was a treasure-trove of radio fodder, pre-digested and waiting to be spoon-fed to the adoring fans of Jack DuVal.

Diane's stomach began to growl. After several hours of intense concentration, hunger was setting in. Lunch was always a conundrum for Diane. She could order in and eat at her desk (an option she availed herself of far too often), she could grab something from the company cafeteria, or she could actually go outside the building. The third option, while certainly the most appealing, presented its own range of options and problems. Those included: the amount of time she could reasonably spend away from the office without being overwhelmed by the volume of missed calls she would need to sift through upon her return; the vast number of restaurants nearby and the decision-making process involved in choosing one; and lastly, should Diane elect to have lunch alone (which she did enjoy), she would have to deal with the slightly less-than feeling (and she was ashamed of feeling this way, or that it was an issue to her at all in this city, in this day and age, at this point in her professional career) of being the lady-who-is-having-lunch-by-herself. Fuck it, she thought, I'm going out. She called Kerri's extension.

"My calendar's clear for the next two hours, no?"

"Looks that way," Kerri replied.

"I'm going out for lunch."

"K. What about calls?"

"Don't forward any."

"K."

On the way out of her office, Diane stopped at Kerri's desk.

"Can I get you something while I'm out? A sandwich? A salad, or something?"

"Oh, no thanks," she answered, diverting her eyes momentarily from the computer screen as an IM alert chimed.

"You're sure?" Diane prodded, "it's no trouble."

"Um, I'm not hungry yet. But I could use some tampons…if you think of it," she said, digging into her purse for money. "Tampax Super," she added.

"Don't worry about it," Diane said, crinkling her nose and holding a hand up as she turned and hurried toward the elevator. Who takes their boss up on an insincere offer of kindness, she wondered, as she pressed L as watched the doors close.

Thirty floors down, Diane walked the two-block distance to a dependable local bistro. She settled in to a small table on a long banquette and turned off her cell phone. A wild and reckless act of rebellion, in her line of work. She perused the menu. It looked familiar, partially because she had been there before, and partially because it offered roughly the same range of options as many if not most of the other restaurants she frequented in town: grilled salmon with some kind of a sauce, a roast half-chicken with mashed potatoes and sautéed spinach, hanger steak with fries, a Caesar salad, so on. Restaurants were starting to seem like those third-generation punks that hung out on Avenue A, bravely going where so many had gone before. She ordered the salmon and opened her bag to look for some suitable reading material.

Diane's bag was more akin to a piece of luggage than a typical purse. In terms of the purpose it served, at least. It was, to be fair, a purse—albeit of the large variety—if having a single strap and having been designed to be carried over the shoulder were the criteria for that distinction. Fully loaded, however, it held over a cubic foot of cargo and weighed in excess of ten pounds. The purse was a source of continual back pain for Diane, and considerable discussion and amusement amongst her friends. The problem was paper. A single piece weighs little. Thousands of pieces, a good deal. And Diane carried thousands of pieces. Magazines, newspapers, books. Tissues, notepads, envelopes. An old Filofax she had owned since she graduated from college, before—she shuddered to think—the Palm Pilot was even invented. Diane loved paper. She avoided electronic devices as much as she was able. Yes, she used a computer, wrote and received e-mails and so forth, but she also still wrote memos to her staff. On paper. If you feel strongly about something, she thought, commit it to a medium that has some longevity. Those ones and zeros so dependent upon electricity, to her way of thinking, were not the place to safeguard thoughts, ideas or history. Or even addresses and phone numbers, for that matter. What if the information on the Dead Sea scrolls, for instance, had only been captured on an 8-inch floppy disc? How would you retrieve it now?

Diane pulled a copy of *InStyle* out of her bag and began paging through the magazine in an impatient, distracted manner. Jesus Christ, she thought, is there any content in this thing? Fifty pages of ads before you get to the masthead. "Fuck it," Diane muttered, closing the cover and thinking, I know more than enough about Kate Hudson for one lifetime.

"Excuse me?" Diane heard a voice say.

She looked up, and glanced toward the direction of the voice. A man—a not unattractive man—sat alone at the next table on the banquette. He was in his late 30s, dressed in a casually fashionable manner (mostly black and brown) and had a full head of dark, wavy hair specked with the odd strand of gray.

"I said *fuck it.*"

"Fuck what?" he asked.

"Um, *InStyle,*" Diane answered, looking down at the tome in her hands.

"*InStyle*, the magazine?" he asked.

"The same," Diane said, holding it up for his perusal.

"I only read it when I have to," the man said, "too many ads."

"Exactly," Diane exclaimed, then asked, "When do you have to?"

"You know, waiting in the dentist's office, getting a haircut, that kind of thing."

Diane laughed.

"I see," she said.

The man introduced himself. He said his name was Roy Eldridge, and he was a documentary film and television segment producer who had recently returned from a six-month shoot in Manipur, India.

"What were you working on?" Diane asked.

"A piece about the relationship between HIV transmission rates and the proximity of the Golden Triangle drug trail," Roy answered.

"Sounds interesting."

"It was."

"Will you go back?"

"Not unless I have too," Roy replied, laughing. "I like comfort."

"That bad?"

"India is a fantastic place. Wonderful people. But so many problems. Poverty, disease, overpopulation. I'm glad I had the experience, but to be completely honest, I'm ready for the next place."

There's something likable about this guy, Diane thought. She listened attentively to his stories about India, and told him bits and pieces about her own work.

"Talk radio," she said, "is like putting a stethoscope to the heart of the country."

"And what does it sound like?" Roy asked.

"Like it needs to stop eating crap."

They talked about the kinds of things they liked to read, and where they looked for inspiration and ideas. Roy was only slightly familiar with DuVal. He said he knew the program by reputation, but not as an actual listener. Talking to this man, who was attractive and smart—and a producer of apparently serious work—Diane felt a rare pang of shame. She had an ongoing internal dialogue about the nature of her work. This dialogue was fueled—and kept forever at arm's length from resolution—by her stubbornly ambivalent philosophy (or more accurately, philosophies) of life: on the one hand, she thought, we're only alive for a very limited amount of time. Every second on earth is precious; each decision made and every action taken has great weight and importance. This line of thinking made her get up in the morning and go to the gym, try to be as honest as possible, and pray once in a while. On the other hand, she thought, we're all going to die, so nothing matters at all. It was this mindset that allowed her to order steak frites at 11 P.M., stay out late at night drinking martinis, and ultimately led to sleeping with married or otherwise unavailable men. Yin and Yang. Dr. Jeckyl and Ms. Hyde.

Diane decided to postpone any further introspection and concentrate on the matter at hand. Her plate half-empty, and what remained cold, she subtly made the air-check hand gesture to her waiter who was chatting with the bartender on the other side of the room. She took a deep breath and turned to her impromptu lunch companion.

"Listen, Roy. I have to get back to the office, but I'd love to continue this conversation. If you don't have a girlfriend or a wife, I'd like your phone number so I can call you sometime."

"I'd love to see you again," he answered. "I was trying to get up the courage to ask you for your card."

Diane tore a piece of paper from her Filofax and slid it and a medium-point Uniball pen across the top of Roy's table.

"Nice pen," Roy said, as he carefully wrote his number on the unlined sheet.

"Thanks," Diane said, "I like pens."

FOURTEEN

DuVal lowered himself into his chair and eased his headphones on—careful not to cuff the sides of his pounding head. He was hung over. Again. And he had left the studio the night before with the best intentions: go home, order dinner in, watch a little TV in bed, and then sleep. It had been a long day; one that involved recovery from a previous hangover, a small degree of remorse over the exchange of harsh words with his ex-wife, and a fair amount of puzzlement about what his post-coital telephone conversation with Diane might have encompassed. On top of everything else, he had struggled through the day with a nagging sore throat. Because of the sore throat, he had decided—when he finally got through his front door—to help himself to a generous snifter of Cognac. Something warm and smooth, a beverage that could ease the soreness in his throat and help the relaxation process begin. And a beginning it turned out to be. The beginning of several hours of solitary drunken reverie where the past was dissected and examined, and the future was imagined as many different paths and permutations. And, of course, the pack-and-a-half of smokes needed to round out a proper session.

DuVal shook a cigarette from an open pack and instinctively reached into his left-front pocket for his lighter. Realizing anew that the cherished object was missing, he gritted his teeth and searched for a pack of matches. DuVal was becoming increasingly annoyed and uneasy. It was not good to start a show in a state of high agitation; this he knew from bitter experience. It could wreck the pace of an entire program. And standing between DuVal and any hope of becoming calm was an unlit cigarette.

"COULD SOMEBODY GET ME SOME FUCKING MATCHES?" he shouted, to no one in particular. In point of fact, he was not screaming at no one in particular. DuVal was still angry that Diane had not brought his lighter in to the studio that morning, especially after forgetting it the day before. He was certain that it was an act of passive aggression, perhaps related to the drunken phone conversation that he couldn't remember. Of course DuVal shouting for *someone* to get him some matches was (if one were to play armchair analyst), an act of passive aggression itself. Because that someone would almost certainly be Diane. But he couldn't bring himself to shout directly at her. It wasn't DuVal's style and, somewhere deep down inside, in a place that hadn't yet broken through to his conscious mind, he knew it was partially his fault for leaving the lighter at her apartment in the first place.

Diane dutifully secured a pack of matches and brought them to DuVal.

"Here you go," she said, and watched as he immediately lit his cigarette and took a long, deep drag, the force of which caused his cheeks to collapse in toward the centermost point of his head.

"Thanks," he said in full voice, the smoke lodged so deeply in the recesses of his lungs that not a whisper of it escaped from his mouth.

"Julie Davenport is in the green room, Jack. When do you want me to bring her in?"

DuVal considered the question for a second, then blew twin cylinders of smoke from his nostrils as he replied.

"Just before I introduce her."

DuVal rarely liked to speak with his guests before or after a show, but it did happen. And Diane could never predict which ones he wanted to grace with actual conversation. Once he had become enraged when she hadn't brought Ralph Nader in early. It turned out DuVal had always had a soft spot for the guy. Who knew? From that point on, Diane figured it was best to just ask.

"Five minutes, then," she said, as she headed for the studio door to make her way down the hall to the Green Room, where Dr. Julie Davenport patiently awaited her turn to be embraced or pilloried by Jack DuVal.

"Fine," DuVal answered, as he exhaled another long breath of blue smoke into the still, darkened air of the studio.

Most guests were aghast at how thick with smoke the studio was when they entered the room. But they fought to get on the show, because an hour with DuVal, even an hour of combative humiliation, could put your book on the *New York Times* bestseller list, or help your movie open, or raise money for whatever cause you might be pushing.

Diane entered the studio and showed Julie Davenport to her chair opposite DuVal. A production assistant had already set a few sponsor-provided bottles of water on the tabletop in front of Dr. Davenport's seat, but Diane asked if she would like a cup of coffee or a soda before the interview began.

"No, water is fine," Dr. Davenport replied.

Though she had already done so in the Green Room, Diane again explained the format of the show.

"Okay. Just to review, Dr. Davenport. DuVal will open with a monologue, then introduce you. There will be a short commercial break, which will be followed by anywhere from 20-40 minutes of interview slash discussion. We'll do another commercial break, and then open up the phone lines to callers."

Over the years, Diane had found that if guests were nervous or unsure, this repetition of the schedule sometimes calmed them. It also saved her from having to make conversation with the guests. It was awkward: Diane usually could predict in advance what type of questions DuVal would ask, and she sometimes felt like an accomplice to an attack.

"Any questions?"

"No, thank you," Dr. Davenport said, as she adjusted her headphones around an abundance of straightened, auburn hair.

"Very well, then."

"Interesting interview with Joy McCorkle last night," Dr. Davenport mused.

"Uh-huh," Diane answered in a non-committal fashion, precluding any possibility of conversation with the guest.

The engineer cued DuVal, and the broadcast began. "Hello America, and good evening. You're listening to Jack DuVal, and I'll be your host tonight and every night here on the American Radio Syndicate," DuVal, announced, then paused to take a long drag from his cigarette. A pensive expression came over his face.

"I was thinking about my parents today, and how difficult it must have been for them when I first came along. They were young—didn't have any money to speak of—and my father had just gotten out of the service. I'm not sure if they ever went hungry, but I know there were many times when they were counting their nickels to pay the rent."

DuVal began a long rhapsody about a youth defined by doing without, and the warm, loving home that his parents had provided in the face of semi-epic obstacles while his father labored and saved to start his own business. It was a good story, and like all good stories, it was based on a true story. He told this story when it would help drive the narrative of the show, and adjusted it to suit the topic. In this instance, he elaborated on the youth of his parents, and their brave decision, in spite of that youth (and the sacrifices they must have known they would face), to bring a new life into the world. It was a familiar story; one that anyone in the audience could easily identify with. And because of Jack's success it had what was apparently a spectacularly happy ending. That DuVal had barely spoken to his father in ten years was, in the end, very much beside the point.

"We have a very distinguished guest with us here tonight. Her name is Dr. Julie Davenport, and she is President of Planned Parenthood. Good evening, Dr. Davenport."

"Hello, Mr. DuVal," Julie Davenport said.

"Please, call me Jack," DuVal said, in a warm, welcoming voice.

"As I was thinking about this show, I got to wondering: Do you ever lie awake at night thinking about the thousands of fetuses that are aborted each year because of your efforts? Because even if I were pro-abortion—and I'm not—I think it would bother me."

"Well, Mr. DuVal, that's an interesting question," Dr. Davenport replied, "our organization, as you know, is devoted to *successful* parenthood. *Planned*, successful parenthood. So, to the extent that we ever make young women aware of their right to safe, legal abortion, we do so as a last resort."

DuVal went on to question Dr. Davenport about her marital history (two marriages, both failed) going so far as to suggest that her inability to commit to a man and the permanence of marriage was somehow related to her affiliation with an organization that advocated the avoidance of one of the most significant commitments human beings make—parenthood.

Dr. Davenport, for her part, gave as good as she got. She refused to answer DuVal's question about her own reproductive history, on the grounds that it was an outrageous invasion of privacy. She also suggested DuVal might be guilty of hypocrisy.

"And what about your marriage, Jack?" she had asked, "I thought divorce was a no-no for the family values crowd. Or does that just apply to other people?"

It was a tense, quietly rousing exchange.

Most of the callers were card-carrying right-to-lifers, but Dr. Davenport found some support peppered amongst DuVal's loyal listener base and those who had tuned in while driving, valiantly searching for something on the airwaves that might keep them from falling asleep at the wheel. Abortion was, after all, as divisive an issue as it had ever been. And even in a time of looming war, corporate malfeasance, and a stock market meltdown, true believers on either side of the argument could be counted on to chime in.

By the end of the broadcast DuVal was shot. He had smoked his way through the better part of an entire pack of cigarettes, and his voice, as well as his energy, was flagging. He repaired to his office after the show, and retrieved a bottle of Bunnahabhain 25 he kept in the lower drawer of his desk. On most days, the fact that he could keep a bottle in his office and have a drink at will was a source of pride and pleasure. But on this occasion, it just seemed necessary. As he poured three fingers of the amber liquid into a coffee cup, Diane appeared in the doorway.

"Well," she said.

"That was a rough one," DuVal replied.

"I thought it went okay," Diane lied.

"It wasn't what I expected."

"What is?" Diane asked, and then told DuVal that unless they needed to discuss anything else, she was going to head home.

"Want to go for a drink?" DuVal asked.

"Not tonight, Jack," Diane said, "I'm a little tired. And anyway, it looks like you've started without me."

"What's on deck for tomorrow?" DuVal asked, ignoring the dig.

"It's in the folder on your desk. It's a story about some Swiss biologists cloning a man from a severed penis."

"What?"

"Just kidding," Diane said, "We've got a gun shop owner who is being sued because a ten-year-old shot himself with a gun he sold the father."

"Jesus," DuVal said, "I think I'd rather have the cloned cock man.

"Oh, really?" Diane said.

DuVal laughed. He opened the top drawer of his desk and pulled one of several unopened packs of cigarettes from within. "Diane?"

"Jack?"

"Try to remember to bring my lighter tomorrow."

"Will do."

Diane said goodnight and shut the door behind her as she left. DuVal picked up the folder, then set it back down on the surface of his desk. He lit a cigarette and refreshed his drink. It had been a long day; he was tired and his throat was sore, but he had nowhere to go and nothing to do. He picked up the folder again and started to read.

FIFTEEN

The night air feels nice, Cheryl Nevins thought, as she crossed DeKalb, working her way towards Flatbush Avenue. She had decided not to cook, opting instead for take-out. It was the second night in a row she had bought, instead of prepared, food. She'd felt a momentary pang of guilt. But after cleaning two apartments in a day it was sometimes hard to find the energy to cook a meal. Besides, she told herself, I've got a little cash in my pocket now; I can afford it.

It was good to walk. The act of breathing in fresh air—or at least the air that was available on the densely populated eastern edge of Brooklyn— was a simple pleasure she had come to enjoy. She'd been off crack for over two years and during the process of getting clean had pretty much relearned how to live life. She had to. And she also had to be careful. This she knew. Cheryl understood that the temptations of the street still pulled at her, especially after dark. Night itself was a trigger for her, and it came every day without fail. It took vigilance to stay off crack. Especially in Fort Greene. People, places, and things, as they said in her NA meetings.

"You gonna hit a room tonight?" her sponsor had asked, when she'd called to check in before stepping out.

"I can't get a sitter."

"Can't, or won't?"

"Can't."

"Don't pick up. Go to meetings."

"Uh-huh."

"I mean it."

"Me too."

"Meeting makers make it."

"I know."

"If your ass falls off, pick it up, put it in a paper bag, and take it to a meeting."

"I know, I know."

"I know, I know, I know. You got Bill Withers disease now?"

"What?"

"Never mind. Hit a meeting."

"I will."

She had left the children alone in the apartment. They would be fine for thirty minutes or so. LaShawna was nearly eleven, and old beyond her years. The eighteen months Cheryl had spent away from the family in rehab had given her a quiet seriousness, and an unshakeable sense of responsibility. In some ways, Cheryl knew, LaShawna's childhood was over. She had the natural maternal instincts that came with being a girl and the oldest child. Those instincts had only been sharpened when she had to fend for herself, her brother and her sister during Cheryl's addiction and her time away. And then there was the matter of trust. It broke her heart every time Cheryl was reminded that LaShawna didn't trust her.

"Where are you going?" she'd asked when Cheryl had announced her intention to go get take-out.

"To get food," Cheryl had answered, "like I told you."

"But where?" LaShawna had pressed.

"Flatbush Avenue," Cheryl had replied, struggling to contain the hurt and anger rising within her as her child questioned her.

"You're coming back soon, right?" her daughter had asked, with a steely look in her eyes.

"Yes, baby," she'd replied, "I promise."

Fort Greene had changed a great deal over the previous two years. Having been away, Cheryl was more keenly aware of those changes than people who had watched them happen in increments as one day gave way to the next. East of Ft. Greene Park on DeKalb, what had once been a liquor store was now a fancy little restaurant. White couples sat inside, eating small plates of food and drinking wine. Beside it was a Moroccan restaurant with long, red velvet curtains in the windows, blocking the interior from view. Two real estate agencies had opened on LaFayette. The prices of the apartments listed on printouts in the windows filled Cheryl with awe. A one bedroom for $250,000! In Fort Greene! Who had that kind of money anyway? And why would they spend it to live here, she wondered? If she had that kind of money Cheryl would get the hell out of Brooklyn. Or at least move to Park Slope.

The projects, as nearly as Cheryl could tell, hadn't changed one bit. She still saw the same people doing the same kind of shit. Boys grew into men (or older boys, in her opinion), they got themselves sent to prison, shot or stabbed. Girls had babies and took care of them on their own. Nobody seemed to learn a thing. A lucky few got out, and they never looked back. More than just about anything, Cheryl wished she could be one of them.

Rehab had given Cheryl reason to hope. She had kicked crack and earned her high school diploma, and now that she was back home she was starting to think about trying to take some classes at City University. Above all, she was determined to get her children out of the projects. She would have to act fast. LaShawna was headed into middle school soon, and Tawanna and Antwon were both in grade school.

At the corner of DeKalb and Flatbush Cheryl took a moment to think. She surveyed her surroundings as trains rumbled underfoot. A line of cars on Flatbush waited for the traffic light to change, as others on DeKalb flew past, engines racing, horns howling. She saw a KFC, a Kennedy Fried Chicken, a Chinese restaurant, a Chinese Mexican food restaurant and a McDonald's all within steps of the intersection. Chinese Mexican food was a new thing to Cheryl. Small Chinese-run taquerias had sprouted up all over town in her absence. They offered decent food at low prices, but she couldn't figure out how it had started. It was a mystery. After considering her options, she decided to go for the old standby—McDonald's. The kids would be happy. They would eat McDonald's three times a day if they had their way. For the rest of their lives. Most of the time, all they really wanted was those little plastic toys. They'd eat half a burger and leave the rest sitting on the paper wrapper.

As she approached the restaurant, an emaciated man in a tattered coat four sizes too large extended a dirty hand holding a cup full of change and opened the door for her. Cheryl dug into her purse and found a quarter, then dropped it in the cup.

"Thank you. God bless," the man said.

Looking briefly at his face, Cheryl thought she recognized him from when she was on the streets. She stepped inside.

"YO CHERYL!" a voice called from a table nearby.

"Yo Anthony," Cheryl replied, spotting a man in a fur-lined hooded parka, baggy jeans, and a too-large sports jersey. A heavy, diamond-encrusted pendant hung from around his neck.

"What up?"

"Getting some dinner for my kids," she said to the man, a neighbor she had known since she was a child herself.

"I feel you. You know my son, Shaquille?" he asked, pointing across the table at a six year-old version of himself, right down to the cornrowed hair.

"Hi Shaq," Cheryl replied, waving and adding, "see you later, Anthony."

"Aahight," he answered as she walked forward to get in one of the lines to place an order.

The lines were long; ten deep, mostly black people. She recognized many faces from the projects. A few white kids in their 20s were clumped together in a bunch. The line was loud with voices—people talking on cell phones, gossiping and disciplining their children. As she waited she started to worry about the kids. Cheryl reassured herself that they would be fine. Looking around, she realized she needed to get a cell phone. She made a mental note to herself to look into it in the morning. Price one out.

Ten minutes later, with a bag of burgers, fries and sodas in hand, Cheryl emerged on to Flatbush Avenue and took a deep breath. She was relieved to be back outside. For a brief moment while she was in line she thought she had seen Antwon's father. She knew that was impossible, that he was long gone, but for that fleeting second her heart had jumped into her throat. All these children with no daddies, she thought. Men.

Cheryl decided to walk back home a different way. Lately, when she was walking to a regular cleaning job she would take different street routes if she had time, just to see new things. It had recently dawned on her that she had lived in New York all her life and she didn't even know her way around Manhattan. There were entire neighborhoods where she had never been. Tribeca and Soho, for instance—because of a loft she cleaned on Greene Street—were new discoveries. She had been to one museum in her life: the Metropolitan Museum of Art on the Upper East Side. It was on a field trip in fifth grade, and it was also one of only four or five times she had been to Central Park. Her life had been lived almost entirely in Brooklyn. And in some of the worst, most depressing parts at that. Bed Stuy, East New York. The projects, the street corners, the alleyways and the crack houses. Where the dealers dealt, and where the addicts used. It was sad. Her life so far had been incredibly small, circumscribed by bad choices. But that could, and would, all change. Now that she was clean, she was determined to see a different side of the city, and maybe even different parts of the country and the world. She wanted that for her children, she wanted that for herself, as well. Anything was possible. That's what they said in the rooms, and Cheryl was beginning to believe it.

She walked west along Flatbush toward the Manhattan Bridge. On any one of several streets past the base of the bridge she could turn right and make her way toward the familiar brick sameness of the Walt Whitman houses. She tried to remember if she would have a nice view of the East River and the Manhattan shoreline as she took that route. Either way, she thought, I'll at least get a glimpse of the skyline.

The skyline without the World Trade Center was a strange thing for Cheryl to behold. It was as if the front teeth of the city had been knocked out. She'd been at Daytop when the attack had taken place, and the residents had all clustered around the television to watch the news. Cheryl was frantic until she was able to talk to her mother and learn that her children were safe, and was only marginally calmer after speaking with her. She had ached to be with her family, to ease their fears, and her own. It was one of the only times she had challenged the counselors in group.

"I gotta go home now," she'd said.

"Now is not a good time," replied Caroline Hurst, a bushy-haired social worker with thick glasses, chronic bad breath, a thick middle, and a robust collection of fanny packs and ankle-length denim skirts.

"Not a good time! When's a fucking good time?"

"When your treatment is complete."

"If it's the end of the world, I don't care about my fucking treatment. I want to be with my family," Cheryl had said, then started to sob.

"The world isn't ending," Caroline had answered, "and you're no good to your family if you relapse."

Michael, a gaunt white junkie from Staten Island, had put his arm around her and held her while she cried.

As Cheryl walked toward the river, there was increasingly less surface light from stores and street lamps. She looked up at the sky and was able to make out a few stars. Upstate at Daytop the sky had been blanketed by stars, and Cheryl had been amazed at what she had been missing all her life. One of the guys in the facility had taken some astronomy in college and told her that the stars she saw in the night sky were actually millions of years old. Even billions. Or rather, the images of those stars that appeared to their eyes were. He said that some of the stars they saw may have even burned out by the time she saw them, standing, as they were, on the surface of the Earth. The stars, even the few that were visible—and even if they had burned out—were a nice reminder of the life that had been given to her by getting off drugs. A life of choices. At least more choices than she had before.

Cheryl crossed Tillary on Flatbush and decided she would head north at the next corner. Nassau Street would take her straight to the Whitman Houses. Under the light of a streetlamp she set the McDonald's bag down and unzipped her purse to find a cigarette. She opened the pack of Newports, removed a cigarette and placed it between her lips. Reaching into the pocket of her jeans, she felt the gold lighter. *Oh shit*, she thought, that lady Diane is going to think I stole it. *Damn.* I'll have to call her when I get home. Explain what happened. She lit the Newport and took a long mentholated drag, wondering how she could tell it so the lady wouldn't think she was lying. She'll never believe me, Cheryl thought, no matter what. *I won't call her. It would only fuck things up.* And if asked, Cheryl decided, she would say she'd never seen the lighter. That was the only way. Shaking her head, she put the lighter back in her pocket. Then, she picked up the McDonald's bag and started back on her way.

The blow hit Cheryl with such force that it knocked her to the ground, spilling the contents of the McDonald's bag. As Cheryl tried to figure out what had happened, she saw burgers in wrappers before her on the sidewalk, and the fries that had been shaken loose from their cardboard containers formed a trail from the sidewalk into the street. Her ears were ringing. She turned to see two heavyset female figures standing over her, one with a baseball bat in her hand.

"YOU FEELING THAT, BITCH?"

Confused, Cheryl started to gather the burgers from the sidewalk. One of the heavyset young women ripped the purse from the prone Cheryl's shoulder, unzipped it, and began rifling the contents. As the young woman located the wallet within, Cheryl lunged to grab the purse from her hand.

"That's my money," Cheryl pleaded, "I worked for it. I need to feed my children."

"It's mine now," the woman said, kicking Cheryl in the stomach, then laughing.

The other figure took a roundhouse swing at Cheryl's head with the bat, connecting across her cheekbone and temple. The impact of the wood on Cheryl's skull made a curious sound, like a watermelon splitting open after a 10-foot drop. Cheryl fell to the ground bleeding from her nose, her mouth and her ear. The last thought she ever had was that she'd broken her promise to LaShawna. Because she wasn't going to be home soon, after all.

The two figures descended on Cheryl's supine body like animals in the wild, quickly and expertly foraging for anything of value they might find. From the left front pocket of Cheryl's jeans, one of the young women pulled the gold lighter inscribed with DuVal's father's words.

"That shit's gold," she said, as they walked off into the darkness of the Brooklyn night.

SIXTEEN

Dave and Jodi Miller had agreed to meet at Le Colonial at eight o'clock. The 57th St. restaurant was a common meeting place for the married couple on days that Jodi was in town. The food was Asian-influenced and good, and the location was convenient to his office and some of her favorite designer shops on Madison Avenue.

Dave was early by half an hour, so he positioned himself at the bar upstairs. As he squared himself on the padded barstool, a woman in her twenties—whose nose had been sculpted to a tapered, sloping form resembling a miniature ski-jump—forced her way into the space between Dave and the next barstool.

"I'd like an, aaaahhhhhhuuuuummmmmmmmmm, applemartini," she said, compressing the pair of words into a single, poorly enunciated stew of soft vowel sounds.

"What's an apple martini?" he asked, as the bartender turned to mix the concoction.

"It's the BEST!" the young woman replied.

"What's in it?" Dave prodded.

"Aaaahhhhhhummmmmm, aaapple and something else."

"I see," Dave nodded.

He waited until the bartender returned and ordered a double Grey Goose on the rocks. He took a look around the room. Thirty versions of the same guy: short hair, well-defined physique, narrow-cut slacks with a fitted shirt worn with the tails out talking to, or trying to talk to, thirty versions of the same girl: tight, low-waisted jeans—flared at the bottom, pointy shoes with three-inch heels, one-to-three inches of waist exposed, straightened hair, straightened noses.

He took his cell phone out of his jacket pocket with the intention of checking his voice mail and returning a few calls, but the music in the bar proved to be far too loud for him to accomplish any work. What is it with the music in restaurants and bars anyway, Dave wondered? It's bad enough that there are no songs, per se, just an endless loop of idiotically simple chord progressions sitting on top of relentlessly throbbing beats; it also has to be played at the volume of a jet engine at takeoff. It stands to reason, he thought. It's like people—the less they have to say, the louder they talk. Popular music, it occurred to Dave in this transcendent moment of clarity, is now officially devoid of ideas. The exact moment that the well had run dry, Dave now realized, could probably be traced back to the day that the first review of a "performance" by a DJ had been published. It's just a matter of time, he remembered thinking, until they start reviewing the projectionists in the movie theaters.

"The music's great here!" Ski-Jump Nose offered, as she waited for her apple martini.

"Yeah," Dave replied, "I could listen to this song all night."

"Me too!" she said, as she gathered her drink and waded off into the crowd.

Dave took the *Wall Street Journal* from his briefcase and tried to read. The room was very dark, but the combination of the light behind the bar and the candles on it enabled him to make out a paragraph here and there. Jesus, the stock market is in the shitter, Dave thought. This realization was a deeply vexing one that popped into his head at least once a day. He had been quietly building up a modest leave-Jodi fund over the past few years. A small sum he could use to rent and furnish an apartment and stay afloat while the marital property could be divided in a divorce. It was all sitting in a self-managed account at Charles Schwab. At the top of the market in 1999 he had over $100,000 and was almost ready to pack his bags and file. But in the last year he'd seen the door of the gilded cage swing shut. He was down to a quarter of what he once had stashed. It was depressing.

Fortunately, the numbers that were being discussed for DuVal's new deal were in a range that could buy him a significant amount of wiggle room. Even if Jodi got half of what was left over after the agency got its cut of the commission. All he needed to do was hang on until the deal was done. Of course, Jodi's father would probably fire him immediately, but if the deal was as big as it looked like it was going to be, he would have his choice of agencies to work for. Dave's reverie was suddenly interrupted by his wife tapping him on the shoulder.

"Did you check with the hostess?"

"What?" Dave asked.

"Did tell the hostess you're here?" Jodi asked.

"No, I came straight up. I thought you made a reservation," he added.

"I did, but you know how they are; they don't mind making you wait, but if you're ten minutes late, they'll give your table away," she said, indignantly.

"Are we late?" Dave asked.

"No."

"Then what's the problem?" he asked, extending his arms with palms upward, and retracting his neck into his torso in a posture of mild exasperation.

It was a typical beginning to a typical dinner for the Millers. Jodi had come into town to check up on a few of her buildings and look at a few others that were on the market. She was struggling with a dilemma, she told Dave, because the market was at the top of a cycle, price-wise, but interest rates were incredibly low.

"I'm going to give it some thought, but I think I'll do okay in the long run if I buy now," she said.

"What are they like?" Dave asked.

"Walk-ups. Solid rent rolls. A manageable balance of stabilized and controlled apartments."

"Chinatown?" Dave asked.

"Henry Street."

Dave was both amazed at, at envious of, his wife's shrewd investment skills. She had started buying real estate on a lark, and was now on her way to building a small empire. His crippling losses in the stock market—if charted on a graph and turned upside down—would be a fairly accurate depiction of the increase in the value of her real estate holdings. She was like her father; she practically shit money.

Seated downstairs in the restaurant, as they ate an expensive meal of small food, Dave tried to remember what had attracted him to Jodi in the first place. His initial attraction to her, Dave thought, was based on her youthful devil-may-care attitude. This attitude extended to everything from her infrequent class attendance to her enthusiastic sexual performances. It was a characteristic that Dave envied, because he was a worrier. Always concerned with consequences. He had fought it all his life, wishing and wanting to be more carefree. He was now convinced that their differences (in that regard) had to do with economic background. If he made a mistake, Dave was always aware, he could lose everything. Jodi, on the other hand, would always have a safety net. Of course the years had worn away the edginess of Jodi's devil-may-care attitude like water passing over the rocks in a fast-running stream. Many of the original facets—lust and passion among them—had also worn away. Now, in Dave's mind, she was just another middle-aged woman. Albeit a still-and-growing-more wealthy one.

"How are things with the DuVal deal?" Jodi asked Dave.

"Good," Dave replied.

"He's not going to fuck it up, is he?" Jodi asked.

Dave quickly glanced from left to right and held a single finger over his mouth, indicating that Jodi should lower her voice. It was a small town and, regardless of how one really felt, you could never disparage the talent—or be seen as tolerating the disparaging of the talent—in public. You never knew who was sitting next to you. And New York waiters were only too happy to call in an ill-advised or out-of-context quip to Page Six.

"He's really doing great," Dave said, in a strong, clear voice, "the ratings are on fire."

Jodi rolled her eyes at her husband's transparent long-distance brown-nosing. "Well, I'm sure it will all work out fine."

Coming out of the Lincoln Tunnel, Dave could see the taillights of Jodi's X-5 several cars ahead. After dinner they had gone to retrieve their separate cars, and though they had parked some fifteen blocks apart, somehow the two vehicles had managed to arrive at the tunnel at roughly the same time. Jodi, in Dave's view, was an erratic, impulsive driver prone to explosive fits of road rage. He didn't like to ride in the passenger seat of her car for that reason. It made him fear for his safety on two levels: that she might kill both of them, him, or someone else in a collision, or that her road rage would cause some aggrieved man to exit his car, drag him from the vehicle, and—unwilling to deliver violence upon a woman—pummel him instead.

Dave retrieved his cell phone from the console of his car and punched in Diane's number. The phone rang multiple times before her voicemail picked up. Dave left a message.

"Hey. I'm just winding up a long day at the office. I was thinking about you."

He flipped his phone shut and drove, thinking alternately about Diane, the DuVal deal, and the unhappy state of his marriage.

Arriving at home, Dave pulled his car into the garage beside Jodi's. She was sitting behind the wheel with her eyes closed. He got out of his car and came around to the driver's side of hers. Through the glass he could hear The Plimsouls' "A Million Miles Away" playing. What ever happened to The Plimsouls, he wondered? Peter Case was so fucking cool. He placed his hand on the door of her car and could feel the vibration. As the song came to a close, she opened her eyes and switched the car's engine off.

"Haven't heard that in awhile," Dave said, as Jodi stepped down from the SUV.

"I got it at Borders today. It's a reissue."

For a moment their eyes locked, and something rare was exchanged. Jodi put her arms around Dave's neck and pulled his mouth to hers. They kissed.

SEVENTEEN

Diane pecked out the five-digit password required to access her mobile phone's voicemail. She was sitting in a wooden phone booth outside the ladies room door on the basement level of the Odeon Restaurant in Tribeca. That afternoon, on an impulse, she had taken the initiative to call Roy Eldridge to ask him to meet her for a drink after work. It was not something she often did, but now in her mid-thirties, inhibition was beginning to loosen—and something like desperation was beginning to tighten—its vise-like grip. Roy had accepted her invitation, and was at that moment seated on a stool at the bar upstairs.

Diane's first concern was that they would not be able to identify each other. She'd met Roy over lunch only a day or two before, but sometimes even a day can be an eternity in New York, where the act of walking down the street exposes a person to hundreds, if not thousands, of new faces in a fleshy blur of humanity. But Roy had been waiting at the curb as Diane emerged from the cab, and had greeted her warmly with a short hug and a kiss on the cheek.

"I'm so glad you called," he'd said.

She had taken the greeting, and the way he had recognized her without slightest bit of hesitation, as a good sign.

"Me too," she'd replied, honestly.

They were on their second drink (his a scotch, hers a gin) when Diane had excused herself. The trip to the ladies room would serve three purposes: one, she had to pee; two, it would afford her an opportunity to examine herself in the mirror, a kind of date half-time, where one retreats to the locker room to refresh, take stock, and generally catch one's breath; and three, she needed to check her voicemail for messages.

Diane's mobile phone, while pretty much a lifeline as far as work was concerned, was still a great source of aggravation and embarrassment to her. It simply rang too much. And though she often needed to speak with whoever was on the other end of the line, she had a hard-and-fast rule that she never answered her mobile when she was engaged in a conversation with another person. Further, she was appalled at people who took calls in her presence. It was a hideous breach of etiquette. In her mental filing cabinet of human types, she placed the abusers of mobile phone etiquette in the same folder as people who clutched their forks in balled fists as they cut meat.

Diane was relieved to discover that she had only six messages. Sandwiched between five calls from publicists was a lone personal call. It was from Dave Miller.

"Hey. I'm just winding up a long day at the office. I was thinking about you," he said.

Diane felt a momentary pang in her midsection. It was a peculiar feeling. The pang, as she thought about it, was a pang of guilt. She felt—if only for a moment—like she was cheating on Dave. Dave, who was married. God, I'm fucked up, she thought, truly fucked up.

Roy was reading a book when she returned. That was another thing about Roy that Diane had taken as a good sign: he liked to read, and he liked to read a lot of different types of stuff—high and low. Because they both carried bags that were perhaps a bit over-full by contemporary Manhattan standards, she had asked him during the first round of drinks if he cared, just for fun, to compare their contents. There were many similarities: both bags held a Filofax day planner (paper) instead of a PDA, each contained copies of the *New York Times* and the *New York Post* (for balance), both bags contained toothbrush and toothpaste (dental hygiene is very important, they agreed), both contained condoms (standard practice, they admitted to each other, no expectations implied), both had a small assortment of pens (Uniball, for her, fountain for him) as well as at least one notebook (hers loose-leaf, his bound) to keep track of random story ideas as they occurred. Each bag contained a mobile phone (a necessary evil, they commiserated—and by the way, can you believe how bad the reception is in Manhattan?) as well as an AC adaptor for said mobile phone (they were both well-prepared). The similarities didn't end there; they each had at least two books they were in the process of reading—a novel as well as a work of non-fiction. Roy also carried clean underwear and socks. He again claimed that this was standard practice, although the presence of these objects afforded them the opportunity to engage in some innuendo-laced banter about how easy he thought Diane was. When in the field or editing, Roy ultimately explained, he was often kept overnight unexpectedly.

As Diane approached the bar, she saw the cover of the book he was reading. It was a novel entitled *Consent*, by Ben Shrank, and featured a painting of two people kissing on the dust jacket. "What's that?"

"I just picked it up," Roy said.

"What's it about?" Diane asked.

"It's about two people who meet and suddenly fall in love," he said, and laughed.

"Oh," Diane said, a bit flustered, "is it any good?"

"Quite, so far."

He folded the flap of the dust jacket into the book to mark his place, then carefully placed it back in his bag. Diane thought about her own books, their pages dog-eared and abused. Roy took a sip from his glass of scotch.

"Any messages?" he asked.

"How did you know I was checking my messages?"

"I know you're far too polite to do it here," Roy said.

"You're kind," Diane said, adding, "just five."

"Five!"

"*Just* five," Diane said, omitting the Dave message even in her casual account. *Fucked up*, she thought, cringing internally.

"Your life must be a living hell," Roy said.

"If you only knew."

They slowly sipped their drinks, each wanting to prolong their time together and neither wanting to appear to be a lush. In the end, after a bit of half-hearted we-really-shouldn't protesting, they decided to have another round. It was the most pleasant time that Diane had spent in conversation with a man in ages. What if he's a lousy fuck, she worried? I suppose I can always teach him, she thought, her mind momentarily lighting upon a girl-magazine headline she had seen on a newsstand earlier in the day: "Your Man: Repair or Replace?"

The night air, as they left the restaurant, was cool and refreshing. And the streets were free of homeless people. The effort to get and keep homeless people off the streets of New York City by the Giuliani administration had apparently been continued by the Bloomberg administration. It gave Diane an idea for a show. She paused for a moment on the sidewalk to extract the notebook from her bag.

"Idea?" Roy asked.

"Maybe," Diane replied.

They walked north a few blocks to the Franklin Street station, where Diane could catch the 1 uptown to Christopher Street and Roy could take the take the downtown train to his apartment in Brooklyn Heights. On the small triangular median near the entrance to the uptown train, they kissed. It was a long, lingering kiss, and one that stirred Diane deeply.

"I'd like to see you again," Roy said, as they reluctantly separated their lips.

"Me too," Diane replied, "call me."

She walked down the stairs of the station, pausing once to look back over her shoulder. Roy was still standing at the top of the stairs. He smiled.

"Good night," he said.

"Good night," Diane replied, turning to walk toward the train that was now entering the station. Her insides were all a-tingle, and her heart filled with a strange sensation that she could barely recognize: true romantic hope.

Ascending the subway stairs at Sheridan Square, Diane's euphoria was replaced by another sensation: one that vacillated between worry and dread. Her period was late, and while she had been able to back-burner the notion that she might be pregnant, the thought kept creeping back and nagging at her. She was nearly a week overdue, and her menstrual cycle was exceedingly dependable. It was cause for concern.

In the drugstore, Diane headed to the feminine products aisle. She scanned row after row of tampons, sanitary napkins, feminine deodorants (who buys that shit?), and lubricants, but was unable to locate any early pregnancy tests. Frustrated, she walked to the next aisle where a young man in a blue smock was replacing stock on a shelf.

"Excuse me," Diane said.

"Whahappen?" the young man replied.

"Nothing's happened yet," Diane replied, "but I was hoping you could tell me where I might find an early pregnancy test."

"EPT? Pharmacy," the young man replied.

In the periphery of her vision, as Diane turned to walk to the pharmacy counter at the back of the store, she was certain she saw the young man quickly thrust his hips forward and back twice in a mock-fucking gesture. Life, she thought, it strips away your dignity one piece at a time.

Diane could clearly see a range of early pregnancy test products behind the counter. It occurred to her that she had never purchased one of these kits before. Not that she hadn't been less-than-careful at times in her life, but she had thus far managed to dodge the bullet, as it were. She asked the pharmacist for a recommendation, and chose a brand that offered two kits for that price of one and a half. Practical.

"I'm curious," Diane asked, "why do you keep these things behind the counter?"

"Shoplifters" the pharmacist—a wiry woman who appeared to be about Diane's age—said in a curt response.

"They steal pregnancy tests?"

"People," the pharmacist replied with a look of distain, as she gave Diane her change. Diane casually hid her naked ring finger, hoping to escape the withering judgment of this complete stranger.

Back at home in the comfort of her bathroom, Diane concentrated and tried to aim a torrent of urine at the stick she was holding between her legs. She felt a little foolish as her pee splashed across the stick and all over her hand. But she felt a lot more foolish sixty seconds later, as she held the stick up to the light of the bathroom mirror and saw the small plus sign appear.

"Shit."

EIGHTEEN

DuVal was seated behind his desk, his chair in full recline, smoking a cigarette. He was reading a copy of the *National Review*, while CNN blared from the flat-panel television screen affixed to the facing wall. Diane knocked on the office door and entered without awaiting an invitation.

"Where's my lighter?" DuVal asked.

"I don't want to talk about that right now."

"What do you mean you don't want to talk about it?" DuVal asked. "I've been asking you for three days to bring it in. Are you really that forgetful, or are you pissed off at me about something?"

"Jack, it's gone. I don't know where it is. It's possible that my cleaning lady took it, but she's never taken anything before, so I don't know. The short story is that I DON'T KNOW WHERE YOUR FUCKING LIGHTER IS! And anyway, I'm pregnant."

A silence hung in the air like a stale fart. DuVal extinguished his cigarette, rose from his chair, and came around his desk to Diane. He took her in his arms and quietly embraced her. Several moments passed without a word uttered between them. It was a tender side of DuVal that Diane was not certain she had ever seen. Involuntarily, tears began to stream down her cheeks.

"Oh, Diane," he finally said.

NINETEEN

Dave Miller rolled over to see his wife's face matted against her pillow. A small circle of wetness, a puddle of drying saliva, had darkened the area beneath and in front of her mouth. The wrinkles around her eyes were more visible in the morning light, but overall the years had been kind to Jodi's face. She had not yet begun the cycle of face tightening that seemed to be so commonplace among women of her social and economic strata. The sad thing, Dave thought, is that the vast majority of these women (and now, of course, men) who get facelift after facelift don't, in the end, look any younger. They just look old, weird, and strangely similar. Perhaps because of the tell-tale, ubiquitous hairstyle they share, the one that covers the area in front of the ears where hair once grew. Skin that had been migrated toward the back of the head, or eliminated altogether. So what, Dave wondered, was the benefit? To let everyone know that you had the money to do the procedure? Or that you were vain and in denial about the inevitable progression toward the grave? It was an odd phenomenon.

Odd too was the fact that Dave had fucked Jodi within the previous eight hours. Odd, because it had become so much easier to get laid by a stranger—and not just a hooker—than it was to have sex with his wife. There was too much history, and too much baggage, that always seemed to get in the way. The disappointment about their inability to have children. The weight of distrust from his infidelities; those that had been discovered, and those that were only suspected. And not to mention the sameness and the drudgery that just naturally came with having been married to someone for nearly two decades. It was a miracle that any marriages survived.

Dave leaned over to kiss Jodi on the cheek.

"Good morning," he whispered, then rolled out of bed and headed to the bathroom.

"Don't pee on the floor," he heard Jodi's sleepy voice reply, "I have to go, too."

Why, he wondered, is her first instinct to always criticize, or to voice the expectation that I am going to fuck up somehow? While the previous night had shaken his certainty for a fleeting hour or two, a single sentence had again strengthened his resolve to divorce his wife.

"Don't worry. I'm practically standing on top of the toilet," he said, knees bracing the bowl, feet cold against the tile.

It was time to go to work. Or at least get out of the house.

On the drive in to the city Dave listened to the car radio. First, he tuned in 1010 WINS for a traffic update.

"We've got 20 minute delays on the inbound Holland and Lincoln Tunnels, and 30 minutes on the inbound GWB. If you're headed in from Long Island, an overturned tractor-trailer on 495 is why you're sitting in traffic."

Having established a benchmark for his commute, he then switched around between the drive time DJs to keep tabs on the talent.

"So Britney Spears hooked up with Colin Farrell."

"Is that what they're saying?"

"That's what I've been told."

"You gotta wonder what that was like."

"Like a wrestling match between a Leprechaun and a love doll."

"Ouch. Which was which?"

Radio was a niche area, but Dave believed it was a good place to be. Not too glamorous, but the talent tended to have a little less ego (DuVal excepted) and longer careers. There also wasn't as much obsession with the physical appearance of the talent, so he didn't have to worry about that as much. God help you if your job is representing a young actress who weighs 115 pounds and loses a job because she looks 'too fat.' He switched back over to 1010 WINS.

"In other news, President Bush today rejected a UN proposal that would have provided Saddam Hussein with additional time to comply with Resolution UNSCR 1441. In a statement released to the press, he said the UN is, quote, running out of options, end-quote. Kofi Annan, Secretary General of the UN, indicated that he fears the US may be moving toward some sort of unilateral action."

This bit of news troubled Dave. The thing with Iraq was becoming worrisome on a number of levels. First, there was personal safety. 9/11 had scared the shit out of him, and everyone else he knew. How do you defend yourself against people who don't fear death? Talk about not having a hand to play. It was ludicrous. And though he was able to keep the fear at bay most of the time, he did occasionally have visions of choking to death on a lung load of Sarin or walking into Grand Central as some fucking maniac detonated a suicide bomb. Manhattan was a target that was as easy as it was logical: the financial and media capital of the world, built on a tiny island with the most porous borders imaginable.

His concern about the war had another element as well. At face value, a war, or even the impending war, was good for radio. Especially talk radio. It gave guys like DuVal a ton of stuff to work with. And normally that would be a good thing. But Dave worried about a loss of focus on the business side. With ongoing contract negotiations, anything that caused the number crunchers (or the markets) to get nervous could be bad news. For instance, if a war made broadcasts run uninterrupted it would kill ad revenues. Then all bets were off. His hope was that the whole thing would either blow over or take another six months to get started.

Once in the office, Dave settled in behind his desk and started his morning ritual of manicuring, then reviewing his e-mail. Even with spam filters he could count on 20 or more superfluous e-mails that could be deleted without even having been opened. Then there were unsolicited e-mails from talent seeking representation. Those were immediately deleted as well. What remained were generally another 25-40 (if he was lucky) messages that actually had to be read and dealt with. Though he had a very capable assistant, after a few unsuccessful e-mail-delegation experiments Dave had resigned himself to the fact that he was going to have to read and respond to his own e-mail. It wasn't a commentary on the judgment of his assistant—the guy just couldn't read Dave's mind. And that, in the end, was something to be thankful for.

Among the e-mails that were left after his initial pass through the list was one with a single-word subject line that read 'Hey.' It was from Diane Healy. Odd. It was unusual for Diane to e-mail him, and even more so for her to e-mail him at his business account. In the event that she did e-mail him, it was typical for it to arrive in his personal account (the one that Jodi was unaware of) at hotmail.com. He clicked the subject line and opened her note.

Dave-
Stop by my office today after you see DuVal.
-Diane

He read the text twice quickly. It was direct and, at the same time, vague. Hmmmm, thought Dave. Something to look forward to? Or not? After taking a few moments to speculate on the deeper meaning of the message, he decided it was useless to do so. He moved on, opening and returning e-mails, answering the phone, and making calls.

Lunchtime came quickly, and found Dave away from the office and seated on a hard slat in a small phone booth-like structure. He was speaking by phone to a woman dressed in a bustier, a g-string and high heels. She was in a phone booth-like structure of her own, separated from the one Dave was in by a pane of glass.

"Pull your nipple up over the top of your bra," Dave said.

"Like this, honey?" she said, as she complied with his request.

"Uh-huh," Dave replied, as he gently stroked his penis, which was protruding from the fly of his slacks.

"Now lick it," he added.

She did.

"Can you rub your pussy for me too?" Dave asked, as he applied more pressure to his cock and increased the pace of his rubbing.

"Like this?" she asked, letting her tongue fall away from her nipple.

"Uh-huh," Dave answered, "now show it to me."

It was just another lunch at Show World Center, a windowless brick building on the corner of 42ⁿᵈ Street and 8ᵗʰ Avenue, and a holdover from the old Times Square. The three-card monte impresarios with their cardboard boxes, the sellers of loose joints, the roving mobs of mugging teenagers, the seedy sights and sounds of the *Midnight Cowboy*-era Times Square were mostly gone, but Show World remained. A palace of porn, internally lit by a combination of neon and old-style incandescent Broadway-sign bulbs, Show World offered a myriad of pleasures for the bored and lonely businessman. Short loops of porn films in single-occupant masterbatoriums, live sex shows, magazines and DVDs to carry out, all under one roof. But the principal thing Dave loved about the time he spent there (and this particular activity) was the perfunctory nature of it. Once he was done, he didn't even have to say goodbye to the woman on the other side of the glass. He just hung up the receiver. Having just done so, he tucked in his shirt, zipped up his trousers and retrieved his jacket from the peg at the top of the door. With his clothes in order, Dave took a quick glance downward to see if any rogue splotches made their way onto his clothing. He looked clean. He'd pay a visit to the men's room on the way out just to make sure.

As he closed the door of the booth behind him, and even in the dim and flashing light, Dave clearly saw Dean Sinclair emerging from a booth directly across the way from his. Dean was a shock jock and a client of Dave's. It was awkward. Under normal circumstances—that is to say, with any other normal human being—Dave simply would've averted his gaze and been reasonably assured that the other party had thoughtfully done so as well. Like a small-scale version of the cold war. An I-didn't-see-you-you-didn't-see-me kind of détente. But Dean, being Dean, walked directly over.

"DAAAAAVVVVVVVVVE!" he exclaimed in his huge, hokey DJ voice.

"Dean," replied Dave.

"I'd shake your hand, but I know it was just wrapped around your cock!" he said.

That's the thing with these DJs, Dave thought, you're always the straight man.

"Perhaps you should just cut out the middleman then, and shake my cock," Dave offered in return.

"Hey, that's funny—but don't quit your day job!" Dean said, waving and sauntering away.

Dave shook his head and watched his client, a forty-five year-old man, balding on the top, with a nub of a last-ditch desperation ponytail, dressed in relaxed-fit jeans, high-top sneakers and a wool-and-leather, waist-length jacket with a huge radio station logo emblazoned on the back, recede into the darkness. This is my life, Dave thought, hearing the banter of Dean's next broadcast unfold in his head.

"Hey! You'll never guess who I saw at Show World yesterday!"

"Who?" his sidekick, Thirsty Rick, would gamely ask.

"Dave Miller, my agent!"

"No!"

"YES!"

"What was he doing there?" Thirsty Rick would ask.

"Well, I don't know! Let's ask the listeners! If anyone out there can think of a reason why my agent would spend his lunch hour at Show World, give us a call."

"Uh, Dean?" Thirsty Rick would ask.

"Yeah?"

"Not for nothing, but what were you doing at Show World yesterday?"

"LOOKING FOR MY AGENT! HA HA HA HA HA."

TWENTY

Diane stood at the window of her office staring out across the city. Only the halo of the sun, peeking between the buildings, was visible above the horizon, and a sea of artificial light was beginning to shimmer and glow in its stead. She was lost in thought. It had taken a tremendous amount of effort to get the evening's show together. Diane had found it exceedingly difficult to concentrate, and over the course of the day she had returned to her office several times to either suppress or welcome a salvo of tears.

The pregnancy was forcing Diane to take an unvarnished look at her life. She had spent a sleepless night thinking about how she'd managed to get to the age of thirty-five and be unmarried, pregnant, and fucking both her boss and his agent. There were bright spots: Roy had serious potential, and she had a good job and quite a bit of money saved. But the very fact that Roy had serious potential made the situation even more unpalatable. She was going to have to sort the whole mess out in short order. Diane had considered—and considered, and reconsidered—a range of equally disagreeable options through the previous long, sleepless night. She could, of course, keep the baby. After all, she was thirty-five, and as she knew all too well from the recent spate of press about the subject, her eggs were fast reaching their expiration date. But Diane was largely ambivalent about motherhood in the first place, and single motherhood was doubly unappealing. Plus, did she really want a lifelong reminder that she had fucked DuVal? Or Dave? And that was another thing. She was 99.9% certain that it was DuVal's baby but, short of a DNA test, there was no way she could be sure. She and Dave had always used a condom, but was that any guarantee? It was a very delicate situation, and Diane knew she was going to have to handle it gingerly. Of course Roy could know nothing about any of this. It was horrifying. If she actually spelled it out to him he would think she was some kind of pathetic cliché from a bad episode of *Sex In The City*.

A sharp rapping on Diane's office door broke her trance at the window. She turned to see DuVal enter the room, cigarette dangling from his lips. He closed the door behind him.

"Not so bad," he said, eschewing any greeting.

"What?!?" Diane asked.

"The show."

'Oh,' Diane said. She was very tired.

"Are you okay?"

"We have to talk," Diane answered.

"K," DuVal answered.

"What do you think we should do about it?" Diane asked, pointing at her stomach.

"What do you want to do?"

"I asked first," Diane replied.

DuVal looked very uncomfortable. His feet were solidly planted, but he seemed to be, at the same time, moving around the room. His upper body was engaged in a slow rolling squirm, and his eyes would only occasionally make contact with Diane's.

"Well," DuVal said, briefly looking at Diane directly, "I guess—I mean we're not married—and we've never discussed actually starting a family—I guess, I mean, if you want my opinion, in light of those considerations, and the fact that we're not exactly a couple, per se, my inclination would be for you to terminate the pregnancy.

"An abortion?"

"Yes, well, I guess I think we would be talking about a procedure. I mean, that would be my inclination."

"That's what I thought too. I just wanted to hear you say it," Diane replied.

A profound expression of relief spread though DuVal's body: his shoulders dropped, and he drew in a long, deep breath. Stepping forward, he reached to embrace Diane. She leaned away.

"DuVal," she said, "could you leave me alone for a while?"

"You sure?"

"Yes."

Diane turned to again look out the window. As she heard the door close behind DuVal, she began to cry. She was angry and hurt, but she wasn't sure she had a right to be, which made it worse. Moreover, she was disappointed. But what had she expected? That DuVal would offer to marry her, move to Connecticut, and start raising a family? Even though Diane didn't want any of that, a part of her had wanted him to offer. To say, "We have to get married, immediately." She wanted DuVal to have wanted her to bear his child. She was also disappointed, but unsurprised, in DuVal's lack of commitment to the views he espoused to millions of people across the country each night. Not that she agreed with them. And in all honesty, she realized, she would have been tremendously surprised if he had said he wanted her to carry the child to term and place it up for adoption, or something similar. He just wasn't that guy. DuVal didn't really believe in anything; she knew that well. Plus, he was singularly focused on his own needs, desires and ambitions. Diane wondered if that was a shared characteristic amongst highly-achieving people. She both admired and resented that quality. Diane actually gave a shit about other people: about what they thought, and more importantly, how they felt. It was quaint. Out of step with the way the culture was moving. Or had moved. And sometimes, she felt, it was also an impediment to advancement in her professional life.

Drying her tears, she retrieved a bottle of water from the small refrigerator in the corner of her office. She took a few sips, then breathed several deep, calming breaths. Okay, she thought, I know where I stand, and I know what I have to do. She would call her gynecologist in the morning and schedule the procedure. She was fairly sure she didn't want DuVal to come with her. She also didn't want to go alone. What to do?

Suddenly, Diane heard a knock at her office door. Who the fuck is that now, she wondered, walking toward the entrance to her office? She opened the door to see Dave Miller. In the aftermath of her conversation with DuVal, Diane had forgotten that she'd asked him to stop by.

"Oh," she said, "come in."

Diane shut the door behind Dave and directed him to sit on the couch. She sat down beside him, a comfortable distance away. She thought it best to start with a few pleasantries.

"How are the negotiations going?" she asked.

"Fine," Dave replied, "we're very close."

"Any idea where we're going to wind up?" Diane asked.

"You might be staying right here," Dave replied.

"That would be nice," Diane said, "I wouldn't have to pack," Diane said, scanning the sparse furnishings of her office.

"The Syndicate looks like they might step up."

"They should," Diane said, "the ratings are great. And ad revenue is strong, despite the downturn."

"You've done a great job—both of you," Dave said, looking a little puzzled.

Diane shifted on the couch. She turned so she was more directly facing Dave. She decided to dive right in.

"Dave, I don't think we should, you know, see each other anymore," Diane said.

"Okay," Dave replied.

There was a long silence. Okay? Is that it, Diane wondered? No why not? No protestations?

"I met someone," she said, "and I really want to see where it will go."

"That's great, Diane," Dave said, "he's a lucky guy."

Another uncomfortable silence hung in the air. It was as if they had never been intimate. And had they? They had certainly seen each other naked, explored virtually every inch of each other's bodies, and tasted each other's sweat; but at that moment Diane felt like she was no closer to Dave than to a stranger on the subway.

"Okay then," she said, "thanks for stopping by."

Dave rose from the couch. He gave Diane a brief hug, kissing her cheek in the manner that Diane would kiss an acquaintance.

"I'll be seeing you," Dave said, giving her one last squeeze and a pat on the ass.

Damn, Diane thought, as she stood at the window once again. What am I? Just some scrap of fuck meat? She needed a drink.

Diane arranged to meet her friend Sarah at the Campbell Apartment in Grand Central Station. It was dark and woody, with 30-foot ceilings and an older, decidedly un-hip crowd. They made a real drink there, and you could talk without the annoying distractions that celebrities and young people often brought. The trade-off was that one could be surrounded by tourists who had stumbled upon old guidebooks listing the bar as a happening place to go.

She'd arrived at the bar nearly half an hour before the agreed-to time, and ordered a martini. Halfway in to her drink and, mostly to keep from obsessing over the matters at hand, she had started a conversation with the bartender, asking him why (although she was certain she knew) the place drew an older crowd.

"A few reasons, I guess," he had answered. "It's pretty expensive here, for one, and we're not the newest, hippest place, for another." Laughing, he added, "Don't get me wrong, you seem hip, and everything."

"Was it always like this?" Diane asked.

"Nooooo," he replied, washing martini glasses two at a time in a sink under the bar. "When we first opened it was all glamour and glory. We got mentioned on Page Six at least once a week."

"Sounds like you miss it."

"A little, I guess. It was busier. But models and kids don't tip."

"Youth is overrated," Diane said.

"You think?" the bartender, who appeared to be in his early thirties, asked.

"Not the physical aspect of being young," Diane said, "which is great. But our culture worships youth to an unhealthy degree, in my opinion."

"I suppose I can't argue with you there," the bartender said, scanning the bar to determine if anyone needed a drink.

"But why, I wonder?" Diane asked, rhetorically, "Name a good film director under thirty. Or a good writer. Or a good band. I mean a really good one; one as good as the Beatles were at that age."

"I can't do it."

"No, you can't," Diane said, "although you might be able to name a couple of good actors under thirty."

"What do you mean? Are you assuming I'm an actor because I'm a bartender?" he asked.

"No," Diane said, "I just meant that there are a few good actors under thirty around, and that one could probably name them."

"Jesus," a voice said over Diane's shoulder, "is she boring you with her anti-youth tirade?"

Sarah had arrived.

"Did she get to the part about advertising demographics yet? How 18-34 is grossly overvalued because all the media buyers are dumb 25 year-olds?"

"We didn't get that far," the bartender replied.

"Hi," Diane said, kissing her friend on the cheek.

Sarah was Diane's best friend in New York. She too hated young people, but that was only because they were a sub-set of the human race. Sarah pretty much hated everyone. Or claimed to. She was a tall, solidly-built brunette with prominent cheek bones and a maniacal glint in her eyes. Sarah was a freelance magazine writer who Diane had met at the gym during her first month in New York. The gym culture in New York was far more aggressive than the one she had left behind in Seattle. People would stand behind you waiting for cardio machines, and if you looked at them in the mirror they would bore into you with their eyes, trying to will you off whichever machine you happened to be on. It was intimidating. Especially with a 30-minute limit during peak hours, which at Diane's gym were between 6 A.M. and 10 P.M. Sarah, of course, took a more direct approach. The day they met Diane had been jogging on the treadmill at a healthy clip when Sarah had purposely hit the emergency stop button at the rear of the handrails.

"TIME'S UP, HONEY!" she had announced.

Diane had found herself speechless.

"You've been on there thirty-one minutes, step off," Sarah had said.

Diane had hurried to gather her things. In her haste to get away from what was clearly a crazy person, she had lost her grip on her CD player. It fell to the floor, and came to pieces. The battery cover, the two AA batteries, and the CD itself scattered in various directions. Sarah had jumped after the CD, picked it up and examined its face carefully. It was a copy of *Idlewild* by Everything But The Girl.

"I love this CD," Sarah had said, as she handed it back to Diane.

"And oldie, but a goodie," Diane had replied.

"You want to go get a coffee or something after the gym?" Sarah had asked.

Bewildered and largely friendless in New York, Diane had agreed. They became fast friends.

Diane settled up with the bartender and the two women moved to a table. Diane jumped in to describing the events of the afternoon, taking great care to accurately characterize both the DuVal abortion conversation and the Dave breakup, as it were.

"First of all, you are such a whore," Sarah said, laughing. "And secondly, I think DuVal is a fucking loser. He's been good for you professionally, but if he won't even come to your abortion—I'm sorry—he's a dick."

"In fairness, I didn't invite him," Diane said, "I don't want him there."

"But he should have offered to come," Sarah replied, "And, he smokes. It's so 20th Century."

"He does have some good qualities."

"Name one," Sarah replied.

"He's funny."

"I'm funny, and you don't have to fuck me."

"He's loyal."

"How so?" Sarah asked, incredulously.

"He's been really loyal professionally. He stuck with me when I was still learning. He believed in me."

"He was fucking you!"

"No, this was way before that," Diane said.

Sarah looked around the room and lowered her voice. "I think you should quit and sue him for sexual harassment."

"As if!" Diane exclaimed, "DuVal is arguably a jerk, but he's always been a gentleman about the sleeping-together part," Diane said, in DuVal's defense.

"I still think it's time for you to find a new job," Sarah offered.

"You may be right," Diane replied, considering anew whether the time had come for her to jump ship. It would be a good time to go; the show was doing extremely well, and the case could be made that she had been the architect of its success. It was something to think about. But it was something to think about after she had taken care of straightening out the fix she was in.

In the cab on the way home, Diane checked her voicemail. There was a message from DuVal. He was two sheets to the wind, and it sounded like he was doing his best to hoist a third. Almost gone. DuVal didn't slur when he drank, but Diane could always tell when he'd been drinking. There was a certain heaviness in his voice, and a hesitancy that was not there when he was sober. It was as if he was gingerly walking through a verbal minefield, careful of where the next foot—or word—might fall.

"Diane, um, I'm sorry about our conversation today. I, uh, well it's, er, inexcusable, er, that I didn't offer to come with you to the doctor, or wherever. I'm sorry. Call me if you want to talk, or just yell at me, or something. I'm home."

Diane smiled to herself. DuVal did have some good qualities. Yes, he was a dick but, like a dick, he could be hard and he could be soft. And sometimes, kind of in the middle. It was difficult to hate the guy with any conviction.

Diane's cab pulled to a stop a car-width from the curb in front of her building. An unmarked police car had occupied the space—directly in front of the building's entrance—that was designated for discharging passengers. Fucking cops, Diane thought. She handed the cab driver a ten, asked for a receipt, and slid out of the seat as her doorman Pete opened the rear door of the cab for her.

"Hey Pete," Diane said, "what are the cops doing here?"

"Looking for you," the doorman answered.

"Ha ha," Diane laughed, "what are they really doing?"

"They're really looking for you," he said.

"What for?" Diane said, gripped by the inexplicable fear that innocent people have of the police.

"I don't know," Pete replied, "but they're in the lobby waiting. And they said they want to talk to you."

Diane walked into the lobby of her building. It was a large, pre-war affair with high, beamed ceilings and an elaborately tiled floor. A table, surrounded by heavy chairs, supported a vase filled with freshly-cut flowers. Two of the chairs held men in ill-fitting, off-the-rack suits. One wore a goatee, the ubiquitous facial-hair choice of men from the boroughs and the hinterlands, the other, a mustache, the time-honored facial-hair choice of men from the NYPD and Randy, the cowboy from the Village People.

"You guys looking for me?" Diane asked.

The men stood. They were both in their mid-40s, and each was roughly 30 lbs overweight. They identified themselves as Detectives Lerman and Ossola. Detective Lerman spoke first, while Detective Ossola took notes on a small pad.

"Are you Diane Healy?" he asked.

"Yes, I am. What's going on?"

"Do you employ Cheryl Nevins as your housekeeper?"

Diane looked flustered. "Yes, but only on a once-a-week basis. Look, I pay her cash because that's how she wants to be paid. I intend to have my accountant send her a 1099 in January."

"Ms. Healy, we're not concerned with tax issues—that's between you and the IRS."

Detective Ossola looked up from his pad and spoke. "Cheryl Nevins was found dead in Fort Greene, Brooklyn last night. It appears she was the victim of a homicide."

"Oh my God," Diane said, covering her mouth with her hand, "Oh, no."

Detective Lerman reached over and placed his hand on her arm. "We're sorry to have to give you this news, Ms. Healy. We found your name—as well as the names of some of her other clients—on a piece of paper in her apartment. We're just trying to get some information about Ms. Nevins so we can begin an investigation."

"This is such a shock," Diane said, "I only actually met her in person once. Our arrangement was that she came once a week to clean. I left keys with the doorman and she would let herself in and lock up when she was done."

"I see. And how did she receive payment from you?" Detective Lerman asked.

"I would leave an envelope on the table in the hall. A hundred dollars. She did a wonderful job."

"Do you know if she had a boyfriend, or if she had been threatened recently in any way?"

"Oh gosh, I wouldn't know," Diane said, "like I said, I only met her in person the one time. Perhaps the doormen would have a better idea about that sort of thing. Oh, God, this is so awful. "

Diane began to cry. Detective Lerman pulled a business card from his jacket pocket and handed it to Diane. "If you think of anything that might help us, please give us a call. I'm really sorry to have to give you this news."

Detective Ossola folded his notebook shut, and the two men walked through the lobby and out the front door of the building. Diane wiped her eyes and looked up to see them talking to Pete on the sidewalk outside. Diane felt beaten down. It was all too much for one day. Her feet felt leaden as she walked to the elevator, and her hand trembled as she lifted her keys to the locks on her front door. Inside, she dropped her purse on the floor, took the wireless phone from its cradle and dialed DuVal's number.

TWENTY-ONE

Diane moved her head an inch to the right to get the sun out of her eyes. Sliced, as it was, into 2-inch strips by the wooden Venetian blinds that adorned the window on her shrink's office, she found that if she positioned her head just so, a thin strip of shade would provide protection from its glaring intensity. She took a deep breath and sunk into the luxurious leather beneath her back.

Diane preferred to lie down in therapy. When she had first met with Dr. Sammuels, she had been offered the choice of the chair or the couch. Or day bed, more accurately. A mid-century Mies van der Rohe affair covered in tufted black leather. Her choice had been largely influenced by Sarah, who'd referred her to Dr. Sammuels in the first place.

"If you sit in the chair, you'll compromise the whole process," she had said.

"Why?" Diane had asked.

"Because you'll be looking into her eyes for signs of approval."

"You think so?"

"I know so."

"Is that bad?"

"Yes."

"Why?"

"Because you shouldn't give a fuck about what she thinks of you— you're just there to get a job done."

Sarah, it turned out, was somewhat of an expert on psychotherapy, having first been introduced to the practice at the age of eleven when she had decapitated all of her dolls and stuffed animals in a single day. Worried, her parents had talked late into the night about the significance of the deed, and what, if anything, they should do about it. The later they talked, the more liquor they consumed. Eventually their voices became loud, waking Sarah from a sound and peaceful sleep. Appearing in the doorway of the kitchen at the moment her mother exclaimed, "I would just like to know if we have some kind of a future serial killer on our hands," Sarah had rubbed the sleep from her eyes, and calmly explained to her parents that the offending act would be more accurately characterized as a *mass* murder. The decision was made to seek professional help.

Dr. Sammuels was an extraordinarily stylish woman in her mid-fifties. Her hair, entirely grey, was cut in a blunt bob that reached the mid point of her willowy neck. She had flawless skin, a perfect figure and wore impossibly fashionable designer clothes. Given that she only charged $150 an hour, Diane often spent a good portion of her session silently speculating whether Dr. Sammuels was: a) independently wealthy, b) well married, or c) hideously in debt. It was a puzzle. And while Diane found Dr. Sammuels to be very helpful as a therapist, she found her to be very intimidating as a woman—which was another reason why she was lying on the daybed staring at the ceiling.

Diane had just recapped the events of the previous day, including a late-night visit to DuVal's apartment.

"The cops were there when you got home?" he'd asked.

"Yes, well, I saw the unmarked car out front, then my doorman said they were there to see me," Diane had answered.

"That must've been scary."

"It was."

"Detectives?"

"Two of them. Ossola and Lerman, they gave me their cards."

"And they told you your housekeeper, Cheryl—"

"Cheryl Nevins."

"That she had been murdered?"

"They said she had been found dead. And that it looked like it had been a homicide," Diane had answered.

"God, that's terrible. You must've been shellshocked," he'd said, rubbing Diane's arm to comfort her.

DuVal had initially calmed Diane's nerves and listening patiently. But had it all been a ploy, she'd wondered? Because he'd then asked if they had found his lighter on her body. To make matters worse, when she had gathered her things to go, he had offered to let her stay the night—and not even mentioned the pending abortion.

"And you felt his offer was a sexual overture?" Dr. Sammuels had asked.

"I guess he may have only been offering comfort," Diane had replied, "but you never know with DuVal. I mean, the other night he's calling the President of Planned Parenthood a baby murderer on the air, and the next thing you know he's telling me to get an abortion."

"I know we've been over this before, but do you think you might love him?"

"No."

"Why do you think you've continued to have sex with him?"

"Convenience," Diane replied.

"Sometimes the easiest thing is not the best thing."

"Well, duh."

'You're angry," the therapist observed.

"Angry. Hurt. Confused? It's all so fucking complicated," Diane complained. "We've been working together for seven years. And we've taken the show from a local nothing to huge, national syndication. It's been amazing for me professionally."

"Yes, it has. It seems to me that you could have almost any job for the asking now. What I'm wondering is, why don't you?"

"I just feel, responsible."

"To him, or for him?" Dr. Sammuels asked.

"Well, both, I suppose."

"Unfortunately, that's all the time we have today," Dr. Sammuels announced, "Perhaps you'll want to spend some time thinking about the responsibility issue for next week?"

Diane rose from the couch and rooted around in her bag for her checkbook.

"It's one-fifty today," Dr. Sammuels said.

"I know," Diane replied.

TWENTY-TWO

Earl Caldwell stood in front of the vending machine perusing the selection of snacks through the glass. There was an array of nuts, chips, chocolate, (in three different forms: Reeses Pieces, M&Ms, Hershey bars), cookies, gum, mints, a few types of hard candies, and a row of beef jerky packages that seemed strangely out of place. He reached into his pocket and extracted his bankroll, peeling off three singles. Using the grid of buttons below the bill-insert slot, he made four selections, watching as each choice was in turn pushed forward by a rotating metal coil and fell gracelessly into the trough below.

"Hungry, Earl?" a low, Caribbean-accented female voice intoned.

"It's for the kids," Earl replied, not bothering to turn around. He knew what his supervisor, Racine LaMonde, looked like, and didn't feel the need to revisit the sight of her barrel-shaped form.

"Un-huh," she replied, walking away.

Earl dropped to one knee to push the plastic, spring-loaded door open and gather the snacks. Standing up, he found himself winded. He would keep the beef jerky, and give the M&Ms, the Reeses Pieces, and the chocolate chip cookies to the kids, he decided. He thought he had made good choices, but it was tough to know when kids were involved. Sometimes they would go berserk if they had to share, and sometimes they were fine about it. With some kids you had to get them each the exact same thing, or else they all felt cheated.

It was a new case: three kids, mother murdered, no father, no relatives yet found. What were their names? Tawanna? Shaniqua? DaShawn? No. Tamika, LaShawna, and Kobe? He would have to check the file again. Earl was bad with names anyway, and dealing with so many children, it was hard to keep track. Lately, also, there seemed to be endless variations of names that had the same vowel sounds. It was very confusing. He was certain their last name was Nevins—that he could remember.

Earl had been with the New York City Administration for Children's Services for nineteen years. He worked for the Division of Foster Care and Preventative Services out of a field office on Bedford Avenue in Brooklyn. He was convinced it was among the saddest places in the world. And not just because the furniture was old, grey, and threadbare, the computers were outdated, slow, and dirty, and the paint was flesh-colored, stained, and peeling. It was a sad place because on a good day—a day when the stars lined up and all the paperwork managed to get pushed through the Byzantine bureaucracy that choked city government processes like a red tide—children were taken from their families and given to strangers. Of course, there was no doubt that many of the children were better off in foster homes. Earl had seen cases of abuse that made him question his faith; after all, how could a loving God let a mother hold a hot iron in the small of her 4-year-old's back, just because he was crying? He had sought counseling at the church, questioning Father Carmichael about God's love, his attentiveness, and his commitment to children.

"Father," he'd said, "I'm finding myself struggling to believe in God with the things that I've seen."

"It's not God you're seeing," the priest had answered, "it's sin. Human sin. But if you pray for God's guidance, he will guide you. If you pray for his forgiveness, he will forgive you. God's wisdom—and his mercy—are great."

The conversation had done little to shore up the cracks in the foundation of Earl's belief.

As he found less and less comfort in the church, Earl found more and more comfort in food. He ate copious amounts of the stuff. And the more he ate, it seemed, the hungrier he was. It was a paradox. If he had a substantial breakfast of three eggs, breakfast meat, toast with jelly, and a tall glass of orange juice, he would find himself ravenous by 10 A.M., visiting the vending machines for a snack, or stopping for a few donuts if he was in the field. This pattern would continue throughout the day. He might have a double quarter pounder with cheese, a large order of fries, a 24-ounce cola, and a hot cherry pie at noon, and a few hours later, again be looking for a snack. Earl spent increasing amounts of his time thinking about what he was going to eat next. In meetings at work he would furrow his brow and nod occasionally to give the appearance that he was paying rapt attention, when, in fact, it was likely that at any given moment he was thinking about pizza. There had been health problems. Finding his total cholesterol level nearing 400, Earl's doctor had expressed alarm, started him on Lipitor, and given him a list of foods he was to avoid. Earl took the medication daily but had been unable to muster the self-control to change his diet. Consequently, his cholesterol levels had plateaued in the mid-200s. His weight, however, continued to spiral out of control. In a country full of overweight people, his weight was such that children pointed and stared. And adults said things behind his back. Only the day before, he had walked into the men's room to overhear a conversation that was taking place between two stalls.

"How do you think Earl sits on a toilet?" one voice said.

"Very carefully," the other replied."

"That's one fat motherfucker."

"Word."

The laughter that ensued allowed him to exit unnoticed. And while that type of comment was cruel and certainly a violation of HR policy in the workplace, Earl couldn't really fault them for what they said. He was fat. Very, very fat.

The children were quiet when Earl returned from his short trip to the vending machine, seated side-by-side along a hallway wall in government-grade chairs covered in some sort of dove-grey colored leatherette. He took a file folder from a desk in the hallway and checked their names. He'd only been in the ballpark: they were called LaShawna, Tawanna and Antwon. LaShawna, at eleven, was the oldest of the three, and carried an air of seriousness that was far too heavy for her years. Children, Earl knew from experience, tended to go down one of two emotional paths when their home environments were chaotic, abusive, or had simply disintegrated altogether: they either acted out in violent and disruptive ways, or they became sad, serious, mini-adults. LaShawna, while clearly upset about her mother's death, had immediately shifted into survival mode. The first thing she had wanted to know was if she, her sister and her brother were going to be separated. Answering that question, which was asked of Earl often, was the single hardest part of his job.

"I, and everyone in this department, will make every effort to keep the three of you together," he told her. And while that was true, Earl knew that the odds of a single family adopting three children were very long, at best.

Earl set the file down and approached the children.

"Who wants some candy?" he asked, now standing directly in front of the three siblings.

Tawanna and Antwon looked to LaShawna for direction. She nodded her head to indicate that it was okay to accept candy from this particular stranger. Earl held the selection out in front of the kids, and they each made a choice.

"You fat," Antwon said, and was immediately slapped by LaShawna.

"Yes, I am," Earl replied.

"Say thank you to the man," LaShawna instructed her siblings.

"Thank you," Tawanna and Antwon had dutifully and unenthusiastically said, in unison.

"Mister Call-well?" LaShawna said.

"Yes," Earl replied, bending down to look her in the eye.

"Antwon need his asthma medicine."

"Antwon has asthma?" Earl asked.

"Yeah," LaShawna replied.

"How bad?" Earl asked.

"Bad," she replied.

Asthma was cause for serious concern. For some reason the condition was epidemic amongst children in the projects, and Earl knew that if Antwon had an attack and was without his inhaler or whatever form of therapy that he was prescribed to use, the consequences could be life threatening.

"Is his medicine in the apartment?" Earl asked.

"Yeah," LaShawna replied, "in the bathroom."

Earl would have to arrange for another social worker to watch the children while he made a trip to the apartment, his second of the day. Past experience told him that if he brought them back with him at this juncture it would be a mistake. They would either become inconsolable, want to remove every personal belonging that they could carry, or refuse to leave the family home altogether.

"I'll just have to go over there and get it then," Earl said.

As Earl drove toward the projects he considered his options. He could stop at a diner and have a second breakfast, but he wasn't really hungry for breakfast. An alternative would be to order a burger or a sandwich at a diner, but that was risky. It was 10:30 in the morning, and most diners were still in breakfast mode. Yes, they could make a burger or a sandwich, but Earl knew that it wouldn't be as good as if it were made at noon. Why this was, he wasn't absolutely certain. His working theory involved shift change and core competencies of the kitchen staff. Regardless, he knew he was unlikely to get a satisfying lunch meal at 10:30. A third option, albeit one that wouldn't sate his hunger immediately, was to go to the apartment to get the asthma medication first, and then broaden the search. After 11 A.M. an entirely different range of choices would open up, and Earl could make a decision based on desire rather than availability. That was what he would do.

In the apartment a new wave of sadness overcame Earl. He knew from reading the file that the deceased, Cheryl Nevins, had been in the system before. She had evidently developed a serious addiction to crack cocaine and sought long-term residential treatment. From what Earl could see, she had been one of the rare success stories. The home was clean and orderly, and there was a good selection of schoolbooks and other reading materials available for the children. It was a shame, Earl thought. Here was someone who got lost and managed to find her way back. From all appearances, she'd worked hard to get clean and straighten her life out, only to have it snatched away on a street corner in a second of violence. It was a real tragedy, and especially for the children.

In the bathroom Earl opened the medicine cabinet and retrieved Antwon's medicine. Because he was unsure of what other health conditions that the children may have been facing, he took every item in the cabinet that had a prescription label affixed to it and carefully placed the amber bottles, along with Antwon's inhaler, in a plastic takeout bag that he had retrieved from the back seat of his car.

Leaving the building, Earl saw a small contingent of teenaged mothers with an assortment of toddlers and babies gathered in the courtyard of the Farragut houses. A boom box sat on the ground nearby, its speakers blaring bass-heavy rap music at a punishing volume. He knew that some of these women, and their children, would most likely wind up as clients. Some soon, some later. He looked away.

Earl drove slowly along DeKalb, scanning the signs and windows on each side of the street for a restaurant that might offer a tasty meal while simultaneously trying to spot an empty legal parking space. The effort required tremendous concentration, but Earl was aided by the street congestion and slow pace of traffic. Spotting a white Cadillac Escalade emerging from a parking spot directly in front of a Chinese takeout restaurant, Earl considered his choice made. It was kismet.

The establishment, Lo Fat #1 Chinese Restaurant, was new to Earl, but familiar in all of its particulars. The entire business consisted of around 400 square feet of space above ground, 3/4 of that occupied by the kitchen. The remainder was devoted to a small, uninviting seating area with two tables that could accommodate four people each, and a foot-wide Formica countertop that ran along the front window and offered a row of five stools for street-view dining. Every surface in the restaurant—from the linoleum floors, to the pock-marked acoustic ceiling tiles, to the thin layer of plastic that covered the picture-based menu on the wall—had been rendered a neutral color of beige by a combination of time and aerosolized cooking oil, the odor of which now filled Earl's nose, and urged his salivary glands into action.

"Orda?" the woman behind the counter asked.

"Garlic chicken, extra spicy, an order of fried dumplings, and two Diet Cokes," Earl replied.

"Eeeh-dolla, niney cen," the impossibly thin woman replied, calling Earl's order out to the two men working the wok line in the back. She took a ten from Earl's hand and gave him change.

"Fi minit," she added, before returning her attention to the Chinese language newspaper that was spread across the counter.

Earl sat at a table and thought about his upcoming vacation. He, his wife Helen, her sister Marie, and Marie's husband Mike would be taking their annual drive to Florida soon to visit the girls' parents. It was an event he looked forward to each year with a mixture of excitement and dread. It was nice to have the time off and be away from the crushing sadness of his occupation. But the high concentration of elderly people in Florida made him feel sad in a different way. Florida, to Earl, seemed like some huge rendering plant. The end of the line. The place where the last vestiges of life were systematically stripped or extracted from people before they were sent off into the dark abyss of eternal oblivion. Also, while the projects and city buildings where Earl found himself day after day were certainly uniformly ugly, the strip mall/trailer park/fast food establishment/theme park landscape of Florida was, in a way, worse. It was a landscape that offered layer after layer of bland lifelessness, which left him feeling neither rested nor refreshed. Earl wished they would go to the Poconos instead of taking the Florida trip. He liked being surrounded by fresh air, trees, mountains, and furry animals. Still, he did like Mike, and there would undoubtedly be happy moments on the trip.

Mike Lerman was with the NYPD, and he and Earl had become very close friends over their years of marriage to the Coleman sisters. While he was a patrolman, Mike had been called to the scene of many domestic altercations. They were always at once tedious and tragic, and sometimes brutally violent. He and Earl had formed a bond based on the common elements of their work: namely, people involved in domestic crises. Now a detective, Mike happened to be working the Cheryl Nevins murder. They had run into each other in the projects earlier that morning as Mike was interviewing the neighbors and Earl was gathering up the children.

"Looks like a robbery," Mike had confided in Earl.

"Yeah?" Earl had answered, knowing from past conversations with his brother in-law that crimes of passion--where a husband, ex-husband or love interest was involved--were easier to solve.

"Gonna be tough to close," Mike added.

"It's a shame for the kids," Earl had offered.

"Yeah."

"Always is."

"Always is."

Earl thought he might give Mike a call after lunch. He would ask him how the case was coming and confirm their plans for the Florida trip.

Earl carried his food back to the table on a plastic tray. He opened the round container of dumplings and ate each one in two large bites, first taking the hot, doughy object between his thumb and forefinger and methodically dunking it into a two-ounce plastic container of soy sauce. Next, he emptied the pint box of white rice into the center of his paper plate, mashing the grain from its squat box shape into a flat plane that would both support the garlic chicken and absorb its rich, viscous sauce. Earl made quick work of the entrée, and sat for a moment to let the massive intake of food settle. After a moment of rest, he opened the glassine envelope containing his fortune cookie. Earl was very full. Uncomfortably so. He summoned a hot, spicy belch to relieve some of the pressure he was feeling behind his ribs. Breaking the cookie in half, he wondered if he could even eat it. But he did want to see his fortune. ALL THINGS IN MODERATION, Earl read from the small slip of paper. Not really a fortune, Earl thought, more of a cliché, or, what was that word? He couldn't remember. He ate half of the cookie and put the other half in the pocket of his jacket.

Back in the car a pain shot down the length of his left arm as Earl turned the key in the ignition. The pain was razor sharp, and in the moment it took for Earl's brain to register its severity, another, even more severe pain developed in his chest. This pain was crushing; it had real weight and gravity to it, like the rear wheel of a loaded dump truck rolling onto his chest. With that pain, and at that moment, as a cold sweat seeped out of every pore in his body, Earl knew that he was going to die.

"Somebody call 911," a passing woman screamed, looking through the window of Earl's car where his lifeless body was slumped against the steering wheel.

"And shut that fucking horn off."

TWENTY-THREE

DuVal sat in the examining room surveying the area around him. It had been several years since he had consulted an ear, nose, and throat specialist, and he had forgotten—deliberately or simply through an honest lapse of memory—about the unique tools that they used to ply their trade. The room had the standard sink/cupboard/counter setup along one wall, next to which sat what could be characterized as a regular, doctor's-office-grade chair (metal frame, pleather cushion) for the patient to sit in and fidget, while he or she began the second stage of waiting for the doctor to be late for the appointment. It was there that the similarities to a general practitioner's office ended. For one thing, rather than an examining table, the room was equipped with an examining chair. It was designed much like a dentist's chair, in that it had a hydraulic lift (at least DuVal assumed it was hydraulic) that could elevate or lower the patient with the push of a button in order to accommodate the doctor's observational needs and style. DuVal knew that terrible things happened in this chair.

He diverted his attention to the other odd items in the room. He first looked at the model of the head and neck that was on the countertop at his side. It offered a cut-away view of the human sinuses, nose, mouth, and throat, and was designed to be used in an illustrative fashion by the doctor as he or she was describing whatever happened to be ailing the patient. At its base was imprinted the logo of a well-known pharmaceutical outfit, and the brand name of a steroid product they were pushing. Christ, they don't miss a trick, thought DuVal.

DuVal was familiar with steroids. When he and Hillary had been separating in Cleveland, he had screamed himself into a case of laryngitis. His doctor had prescribed a low dosage of steroids to speed his recovery. As he recalled the incident, he realized that then was also the last time he had consulted an ear, nose, and throat specialist. This occasion was a bit more vexing, as DuVal was unable to make such a simple connection between cause and effect. He had developed a sore throat during a bout with a cold. The cold had gone away over two weeks before, but the sore throat was hanging on. Worried, he had decided to do the responsible thing and pay a visit to the doctor.

DuVal looked at his watch. Jesus, he thought, the fucker is half-an-hour late. Doctors. He realized his palms were sweating, and as he rubbed his hands on the upper thigh area of his pant legs to dry the moisture he heard the door open. Dr. Meltzer, a lean man wearing an expensive suit shrouded in a white exam coat, entered the room. He was carrying a file in one hand, and studied it for several moments before looking up at his patient.

"Hello, Mr. DuVal," he said. "What can I do for you?"

DuVal extended his hand. "You can call me Jack, for starters," DuVal answered.

The doctor, either not seeing—or choosing to ignore—the opportunity to shake his patient's hand, removed the metal top of one of the glass cylinders on the counter and withdrew a wooden tongue depressor. "Okay, Jack," he said, sniffing the air around DuVal as he pivoted back to face the patient, "Are you a smoker?"

The doctor motioned for DuVal to open his mouth, and placed the tongue depressor firmly on the patient's tongue. DuVal struggled to form words.

"Uh-huh. Ahhhhhhh," he replied.

"Terrible habit," the doctor announced, removing the tongue depressor from DuVal's mouth, "terrible."

"I've had a sore throat for a few weeks now," DuVal told the doctor.

"I see. Any cold or flu?"

"I had a cold, but all the other symptoms disappeared a couple of weeks ago."

"Uh-huh. Any raspiness in your voice?"

"A bit, not too bad."

"I see. Have you ever had nodes on your vocal chords?"

The concerned expression that had overtaken DuVal's face deepened. "No. Why? Do you think I might have nodes?"

"I don't know. I'm just wondering if you have a history of nodes," the doctor explained.

"No. I don't think so. Not that I know of," DuVal replied.

Dr. Meltzer reached into a cabinet and produced a spray bottle with a small hose attached to the nozzle.

"I'm going to spray this solution up your nose to numb your throat a bit," he announced.

"Okay," DuVal replied, "How come?"

"I want to get a better look at what's going on down there," he answered, in a matter-of-fact way.

Dr. Meltzer sprayed the crisp, stinging solution into each of DuVal's nostrils. DuVal shook his head, an involuntarily reaction. The solution had a bitter taste, and its immediate effect was similar to the sensation he had experienced on the occasions he had briefly flirted with cocaine use in the late 1980's. His throat numbed.

"Do you think something is wrong?" DuVal asked.

"I don't know," Dr. Meltzer replied with his studied, clinical demeanor, "We should have a better idea after a thorough exam."

The specialist then turned on a machine on a rolling cart that sat to the right of DuVal's examination chair. The machine consisted of a box-like component that housed its inner workings—the face of which circumscribed a small television screen—and a long, thin, black hose, which (DuVal was soon to learn) held a fiber-optic camera at its tip. As Dr. Meltzer switched the machine on, the television screen came to life.

"I am going to insert this tube in your nostril, Mr. DuVal, so I can get a better look at what is happening in your throat. You may feel a little discomfort."

"Why does it go through the nos…" DuVal started to say, before gagging a bit as roughly a foot of the rubber hose disappeared into his nose.

Dr. Meltzer told DuVal to try to relax, and urged him to look at the television screen to get an understanding of the architecture of his throat. DuVal glanced to the side. On the screen was a dark, meaty tunnel, which expanded and contracted with his every convulsive breath. What color remained in DuVal's face quickly drained, leaving his complexion an ashen shade of gray. He closed his eyes, deciding it might be better for all concerned to let the doctor continue his examination unobserved.

"Hmmm," Dr. Meltzer intoned several moments later, as DuVal felt an indistinct tugging sensation in his throat.

"Whaa?" DuVal tried to say, as he opened his eyes to see the doctor placing a small piece of flesh into a glass container.

The doctor pulled the black hose from DuVal's nostril. "You may experience a little soreness in you throat for a few days," he announced.

"What the hell was that all about?" DuVal asked, now able to speak in some semblance of his normal voice.

"I saw something that looked a little suspicious."

"And you took it out?!?"

"I removed it, yes. I want to do a biopsy of the tissue."

"Jesus, do you think you could've given me a little warning?" DuVal complained.

"Look, Mr. DuVal, I'm not going to lie to you. I don't like what I saw."

DuVal's palms were again beginning to sweat. "What are we talking about here?"

"I'm not sure," the doctor replied.

"What do you mean you're not sure?"

"I mean, I can't be 100% certain until the pathology comes back. My recommendation is that you not worry about it until we have the results."

"Not worry about it! How the hell am I supposed to do that?"

"Just go about your regular activities, Mr. DuVal. Except for the smoking, of course. I would urge you to stop that post-haste."

"Do I have cancer?" DuVal asked, his momentary flash of anger replaced by a sort of stunned sheepishness.

"I honestly don't know, Mr. DuVal. But don't worry. If you do, there are a range of new treatments available that have greatly increased the survival rate of throat cancer."

"Jesus," DuVal said, "what about my voice."

"Again, Mr. DuVal, I would urge you to go about your regular activities until the pathology comes back. And try not to worry. The preponderance of biopsies produce benign results."

DuVal emerged onto East 72nd Street into the harsh glare of sunlight. He felt shaky and a little weak at the knees. As the door closed behind him, he reached into his jacket pocket for his cigarettes, and expertly shook one loose from the pack. He then slid a hand into his left-front pants pocket, reflexively searching for his gold lighter, something he had found himself doing again and again throughout each day that had passed since he'd left it at Diane's. A pack of matches with an advertisement for a phone sex line was there in its stead. Hands shaking, he worked to make the flame at the head of the match find the tip of the cigarette that protruded from his mouth. As the flame met the dry, compressed tobacco leaves, DuVal took a long, deep drag, closed his eyes, and exhaled a thick stream of smoke into the crisp autumn air.

TWENTY-FOUR

"So wait. Is he pro-war or anti-war?"

"Oh. Un-huh."

"Oh. Which side?"

Kerri was speaking to a publicist and typing a synopsis of the conversation into the keyboard of her lamp-shaped, iMac computer. The conversation concerned a client and his newly-published book, and the publicist thought its topic was ideally suited to DuVal's show. An IM window also sat open on Kerri's desktop. Within the frame of the IM window was the thread of a conversation she was having with her friend Kristen, who was working as a temp at Conde Nast. Kristen was giving her the rundown on the locations of all the sample sales that would take place that week, but the thread was also punctuated with exclamations about how anorexic and cunty various women in the office were. Kerri was having trouble focusing on the phone call. The publicist's client was named Mohammed something-or-other, and was apparently a professor at Columbia University. The book was entitled *Jihad: The Worldwide Islamic Revolution*, and was—as nearly as Kerri could tell from the publicist's description—some kind of anti-American diatribe. Kerri concluded the conversation and tried to edit her notes into a shape that Diane would be able to understand without having to ask Kerri the kind of questions that were designed to make her feel stupid. Diane could be so fucking uptight sometimes.

The whole impending war thing bummed Kerri out. Her little brother had joined the National Guard in 2000 to help pay his way through college, and he'd already been called up once after 9/11. She was worried that he might be called up again if war broke out with Iraq or if there were more terrorist attacks in the US. God forbid he had to go to the Middle East. It was totally unfair.

The sound of an incoming message chimed in Kerri's headset. She looked on her screen to see a new message:

SexyK79: OMG! This grls thighs r smallr thn my wrists!!

DuVal leaned over Kerri's desk and looked at her screen.

"OHMYGOD, OHMYGOD!" he said.

Kerri was startled.

"Hi Mr. DuVal," she said, "just trying to get Diane's messages in order."

"I see that," Jack replied, "is she in yet?"

"Yeah, she's been in for a while."

"Did you hear what happened to the woman who cleans her apartment?"

"Yeah," Kerri replied, "it's so sad. And kind of scary."

Kerri was concerned about the incident. And not only because Diane was upset about it, and Diane was her boss and almost always nice to her except when she was making her feel stupid. Kerri technically lived in the same neighborhood as Cheryl Nevins: Fort Greene. But Kerri lived just to the East of Fort Greene Park, in the part that was quickly becoming gentrified. Still, a bartender had been murdered on his way home a few months before. She did take precautions, like always taking a cab home if it was late. But she couldn't really say if that increased her safety; her landlady had been mugged as she turned the key in the front door of the building.

"Did that woman have any family?" DuVal asked.

"I'm not sure," Kerri said, "Diane didn't mention it."

"Can you find out? Because if she had any kids I'd like to send a check to help them out."

"That is such a good idea," Kerri replied.

"Why don't you get the number of the detectives from Diane, give them a call, and ask."

"I will, Mr. DuVal," Kerri said, in earnest.

"And listen. When you talk to them, ask if she had a gold lighter when they found her."

"What?"

"Do me a favor, just ask," DuVal replied, lighting a cigarette with a match.

"You're not supposed to smoke in here," Kerri offered, sheepishly.

"And you're not supposed to spend the whole day IM-ing your friends," DuVal said, as he walked away.

Kerri shot the finger to DuVal's back, then typed "NYPD Ft. Green Brooklyn precinct" into the search field of her browser.

TWENTY-FIVE

Diane stood in her office, listening through the door to the conversation between DuVal and Kerri. That guy and his fucking lighter, she thought. Of course he assumed Diane's housekeeper had stolen it, probably because she was black. And, unfortunately, as nearly as Diane could tell, Cheryl Nevins had, in fact, stolen the lighter. But she was dead, for crying out loud. Give it a rest.

Diane did feel guilty that she hadn't found out if Cheryl had any kids, or if she could make a contribution of any kind. But she'd been really busy at work trying to get everything buttoned up so she could take a couple of days off to get the abortion and recuperate. DuVal's heart may or may not be in the right place, Diane thought, but his suggestion to follow up with the detectives was a good one. She returned to her desk, dug the detective's business card from her purse, and called Kerri.

"Kerri?"

"Yeah?"

"I need you to call those detectives who came by my apartment the other night," she said.

"K," Kerri replied, wondering if Diane was psychic or had overheard her conversation with DuVal. Either way, she decided, it was creepy.

"Find out if my housekeeper, Cheryl Nevins, had any family, and where we can send things if she did."

"K," Kerri replied, closing her browser window and writing down the number that Diane read to her, then reading it back to make certain she had it right.

"And do it first thing, please."

"K."

Diane placed the phone receiver back in its cradle and started packing up. She shut her laptop down, unplugged the AC adaptor from the wall, and carefully coiled the cord around the adaptor itself. She then slid the computer and the cord into her bag, along with some file folders and other materials she'd need over the next few days while she was resting at home. Diane had e-mailed DuVal from her Hotmail account to let him know that she had scheduled the abortion, but she wasn't certain if, or how often, he checked his personal e-mail. It was not the type of information she wanted to leave hanging around on the servers at work. She'd also covered off all of the arrangements needed to ensure that the show would run smoothly in her absence.

On the way out the door she left final instructions with Kerri. Diane had told her the day before that she would be having a minor medical procedure done, and Kerri had been tactful enough to only probe in a circuitous fashion about its nature.

"Is everything okay?" she had asked.

"Everything's fine," Diane had replied, "Don't worry, I'll be back in a few days.

"It's nothing serious, I hope."

"Nothing to worry about."

"K."

Kerri, for her part, had speculated wildly about the nature of Diane's mysterious impending absence. She and Kristen had engaged in a furious spate of instant messaging devoted to the topic.

KerriRules: dianes getting surgery

SexyK79: plastic?

KerriRules: dunno she's kinda old maybe eyes doesn't need lipo.

SexyK79: boobs?

KerriRules: don't think so

SexyK79: OMG helen g brown

KerriRules: ???

SexyK79: Cosmo lady like 1000 yrs old

KerriRules: abortion?

SexyK79: ???

KerriRules: possible

SexyK79: old people do it

KerriRules: stop

SexyK79: my parents do it alot

KerriRules: eeewwwww

In the end, Kerri and Kristen had decided that abortion was, in fact, the most likely surgical procedure for Diane. This, despite Kerri's inability to picture Diane actually having sex with a man. Or a woman, for that matter.

"I should be back in on Monday," Diane announced, "you have my numbers if you need them."

"I do," Kerri answered. "Feel better," she added, awkwardly.

"Thank you," Diane replied, wondering—at the exact same moment her assistant was—if "feel better" was the appropriate thing to say in such a circumstance.

Downstairs, Diane hailed a cab and told the driver exactly how she wanted to get to her Christopher Street apartment. She needed to drop off her work-related things and change into loose, comfortable clothes (the kind she wouldn't be caught dead wearing to work) before heading to the hospital. She spent the cab ride reflecting. Her gyno had told her it would be best if she had someone to help her home after the procedure, but Diane had been loath to ask Sarah. First of all, she would most likely go on another diatribe about what a shitheel DuVal was. Her opinion, of course, was valid, but it still didn't change the fact that Diane had fucked the guy (a lot) and she still had to work with him for the foreseeable future. In short, it would bring Diane's judgment into stark relief, which she didn't need on an occasion like this. She knew that Sarah's intent would have been to be supportive, but Diane wasn't sure she wanted the-we're-girls-let's-circle-the-wagons type of support just then. Secondly, Diane was very reluctant to ask people for favors, even if she'd done them favors in the past. She had dissected this reluctance in therapy, and had determined that it stemmed from the twin fears that people would: a) say no, in which case she would feel rejected; or b) say yes, in which case she would feel beholden to them. Either way, as Diane saw it, she would find herself in an uncomfortable position. In the end, she had e-mailed Sarah the date, time and location of the procedure, and asked her to call her apartment and check up on her that evening, or go to the hospital and identify her body if she didn't answer after a day or two.

Diane experienced her first nervousness about the actual procedure itself en route to the hospital. Having never undergone surgery of any kind, she was worried about the pain, as well as the risk associated with setting foot in a medical facility in the first place. As an avid reader of the Post, she had been exposed to many hospital-related horror stories. Stories with headlines like **STUMPED: DOCS CUT OFF WRONG LEG**, and **FLESH EATING BACTERIA MAKES A MEAL OF NURSE**.

Diane's gyno had assured her that there was little chance of anything going wrong during a procedure as commonplace as an abortion, but a twinge of fear remained. Partially because she had also advised her (as a woman and a doctor who was clearly pro-choice) that it would not be unusual for Diane to experience some psychological trauma before and/ or after the operation. And although she would not necessarily describe it as trauma, as the cab crawled through the crowded streets Diane did begin to feel alternating pangs of guilt, apprehension, and regret. By virtue of having been born a female, she had been given the incredible ability to incubate life. This ability, as Diane saw it, was both the most common, and miraculous, thing in the world. On a certain level—perhaps out of curios-ity alone—Diane longed to experience what it was to give life to another human being. And, of course, she wondered what the baby might look like. At the same time, she was certain that she had made the right decision. She was (Diane reminded herself) completely ambivalent about having chil-dren at all, and knew that carrying DuVal's (or Dave's) child to term would be a colossal mistake. She took a deep breath, and wiped a tear from the corner of her eye as the cab pulled up in front of the hospital.

A short few hours later—after first enduring an hour of paperwork and waiting—Diane lay in the recovery room with a nurse at her side, her warm, meaty hand wrapped around her wrist. Diane, groggy from whatever narcotic had been administered to numb the pain, looked from the hand up to the nurse's face.

"Anyone meetin' ya?" the woman asked in a lilting Caribbean accent.

"No," Diane said.

"You'll wanna sit for awhile den," the woman said.

Diane began to cry. She had no intention of doing so, but the tears had suddenly welled in her eyes, and—to her horror—a sob had escaped.

"Der, der, darlin," the nurse said, removing her hand from Diane's wrist and placing it on her shoulder, "you'll feel better in a day or so."

"I'll be okay," Diane said, unconvincingly.

"Of course you will, darlin," the nurse said, "all God's children will be."

As the nurse left the room, Diane wondered if the final comment had been intended as some sort of a condemnation. She was too tired to figure it out. And then suddenly, the door of the room swung open and Sarah appeared.

"Jesus, who do you have to fuck around here to see a patient?" she said, rushing to help Diane.

"You came," Diane said, beginning to cry all over again.

"Of course I did," Sarah replied, "I'm the best friend you have in this shithole of a town. And I'm a sucker for an abortion."

TWENTY-SIX

Helen Caldwell broke down. Only now, in the back seat of the limousine with her sister Marie and Marie's husband Mike, did she feel that she could cry again. As the black car crept slowly along the winding road that bisected acre upon acre of rolling green lawns with row after row of neatly planted headstones, Helen sobbed, and her body shuddered with the expression of her unbearable sorrow.

"Let it out," Mike said.

"Oh honey," her sister added.

The truth was that she had done little but cry since Earl's death. Alone, and with her sister and brother in-law as they sat with her in the hours immediately after she heard the news that they had found Earl dead in his car. But she had been afraid to cry at the funeral for fear of collapsing entirely. For fear that once she started, she wouldn't be able to stop. That the tears would come in torrents, and somehow carry her away in a river of grief.

It had been Mike who had come to tell her the awful news. That morning he'd been driving down DeKalb with his partner and spotted the ambulance beside Earl's car. Stopping to check things out, he had seen his brother in-law's lifeless body slumped over the steering wheel. The EMT personnel on the scene had already pronounced him dead. Mike had then sped to Helen's house so she wouldn't hear the news from someone else. It was a terrible task, even if it was one he was accustomed to from his work. But Earl and Mike had been close, and his sudden death was a devastating blow to him as well.

"Helen," he'd said, "it's Earl. He's gone."

"Gone? Gone where?" she had replied. Then, seeing tears beginning to well in Mike's eyes, she'd understood.

"Why?" she'd cried, "How?"

"Heart attack, looks like," he'd said, "I'm so sorry."

Mike looked out the side window of the car, saying a silent prayer for his lost friend, and wondering at how you had to go to a cemetery these days to see men in suits in Brooklyn. He listened to his sister in-law cry and thought of the strength it must have taken to keep her composure during the wake. The wake had started in her apartment at noontime two days before, and stretched into the early morning hours of the next day at the corner bar. All of their friends had come to express their condolences, as had most of the people from Earl's office.

"So sorry."

"You're in our prayers."

"He really cared, and the kids loved him."

"If you need anything, anything at all..."

But what, really, could anyone say? Anything that would make a difference, anyway?

In the late afternoon, to the amazement of the entire neighborhood, the Mayor had shown up. True, he'd only stayed long enough to have his picture taken with Helen, but it was a nice gesture.

Earl's death, it seemed, now had a life of its own. A life that was peculiar to the city. It had started with the *Post*. Perhaps because it was a slow news day, or because they knew their readership well, Earl's death had received front-page billing. The headline, **SOCIAL WORKER DIES DELIVERING ASTHMA MEDICINE TO BOY**, set off a frenzy of media attention that had fostered a citywide outpouring of support. This support had manifested itself in a seemingly endless parade of flower deliveries and the now-daily arrival of hundreds of cards and letters, many of which contained checks. And while all of the support, caring, and attention was nice, it did nothing to ameliorate Helen's emptiness and incalculable sense of loss. She felt that her life was over, that she would always be lonely, and that she would never know happiness again. She knew with absolute certainty that she would have to move from their apartment, because the pain of coming home to it, empty, day after day, would simply be too great. Sleeping alone in the bed for the past few nights had been impossible. Her arms reached for him again and again, and when she had been able to doze off for a few minutes or an hour, she awoke to feel a rebirth of her loneliness. And like a newborn, her loneliness fussed, fidgeted and howled.

"Twenty-seven years," Helen blurted out, to no one in particular, as the limousine eased out of the cemetery and into traffic.

"What?" Marie asked.

"That's how long we were together."

"Oh. Right."

"What was it, your twenty-second anniversary coming up?" Mike asked.

"June."

They had met in high school, when Earl was a junior and she was a sophomore. Earl had resembled Dee Dee Ramone then, a look he had worked hard to affect by cutting bangs and dying his hair jet black. He was pencil thin in those days, wore faded Levi's torn at the knee, and was seldom without his black leather motorcycle jacket with a Gabba Gabba Hey! button fastened to the lapel. Bad acne aside, Helen had thought he was one of the cutest boys in school. And while Earl was perhaps the biggest Ramones fan in their school, other than the uniform, he assumed little in the way of a rock and roll lifestyle. He was shy, bookish and polite, and except for occasionally smoking pot, stayed away from drugs.

"So um," he had said, the first time he had approached her, "would you wannna go to a concert with me? The, um, Ramones?"

His manners and somewhat cautious lifestyle had attracted her to him. So many of the other boys in their school spent their nights in the subway yards, high on the fumes of spray-painted graffiti, or crossing the bridge into Manhattan to cop heroin in Alphabet City. She felt safe with Earl.

They dated through the remainder of high school, and continued during the years Earl took classes at CCNY, commuting by subway from his parents' apartment to the Harlem campus. Helen studied cosmetology at a vocational school and took a job at a salon. They were married in the summer of the year of Earl's college graduation, and flew to Cancun to honeymoon. It was the first time either of them had ever traveled by air.

While they had the common marital disagreements (money, chores), Helen and Earl had been truly devoted to each other. They enjoyed spending their time together, and looked forward to evenings at home watching television or playing Scrabble as much as those they spent out with friends. Now, as the funeral procession became lost in a sea of traffic, Helen imagined her future alone as a cold, dark abyss.

"You had a good marriage," Marie said.

"I miss him so much already," Helen replied, sobbing anew.

Marie considered her sister as she grieved in the car seat beside her. Younger, and without question the prettier of the two, she had always received more attention. And now this. It was hard not to be jealous. The cards, the letters, the visit from the Mayor. Marie would have been satisfied just to know the kind of love her sister and Earl had shared.

Looking at her husband, Marie considered her own marriage. She had gotten together with Mike mainly because Sal Terranova, the boy in school she was really crazy about, wouldn't even be seen in public with her. Or that's what it felt like to Marie, after agonizing over the situation and crying herself to sleep on too many occasions to count. They would meet at his parents apartment after school to have sex, and then he would act like they were just acquaintances or, at best, buddies, when they saw each other between classes or in the neighborhood at night.

So she had agreed to marry Mike after dating him for only a few months in the year after high school. He was a nice guy from the neighborhood. The son of a cop attending the police academy. But she'd never had the feelings for him that she'd had for Sal. Or, for that matter, that Helen had described feeling for Earl. Of course Earl was dead now, and her sister was suffering terribly. But as Marie felt the leather seat of the limousine shake with the force of her sister's sobs, she wondered how the suffering of losing someone you loved so deeply compared to the suffering of spending a lifetime with someone you didn't. Or if her own suffering, like the rest of an existence spent in her sister's shadow, was somehow second rate.

TWENTY-SEVEN

DuVal fidgeted at the table. Dave was late. Only by five minutes so far, but it was still disrespectful. They had chosen Le Bernadin because it was close to their respective offices, but Dave, somehow, couldn't get there on time. The food at Le Bernadin was undeniably great, but DuVal found the décor to be cold, sterile, and corporate. Devoid of warmth. It is the perfect ambiance for this clientele, DuVal thought; these corporate fucks are about the only people who can afford to eat here. Pump up the stock price, waddle up to the bonus trough, and expense a $50 piece of fish every day for lunch. He looked around the room to see a parade of the self-satisfied on display: bankers, high-level media executives, and the odd table of the ladies-who-lunch peppered in for good measure.

Dave's probably meeting with one of his other clients, DuVal thought. Carrot Top, or somebody like that. In truth, DuVal didn't even know who was on Dave's roster, and he didn't care. He didn't really think Carrot Top was represented by Dave, but he had heard Dave mention him once in something like a longing fashion. It had been at an agency cocktail party, and he'd overheard Dave talking to one of his younger colleagues.

"I'd rep him in a second," Dave had said.

"Carrot Top? The prop comic?" the younger man had replied, incredulously.

"You can put four kids through an Ivy League school with a client like that," Dave had replied, "just commissioning his Vegas work."

"Maybe, but that fucker is scary looking. Red on the head like the dick on a dog."

"His is that," Dave agreed.

"And the eyes," the younger agent chimed in, "who did the work? His brows are up near his hairline."

"Who cares? So he looks like he's very surprised, big deal," Dave had countered.

"That act? Working for twenty years? I guess I'd look surprised too."

They had both laughed long and loud. And that was the thing with agents. To them, DuVal knew, you were just a fucking dollar sign. It didn't matter what you did, or who you were, it was all about the commissions you could generate and the length of time that you could generate them.

As DuVal studied the menu and considered ducking outside for a smoke, he heard Dave's voice.

"Jack, sorry I'm late. Client meeting," he said, taking a seat in the chair across from DuVal.

"Carrot Top?" DuVal ventured, prodding.

"I wish," Dave replied.

DuVal looked up from his menu and gave Dave a forced smile. At the corner of Dave's mouth, he noticed, was what appeared to be a slight blur of lipstick. His shirt, too, seemed to be a little less pressed than was typical. Christ, DuVal thought, even my agent gets more pussy than I do.

"What are you going to have?" Dave asked, "Have you decided yet?"

"I think I'm going to have a smoke right now," DuVal replied, "I'll be back in a minute."

DuVal rose from the table, taking the napkin from his lap and placing it on the empty plate before him. A waiter appeared suddenly out of nowhere and folded the napkin into a small tent.

"You should really have the salmon," Dave ventured, "great for your heart."

"I don't have a heart, Dave, and I didn't think you did either," DuVal replied.

"Still," Dave replied, as DuVal made his way through the dining room to join the other smokers huddled on the sidewalk.

Outside, DuVal shook a cigarette from the pack and lit up with a match from a book that he'd taken from the bar. It's weird, he thought, you can't smoke in restaurants anymore, but they all still have matches. Wonder how long that will last? This thought, and the act of smoking, triggered a rapid chain of free-association in his mind: I wonder where my lighter wound up? Pawn shop? Some crackhead's pocket? Or is it sitting in Diane's housekeeper's apartment on a dresser, waiting to be claimed? Have to ask Kerri what she found out from the police. *If* she called them. Wonder if she called them yet? I need to send some flowers and a check too: don't want to come off like a dick. Damn, my throat hurts. If I have cancer I'm fucked. Fucked. If they had to cut my larynx out I'd kill myself. How would I do it? Gun to the head? Too messy. Hate for anybody to find me like that. Pills and booze? Cleaner, but where do you get the pills? Can't just tell your doctor you want enough sleeping pills to kill yourself, can you? What if you live? What if you live, but you're in a coma? Or do some brain damage and wind up half an idiot? Maybe I could gut it out. Doctors, Christ. How the fuck are you supposed to not worry? Jesus, why is all this shit happening? Right when I'm trying to negotiate a fat new contract, too. Something always comes along to shit on a great moment. Wonder who Dave is fucking? Surely not his wife. Maybe, though, who knows? Never liked to fuck mine much.

With that thought DuVal dropped his cigarette to the ground and tamped the butt out with his right foot. Looking up, he found himself face to face with Carrot Top, who was apparently, as fate would have it, dining at Le Bernadin for lunch.

"Jesus," DuVal muttered, as Carrot Top's entourage passed through the door, "what a world."

DuVal followed the group in and headed back to his table. Dave, for his part, was no longer seated, having taken DuVal's absence as an opportunity to work the room. DuVal caught his eye and waved him back to the table as if he were a wayward child, or a waiter.

"Sorry about that," Dave said, as he sat once again across from DuVal, "my father in-law."

"Bummer," DuVal countered.

"No," Dave protested. "we get along fine."

"I'm just saying," DuVal answered, "I'm not sure I'd want to work for my wife's old man. I think it would make me feel, uh," DuVal paused to search for the right word, "owned."

Dave and DuVal both looked across the room at Mitch Sanders, Dave's father in-law. At that very moment, Sanders was looking over at them. It was slightly awkward. Seeking to diffuse the awkwardness, the three men each chose the same tactic: a forced smile coupled with a single upward nod of the head. DuVal turned his attention back to Dave and cocked an eyebrow.

"Anyway," Dave said, "we should order."

Predictably, Dave ordered the salmon on his own recommendation; DuVal opted for a piece of halibut. Neither wanted an appetizer. They briefly considered a bottle of wine, but thought better of it, deciding that the importance of the business at hand called for sober reflection. As they arrived at their decision to abstain, the waiter, a middle-aged French man, ran through a series of facial expressions that betrayed impatience, contempt, disappointment, and finally, resignation. Fuck him, thought DuVal, as the Frenchman walked away. The guy probably makes more money than the average high school principal; he can live without 20% of a $175 bottle of wine.

DuVal snapped out of his mental calculations as Dave began to update him on the nuances of the two competitive offers that were on the table. Both would pay in excess of $10 million per year, but one had a back-loaded structure that offered less money in the near-term, but more overall.

"Which one should we take?" DuVal asked.

"Tough choice," Dave replied, "each has its advantages. Both are five-year deals, with options for two-year extensions. You can stay put, and earn five, seven point five, ten, twelve point five, and then a balloon of twenty in the last year. That gives you fifty-five million over five years. King is offering a straight ten per year for five years, which would give you a neat fifty."

"I'm going to have to talk to my financial guy before I can make a decision," DuVal said. "With the market and interest rates where they are, it's a little more complicated."

"Of course," Dave replied. "The main thing is that you're happy wherever you wind up."

DuVal wondered what Dave really thought. He assumed that Dave would prefer that he take the $10 million per year deal from King. It would provide larger commissions to the agency in the near term and make him look like a big swinging dick around the office. DuVal was on the fence. He wasn't a big spender, so any increase in salary would go, if not unnoticed, pretty much straight into his investment portfolio. For DuVal, money was respect. Not personal respect, because the guys who ran these companies had so little integrity that DuVal found it extremely hard to give a shit what they thought of him. But the money—and the larger the amount the better—meant that they were transferring to him the only thing they recognized as having value or meaning. From their pockets to his. Or if not their pockets, from the available pool of revenue from which they could derive bonuses. DuVal hoped it hurt them a little bit.

Dave was doing some wondering of his own. Which way would DuVal go? He didn't want to seem like he was pressuring him one way or the other because that would be a mistake. But Dave was hoping against hope that DuVal would take the deal with more money up front. Either deal was going to give him some juice in the business, and he would likely be able to go wherever he wanted to go after it went through. But his slice of the first-year King deal commission, he calculated, would allow him to leave Jodi. Even if he had to give her half of it in the near term. The fact that Jodi had a trust, and earned substantial income of her own, meant that Dave would most likely not be saddled with any alimony in a divorce. But you never could tell. And, he knew that no matter what, a divorce was going to be bruising and expensive. He'd seen friends and colleagues go through divorces and it wasn't pretty. It was like a carnival of rage and pettiness. Screaming mid-day phone calls about who-did-what, and bitter arguments over the division of paperback books that nobody would ever read again. For one thing, Dave knew he would be saying goodbye to the house and most of what they owned. He would essentially be starting from scratch. New furniture, new home entertainment gear, pots, pans, sheets, towels, the whole bit. It wouldn't be cheap. And he was too old, and too accustomed to nice things, to buy crap. It's a good thing we don't have any kids, Dave thought, because that would open up a whole other world of hell.

"Dave," DuVal said, snapping him out of his divorce fantasy, "I have to get back to the station."

"Of course, Jack," Dave replied.

DuVal stood, and raising his eyebrows, pointed at the small leather folder the waiter had placed on the table. Dave put his hand over it and shook his head. DuVal nodded.

"I'll get back to you on this in a day or two," he said, and turned to leave.

"Great," Dave said.

Dave watched DuVal walk out the door of the restaurant and immediately light a cigarette. What a habit, he thought; it'll probably kill him one day. He opened the leather folder, slid his credit card inside, and motioned his waiter to the table.

On his way out of the restaurant, Dave headed to the men's room. His office was only a few blocks away, but nothing was worse than needing to take a leak on the streets of Manhattan. There were no public toilets anywhere. Finishing, as he shook the excess water from his penis with his right hand, his thumb grazed an area that felt strangely tender and irritated. Concerned, he looked around to make sure he was alone, then delicately twisted the skin of his penis in a clockwise direction and bent over to examine the area more closely. There, in the dim overhead light, he saw what appeared to a pus-weeping blister. Fuck, Dave thought. Fuck, fuck, fuck.

TWENTY-EIGHT

Diane squirmed in bed, flipping rapidly through the pages of *Us*. For two days she'd been alternating between reading trashy popular culture magazines and clicking back and forth on the television from the Animal Channel to various reality programs and a wide array of talk shows. There was a long list of things she was trying to avoid, and doing so was proving to be difficult. She was avoiding any pictures of pregnant women in magazines. She was trying to avoid any births on the animal channel (which, she was learning, was nearly impossible to do). And she was also trying to avoid any images of babies and mothers on the various talk shows she was skipping back and forth between. That, too, was a challenge, because the bread and butter of those talk shows (at least the ones that were any fun to watch) was the woman-impregnated-by-friend-of-husband-or-boyfriend scenario.

But at the top of her list, above all of the images of human and animal reproduction, the single thing she was trying hardest to avoid was calling Roy. She felt a little guilty about it. Or rather, she felt that she should feel guilty about that fact that her preoccupation with Roy transcended her feelings about the abortion. They had only been on one proper date (and Diane was experienced enough to know that one date does not a relationship make) but her thoughts kept returning to him again and again. It wasn't that he was handsome (although Diane did find him extremely attractive), or that he was nice (which he was), or that he was considerate, so much so that he had sent a card (understated, fine stock, no image) after their date to thank her and say how much he had enjoyed their evening out; it was all of those things, together with his wit, intelligence, and love of reading that made Diane think he might actually be the one. Of course she knew it was stupid and dangerous to go down that path in her mind. What is it with women, she wondered? One date and we're buying the wedding dress. No wonder men are afraid of us.

Diane had mocked herself for building a fantasy future with Roy, but as she tried to fill her time by scanning page after page of MTV Movie Award fashions, and watching television footage of lions on the savannah or socially retarded bachelors and bachelorettes, her mind kept circling back to Roy, the man she had met—randomly, impossibly—in a restaurant.

It was a strange time for dating. Ten years earlier, the notion of taking out a personal ad in a magazine would have been unthinkable for most people. It would have been seen as a final act of desperation, a public declaration of bankruptcy in the dating economy. But inasmuch as the Internet had served to commoditize everything from home electronics to home mortgages, so too had it commoditized the dating process. Now, almost every woman she knew had placed her picture on Match.com or some similar dating site. Most of the single men she knew had done so as well. While Diane had resisted the temptation, Sarah had been an early adopter, quickly getting an article—if not more than a few paramours—out of the experience. She had described the process (both to Diane and in the pages of *Cosmo*) as similar to shopping at Costco: you always ended up with more objects in your basket than you had intended. For most women, an initial rush of euphoria at the sheer volume of responses was followed by a vast number of dates. That phase, in turn, was followed by somewhat predictable disappointment at the abundance of men who were either nothing like their descriptions and pictures (or, equally disappointing, nothing more than their descriptions and pictures), which was followed by the realization that dating is, alas, more than just a numbers game. Still, Sarah was not above using the service when she needed to get laid. For that, it was like Amazon.com: one-click checkout.

That Roy had been out of town doing research for the past several days was a stroke of good fortune for Diane. His absence had helped her avoid a conversation about why she wasn't at work. Not that they would have definitely spoken, or tried to arrange a date, but still. In the thick of cutting his piece on India he'd taken a break to fly down and visit some bingo halls in Austin, Texas. The six months he'd spent on the other side of the globe among the desperately ill had convinced him that his next project needed to be lighter fare, and relatively local. So when an old friend from Austin had told him that Texas bingo might make a nice subject for a piece, Roy had decided he could spare a few days away from the editing room.

It was 10:05 P.M. and Diane glanced over at the phone on her bedside table. Too late to call Roy, she thought, talking herself back from the ledge. She turned her attention back to the article she was reading about Justin Timberlake. Diane had a hard-and-fast rule, ingrained from her midwestern upbringing, that it was unacceptable to call anyone after the hour of 10 o'clock. But it's only 9 in Austin, she realized. Central Time. She considered an unpleasant notion: what if she called and he was with somebody else? A road wife, if you will. An ex-girlfriend. Or maybe somebody he just met. Worse yet, what if she called him in Texas and he thought she was some kind of stalker? An obsessive. Calling him would be a mistake. On the other hand, he might be happy to hear from her. He could be lonely. He probably was. Maybe he would be thrilled to know that she'd been thinking about him. It could go either way, of course. Who knew? That's the risk. Diane set her magazine down. I'll call him on his cell, she thought. What the heck? If he sounds weird I'll feign surprise and tell him I forgot he was out of town. As Diane set her hand on the telephone receiver, she was startled by the noise and vibration of it ringing in her hand. She examined the Caller ID screen on the telephone's face. Private Caller, it read. Answering would be dicey. It could be anyone: Dave, DuVal, even a publicist. Some of the heavyweights were not above calling Diane at home. Even after 10 P.M. But Diane was bored. After two days at home in bed, she was going stir-crazy. On the third ring, she decided to answer.

"Hello?"

"Di___ne," she heard a voice rendered barely decipherable by a bad cell connection say.

"Hello?" Diane replied.

"It's __oy," the caller continued, "__exas."

"I can barely hear you," she replied.

"___ove around, ____et more bars," he said, then more clearly, "Can you hear me now?"

"Roy? How are you?" Diane asked.

"Good. I'm good," he replied.

"How's the bingo?" Diane asked.

"Good. Really fun," then, "I wish you were here to see it."

"That's a nice thing to say," Diane replied, not knowing how to reply, or to keep from showing her hand prematurely.

"I can't stop thinking about you," Roy said.

The butterflies that had appeared in Diane's stomach upon realizing Roy was on the other end of the phone call now took flight. For the first time in a long time, or maybe since that night, she felt a twinge of the feeling she had experienced when her father had opened the front door of their house to greet David Bologna, the first boy who ever took her on a date in a car.

"I'm so glad you called," Diane gushed, "I really wanted to talk to you tonight."

"Me too. I was on the fence about it, thinking you might not be home, or, you know."

"Uh-huh," Diane said, wondering at how they seemed to think similar thoughts. "So, how is it? Tell me details."

"The bingo?" Roy asked, "It's so much more exciting than you might imagine."

"How so?"

"It's hard to describe, but the place gets charged with this incredible tension towards the end of every game when a bunch of people have four of the numbers and they all think they might win. The prizes are pretty big: $500 to $2500 a game. And there are several games a session."

"Have you been playing?

"Oh yeah. I love it. A few times I've been one number away from winning, and on the edge of my seat thinking I might win."

"You're joking."

"I'm not. It's really exciting. And fun."

He talked about nondescript rooms with folding tables arranged in rows, and how people walked up and down between the rows hawking new game cards in the minutes before each game began. And how he had found lightheartedness where he had expected despair.

"It'll make a great piece. An hour, maybe for television," he said, adding, "Now I just need to find some money."

Roy then told Diane about Austin. How it was hilly and green, unlike other places he'd been in Texas. He described the abundance of good music, barbecue and Mexican food, and the laid-back feeling of the town.

"Everybody says it's not as good as it used to be, but it seems pretty great to me."

"It sounds fun," Diane said.

"What have you been up to?" Roy asked, sounding genuinely curious.

"I've been home sick for a few days, believe it or not," Diane said, hoping against hope that Roy wouldn't ask the particulars.

"You? I had you down for one of those people who never took a sick day."

"Yeah, well."

"I hope you're on the mend."

"I'm starting to feel a lot better. I'll probably go in tomorrow."

Having spent nearly a half-hour on the phone, Roy apologetically announced that he needed to cut their conversation short to head to a late game in South Austin.

"I'll call you tomorrow," he said.

"Do."

"And let's get together as soon as I get back."

"Okay."

"Okay."

"Goodnight."

"Goodnight."

"Feel better."

"I will," Diane said, then, "I do."

"Goodnight, then."

"Goodnight."

Diane set the phone receiver on her bedside table and glanced at the clock. It was 10:30, and she was now wide awake. More awake than she had been in a while, it seemed. And even though she knew it was a preposterous notion, and one that was unsupportable by a rational mind, she had the feeling that she might be falling in love.

TWENTY-NINE

"Hello America, and good evening. You're listening to Jack DuVal, and I'll be your host tonight and every night here on the American Radio Syndicate. Our topic is Jihad: the holy war that various fundamentalist Islamic groups are waging against America, Americans, our allies, and friends who support democratic ideals around the world. As always, we'll be opening the phone lines up later for your questions, but first I'd like to introduce to you our guest for this program. He is the author of a controversial new book entitled *Jihad: The Worldwide Islamic Revolution,* and a distinguished professor of history at Columbia University here in New York City. I am pleased to welcome Dr. Mohammed Farooq to the show. Good evening, Dr. Farooq."

DuVal took a long pull from his cigarette and looked across the studio desk at his guest. Mohammed Farooq was a fit man in his late 30's, dressed in a well-cut charcoal-colored suit with a blue shirt and a solid gray tie. His face was clean-shaven, and defined by brooding, dark eyes nested beneath thick eyebrows. Stylish glasses with frameless lenses balanced on the bridge of a pronounced nose. When he spoke, it was with a refined British accent.

"Good evening, Mr. DuVal."

"Let's first talk about the word Jihad. What exactly does it mean?" DuVal asked, fine trails of smoke creeping from his nostrils.

"Well, I suppose that would depend who you ask. It can be defined as striving in the cause of Allah. It can also mean a holy war in the cause of Allah, in the…"

"So a holy war," DuVal said, interrupting and leaning slightly forward toward his guest.

"Yes."

"And where does this word, Jihad, come from?"

"Jihad is derived from the Arabic verb jahada, which means, literally, to strive, or do your utmost. In the *Koran*, this notion of Jihad is really about the need to do good and suppress evil. Especially in the sense of believers struggling against idolatry, or religious persecution."

"So how do we go from the need to do good to a 'worldwide Islamic revolution' that produces someone like Osama Bin Laden and the attacks on the World Trade Center?"

"Right. Well, that's the big question. I teach a year-long seminar on that very topic…"

"Don't worry, professor," DuVal said, "you won't be graded on your answer," DuVal said, giving the slightest nod toward his guest to indicate that it was all in good fun.

"Right. Well, in the simplest sense, you have a group, or more accurately, groups, of people—Muslims—spread around the globe, who feel that their way of life, and their most deeply-held beliefs, are under attack."

DuVal again sat forward in his seat.

"Enlighten me a bit. Give me some examples of what these people might see as an attack on their way of life, or their beliefs."

"Well, certainly the treatment of the Palestinians in Israel over the past half century or more, would be one."

"It's my perception that the Israelis have been under fairly constant attack by the Palestinians during that period."

"And that perception is shared by many people. But there are two sides to every story. Three, if you include the truth, as they say. But that might not be your perception if you were a Muslim. And that certainly wouldn't be your perception if you were a Palestinian."

"All right, I can understand the Palestinians. But what about Bin Laden? This is a guy who grew up rich in Saudi Arabia."

"Bin Laden is a complex man. Wealthy, well educated—trained as an engineer in fact. And the 17th of his fathers's 52 children. But he also fought in Afghanistan against the Soviets. In the trenches, so to speak."

"But we supported the Afghanis," DuVal offered, "so we were on the same side."

"You might think so," Farooq countered, "but Bin Laden would say it was a marriage of convenience, at best. His struggle is, and always has been, against anyone who would oppress Islamic people. The immediate threat at that time was the Soviets. Now it's the US."

"Back up a second," DuVal said, "what about our relationship with Saudi Arabia?"

"Bin Laden believes, and has said as much, that the US has effectively colonized Saudi Arabia. That it is the duty of all Muslims to drive America, and Americans, out of the Holy Land."

"It doesn't seem like the Saudi Government shares his views," DuVal said.

"Perhaps not. And that's partially why we see this struggle, for Bin Laden, and others, take the shape of a guerrilla war," the professor said, pausing for a moment to lift his glasses from the bridge of his nose and rub a finger in the corner of his eye.

"Go on," DuVal urged, and took another long drag from his cigarette.

"Whether there is state sponsorship for this Jihad or not—and there may be in some instances—in the larger sense, at least for Bin Laden and other fundamentalists, the Jihad transcends tribal or national affiliations. It's larger than that."

"Okay," DuVal said, gesticulating with his cigarette-holding hand, "so it's a religious war. I accept that. But here's where I'm having a discon-nect: if this is a religious war, then how can so-called righteous men fly fully-fueled jet aircraft into buildings full of innocent civilians?"

"Going back to how we defined Jihad," the professor explained, "these people believe it's their duty to suppress evil. Because the *Koran* tells them so. And they see the US as evil. As perpetrators of, or accomplices in, widespread persecution of Muslims."

"Fine. So strike our military installations."

"But Bin Laden would say that turnabout is fair play. In 1996 he was quoted in Nida'ul Islam magazine on this very topic."

"Enlighten me."

"He said that America and Israel have killed women and children in the Muslim world repeatedly."

"Maybe as collateral damage," DuVal said, "but,"

"Does it really make a difference?"

"Of course it does!" DuVal exclaimed.

"Death is death, Mr. DuVal. And what these people see is a military and industrial giant who has invaded their holy land, killed women and children, co-opted and secularized governments, and planted the seeds of moral corruption in their people. What would you have them do?"

"Not kill civilians, for starters. It seems to me that if these folks have a problem with where their governments are leading them, they should start there. Work from the inside."

"Right, then. And that's what they would say they are doing, working from the inside. Inside their *souls*. Because they believe, in their souls, in their hearts, and in their minds, that Allah has called them to wage holy war. And it's very difficult to argue with the word of God."

"Or their interpretation of the word of God. Look, I'll be honest with you, I haven't read the *Koran*," DuVal said, his voice beginning to rise a bit, "but for the record, I think Bin Laden and his gang are nut cases. And if the *Koran* inspires people like him to incinerate thousands of innocent civilians, I would really have to begin to question its value as a religious document. Or at the very least, question the fundamentalists' reading of the *Koran*."

"Muslims make up more than a fifth of the world's population," the professor said, visibly stiffening, "and the proportion of fundamentalists is growing."

"And just a few centuries ago, the majority of people on earth believed that the world was flat. They were wrong," DuVal added, now relishing the role of devil's advocate, "I mean, don't you think it's healthy to question things every once in a while, Professor, especially if those things seem to be leading people down the wrong path."

"Again, Mr. DuVal, I would say that is a matter of perception. And I would add that you're fortunate that you live where you do," the professor went on, "because people have been put to death in the Middle East for that type of questioning."

"That sounds a little like a threat, professor," DuVal said.

"Did it? I certainly didn't mean it that way. But there are vast differences between cultures, and understanding that, I believe, is the key to beginning to understand this Jihad, and events that are taking place in the Middle East, in Indonesia, on US soil, and elsewhere."

And so it had gone. DuVal and Dr. Farooq had jousted and parried for the better part of an hour, the professor—when given an opportunity—plugging his book. They had then opened up the phone lines to DuVal's listeners, most of whom believed, predictably, that the solution to the problem of this Jihad lay in the considerable weapons stockpile of the US armed forces.

DuVal watched as the empty beer can shivered at the edge of the terrace wall. The wind had risen in the hours after the sunset, coming from a northeast direction, and bringing with it a true autumn chill. DuVal loved the autumn. He had loved almost all of the autumns of his life, but especially those he had spent in Oklahoma, and later in Kansas, working at stations on or near college campuses. It was a time of excitement and renewal, when the jet stream carried cool, fresh air from the north, from Canada and beyond, and with it, a sense of limitless possibilities.

New York had plenty of colleges, but little of the collegial atmosphere that populated DuVal's memory. The pierced and tattooed kids in Washington Square Park, the ones who spent hour after hour trying (with limited success) to make skateboards flip in mid-air, may or may not be

NYU students, it was hard to know; either way, they had little in common with the vibrant, enthusiastic students that lived in DuVal's memories of college campuses in the fall. Of course, times had changed. For all DuVal knew, the kids at Oklahoma State University were skateboarding around Gallagher Hall at that very moment in dungarees that were too long to be shorts and too short to be pants. He hoped not. But since he hadn't been back in well over a decade and had no intention of returning soon, it probably didn't matter anyway.

DuVal's momentary ride on this wave of nostalgia had been preceded by a more prolonged period of thought and reflection. He had returned to his loft after the show and ordered food in, eating alone in front of the television set while watching reportage of the plodding war build-up on CNN. Shit or get off the fucking pot, he thought, as he saw images of Colin Powell and George Bush warning that time was really, really (and this time we mean it) running out. He had turned the television off in disgust, retreating to the terrace to drink and smoke cigarette after cigarette.

DuVal collected his beer can from the terrace wall, took a last sip of the backwash, and crumpled it in his hand. He dropped the dented aluminum cylinder into a large ceramic urn where several others like it had gathered over the course of the previous hour. He lit a new cigarette from the burning ember at the end of the one he was smoking and was struck with a searing second of certainty: he had cancer, it was in his throat, he was going to lose his voice, and that would lead—in one way or another—to his death. Work had allowed him to divert his attention (if only for the duration of the show) from this recurring line of thinking. Home alone, he didn't have that luxury. The doctor had told him that it would be at least another day until the results of his biopsy were available, and the waiting was eating DuVal alive. He could think of little else.

He thought back over the events of the previous weeks. Why, he wondered, during what should have been one of the best, and most exciting periods of his life—negotiating the mega-contract that would make him a wealthy man—was he concurrently experiencing this run of bad luck? It had started with the lighter: his cherished gold lighter, left at Diane's apartment, never to be seen again. Even Kerri's gentle prodding of the police investigating Cheryl Nevins' murder had produced no evidence of his prized talisman. Then there was Diane, suddenly freezing him out. Granted, their arrangement had been too good to last; but still, why had the pregnancy and its resultant ill will happened now? And finally, the sore throat, biopsy, and interminable period of waiting to find out if he had cancer. It was almost more than DuVal could bear. He wished he had a real friend in New York, somebody he could talk to and confide in. He wished he had some real friends anywhere. DuVal realized—at that moment and for the very first time—that because of the nature of his work and his frequent moves, or maybe because of the type of person he was, that he only had one friend: Diane. And it looked as though he had damaged their friendship, perhaps beyond repair.

THIRTY

Helen Caldwell and Marie Lerman sat together eating. The sisters usually met for lunch at least once a week, but since Earl's death Helen had wanted to see her sister every day. The loneliness was too much to bear. She hadn't been able to sleep for more than a few hours at a stretch since his passing. The bed that they had shared, once a refuge, had become a dark, lonely place inhabited by relentless fears of an uncertain future.

"I just can't imagine," Helen said, picking at her food and staring out the window into the distance, "a life without Earl."

"It's just going to take time," Marie said, offering a subtle variation of the same line of comfort she had been doling out to her sister since her husband's death.

"I know it must seem like I'm repeating myself," Helen said, "but I lived my whole life around Earl. What I cooked for breakfast in the morning, when I used the bathroom before we went to sleep, every little decision involved thinking about how it would affect him."

"I know," her sister said, "I know."

"*Do* you?!" Helen said, stifling a sob. "I'm sorry. I just can't, I don't know what I'm going to do."

"Well, you don't have to do anything, Helen," Marie said, "for now."

In point of fact, Marie was beginning to realize that she didn't know what *she* was going to do. Because even as she listened to her sister so obviously suffering, Marie was consumed with envy. With every card and flower delivery that her sister received, she felt diminished. And people were sending money. In less than a week, Helen had deposited checks totaling in excess of $100,000. The mayor had even given Earl a posthumous promotion so that Helen's death benefits would be as great a sum as possible. She would never have to work again. Why couldn't it have been Mike who died on the job, Marie wondered? And though she felt a pang of guilt each time that thought entered her mind, she also couldn't keep it at bay. There had certainly been close calls. He'd been shot at, knives and hypodermic syringes had been pulled on—and violently thrust toward—him. Trash cans, bricks, rocks, bottles, telephones, toys, and television remote controls had been hurled in his direction. He'd been kicked, punched, scratched, slapped, and bitten at one time or another. Cars had been driven his way. He'd been in some very dangerous situations. But somehow, time after time, Mike managed to walk away (except for the odd scratch or bruise) unscathed.

In reality, Marie and Mike had never been anywhere near as happy as Helen and Earl. There were periods of contentment. But for Marie, there had never been real passion, or true love. And her sister's relationship with Earl had been an ever-present reminder of the emptiness she felt. It was the gnawing sensation that she had settled, and that there had to be more. It was sad. She'd fantasized about what she would do if Mike were killed on the job. After all of the cards and flowers, the department funeral (and an acceptable period of mourning), Marie thought she would move. Florida maybe. Somewhere sunny and clean, where she could start over and find someone who made her feel as if she wasn't missing out. Maybe Sarasota, the west coast. In her fantasy she wasn't too close to her parents.

"Are you okay?" Marie heard her sister say.

"What?" Marie replied.

"Are you okay? You looked like you somewhere else," Helen said.

"I'm fine. Just thinking," she added.

"Open your cookie," Helen said.

"Oh, it came," Marie said, reaching for a black tip tray with a check and a fortune cookie on top of it.

"Let me get lunch today," Helen insisted, "you've paid for the last three days."

Marie took the fortune cookie from the tip tray, removed it from its glassine envelope and broke the crescent in half, revealing the small strip of paper within. She pulled the paper from the cookie and stretched it between the thumb and index finger of each hand.

"What does it say?" her sister asked.

"BE CAREFUL WHAT YOU WISH FOR, IT MIGHT COME TRUE," Marie read.

"That's funny. Mine says 'Good fortune will smile upon you,' but I don't feel so fortunate right now," her eyes again welling with tears.

Marie reached across the table and clutched her sister's arm. "Oh Helen."

As they stepped outside the restaurant, the sisters buttoned their coats against the wind. The days were getting shorter and cooler, and the thought of autumn giving way to winter made Helen even more melancholy. She clenched her jaw and said a silent prayer, asking God to take care of Earl, and to give her the strength to carry on until she could join him.

"Do you want to have lunch tomorrow?" Marie asked.

"Could you?" her sister pleaded.

"Sure. Of course."

"I'll call you in the morning."

"Want me to walk you home?"

"No," Helen said, "I'll be all right."

"Call me later if you want to," Marie said, hugging her sister, adding, "and stop by for dinner if you want. Mike would love it."

"I'll call."

The sisters parted company and began walking toward their respective apartments, separated, even in midlife, by less than a half mile of Brooklyn streets.

As she walked, Marie tried to temper the envy she felt for her sister with some empathy. Helen was genuinely devastated. And while she hadn't mentioned suicide, or an unwillingness to go on, she had said again and again that she wasn't sure how she could. She really didn't know how to live life without Earl. Her loss was total. Complete. And other than listening to her, Marie didn't know how to bring her sister any real comfort. Her heart was broken in a way that only time, if even time, could heal. But as bad as she felt for Helen—and deep down she did feel bad for her—the very depth of her sister's misery made Marie envious. Why couldn't she love Mike like that? In an all-consuming, life-or-death kind of way. Marie knew she wouldn't be as heartsick if it had been Mike who had died. She'd certainly be sad. But her loss, and the effect it had on her, would be—like so many things in their lives—smaller, and somehow less than her sister's.

To be fair, Marie thought, she and Mike had it pretty good. True, he was not the love of her life, but nobody could say he wasn't a good man. Friends and acquaintances often reminded her how lucky she was. In almost twenty years of marriage, Marie could count on one hand the number of times he had raised his voice to her. He didn't drink much, only socially; he went where he said he was going, and came home when he said he would. They had a nice apartment, and a little money in the bank. Their sex life, while not what it was when they were younger, was still passable. It could be a lot worse. The stories she heard from some of the cops' wives were enough to curl your hair. Drunken fights, crying jags, a whole gamut of shitty behavior that Marie, when she really gave it some thought, was glad not to have to put up with. Then again, without passion, what is a marriage? And what is a life? Pondering these philosophical questions, Marie passed a nail salon with a sign above the door reading: Nail's Noble. She stopped and cocked her head an inch to the side, trying to figure out if the apostrophe was in the right place and, more important, if she needed a manicure. Yes, and yes, she concluded.

Inside and underway, the manicurist was less than delicate with Marie's cuticles. More than once, Marie found herself jerking her hand back as an unexpected, sharp pain shot up one of her fingers.

"Doh-moo-yo-han," the manicurist barked on each of these occasions.

"Sorry," Marie responded, thinking, if you'll stop jabbing my cuticle maybe I'll stop moving my hand, idiot.

She surveyed the room. While Marie had asked for a simple French manicure, many of the women in the chairs nearby were having false nails of extravagant length applied, nails that were then festooned with garish color, and wild appliqués depicting tropical scenes, shooting stars, product, or even sports franchise logos.

"Do you still do lots of those appliqués?" Marie asked.

"Oh yeah, vey popula," the woman answered, her gaze fixed on Marie's fingers.

"Really."

"Yeah. Maybe you should try one time."

"No, thank you."

"French manicure too boring," the woman said, finally looking up at Marie, then adding, "you finish."

Facing the street as her hands sat under the row of nail dryers, Marie considered the clothing of the passers-by. It was getting cooler, and new leather coats, bought on sale in mid-summer, were making their debut appearances. I should call to get my mink out of storage, Marie thought, Mike can pick it up.

Nails dry, Marie paid for her manicure, deciding to tip the woman who had done the work (because she'd been both rough and rude) only a dollar. Outside again, she considered riding the bus, but decided instead to walk. It was Saturday afternoon, Mike was working, and she was off. She had no time constraints, their apartment was only six or seven blocks away, and it would soon be too cold to spend much time outdoors.

A few blocks down the avenue, Patti Caiati, a woman from her street, came out the front door of Starbucks with a large cup of coffee in her hand. Though they'd lived less than 100 feet from each other for over a decade, the two women had seldom spoken, other than exchange greetings and pleasantries.

"Marie!" Patti exclaimed.

"Patti." Marie responded.

"Three-eighty-five for a cappuccino, can you believe it?" she complained, falling into step beside Marie.

"They shouldn't be able to charge that in Brooklyn."

"It's a crime, we should send your husband over there."

"Yeah," Marie said, forcing a laugh.

"It's the yuppies. They've ruined the neighborhood," Patti said, gesturing broadly with her Starbucks cup, "Nobody can afford to live here anymore. My brother had to close his store, the landlord wanted to quadruple his rent."

"What are you gonna do?" Marie replied.

"Frank and I pay $900 for our place. The couple downstairs pay $2800 for the same. What's gonna happen?"

"Who knows?"

It was the principal topic of conversation amongst anyone who had lived in the borough for more than a decade. Tens of thousands of refugees from Manhattan were invading Brooklyn, bringing high rents, fancy restaurants and spoiled children. What would become of the regular people? The teachers, cops and administrative assistants? The Franks, the Petes, the Maureens and the Donnas? Where would they go? For now, she and Mike were okay: he got detective pay, and she made a decent salary at the travel agency. But how long her job would last was anyone's guess. With each passing week, Travelocity, Expedia and Orbitz eroded their customer base. The only thing keeping them open was that many of their long-term customers were either computer illiterate or afraid to use credit cards online. The entire industry was on a deathwatch.

"I was so sorry to hear about your sister's loss," Patti said, placing her hand on Marie's forearm.

"Thank you," Marie said, wondering if this was a genuine expression of sympathy, or if Patti was simply fishing for gossip.

"What a tragedy. On the front page of the Post and everything."

"Earl was a good guy," Marie said, "He'll be missed by a lot of people."

"I never got a chance to meet him," Patti lamented, as they turned the corner onto their block.

Marie and Patti looked ahead, seeing a familiar row of brownstones, their heavy brick and concrete staircases and stoops reaching from what were once parlor floors (and now one-bedroom apartments) down to the sidewalk. A couple of boys, perhaps eleven or twelve years old, were tossing a football to another boy on the other side of the street.

"Yo! Catch it, bitch!"

"Throw it, nigga!"

"FRANKIE!" Patti called to one of the boys, "WHERE'S YOUR JACKET?"

She turned to Marie.

"He don't listen."

But Marie's attention was elsewhere. At mid-block, double-parked in front of her building, she spotted an unmarked police car. Perhaps Mike had forgot something this the morning, she thought, or stopped by the house for a snack. She wondered for a moment if she had left the apartment a mess. Sometimes, while getting ready—especially if Mike wasn't at home—she could be a bit careless, leaving discarded clothing selections draped across the bed or hanging from doorknobs around the apartment. It was one of the few things that drove Mike crazy. He hated to try to open a closet door with a cardigan or a blouse on the doorknob.

"Did you want me to hang this up?" he would ask. "I'm happy to do it," he'd add, hinting at his displeasure.

Suddenly—for reasons she could never explain but would question and discuss with friends and family in the remaining years of her life—a feeling of great unease came over her. She felt afraid, panicked even, and began to jog down the sidewalk.

Patti, left behind on the sidewalk, called after her.

"MARIE!?"

But Marie was already past Frankie and his friend, and nearly to the unmarked car. As she came closer, the driver's side door opened and a plain-clothes officer emerged. Tucking his shirt into the front of his slacks, he came around the back of the car to face a hard-breathing Marie.

"Marie?"

"What happened to him?" Marie asked the man, whose name—though she'd met him many times before—she could not remember. "Something happened. I know it."

Marie felt a hand on her shoulder. The plain-clothes officer had placed it there. She saw his mouth move in slow motion, and as the words came out, it sounded as if his mouth was stuffed with cotton balls.

"Mike's been shot, Marie," he said, "He's in King's County hospital. We gotta go. Now."

THIRTY-ONE

Traffic started to break up as Jodi Miller came though the Lincoln Tunnel heading westward into New Jersey. A few cars veered right toward Hoboken and Weehawken, which opened even more space for the stout BMW to power into the long curve that would put her on 3. It was early, still before 11 A.M. Jodi had driven into Manhattan for an 8:30 appointment with her gynecologist, whose office was on the Upper East Side. It was the same office she had been visiting since her early teens, but the old Dr. Rosen had retired, and his daughter, Wendy, had taken over the practice. Wendy had been in Jodi's class at Spence, before Jodi had been asked to leave the school. They'd smoked pot together at an Elvis Costello concert, if Jodi's memory served her. She couldn't remember if it was the *This Year's Model* tour or the one that followed: for the first four or five years after *My Aim Is True*, he'd come through New York a few times a year, and Jodi had seen many of the shows. In any event, she remembered what she was wearing: a short plaid skirt with a black motorcycle jacket over a white blouse. She was fairly certain that she also had high-top Chuck Taylors on her feet, but whether they were black or red was anyone's guess.

Jodi and Wendy had both come from that privileged class of largely unsupervised kids from the Upper East Side who, during their high school years, got to see every band that they wanted to see. Jodi now realized that it had been—even taking into account the anger and rebellion that led to so much trouble at school—one of the happiest times of her life. Especially in light of current events. Back then, throughout her teens and into her early twenties, she had virtually no responsibility, and the world had seemed like a limitless expanse of fun, promise and possibility.

In over a decade of practice, Dr. Rosen, the younger, had developed a bedside manner that was a studied mixture of her father's calm, authoritative physician persona and the I'm-still-hip city girl who had watched *Sex And The City* from the first episode and caught every trend on either the initial wave or the one in its shadow. As evidence, Jodi needed look no further than the back of Wendy's office door: there, the requisite Burberry scarf, raincoat or hat had been replaced by a yoga mat. Jodi wondered how long the yoga fad would last. Of course it wasn't a fad to some people, but she predicted that Wendy Rosen's yoga mat would soon find its way into a closet that held a long-neglected Thighmaster and the Tai-Bo tapes.

The fact that Jodi had known Wendy since childhood had done nothing to shorten the time between having had her vital signs taken by the nurse practitioner and Wendy's appearance in the examining room.

"Hey girl," Dr. Rosen had greeted her, annoyingly, when she finally arrived.

"Hi Wendy."

"Are you still taking the folic acid?" the doctor asked, looking at Jodi's chart and referring to the supplement that would supposedly increase the chances of she and Dave getting pregnant.

"No, I gave up on that."

"Oh really?" the doctor asked, probing gently into what, for Jodi, was a sensitive area, and one which, if she remembered correctly, had been discussed and dismissed during her last visit to the office.

"Yeah, we went over that last time," Jodi replied.

"Okay, okay," Wendy said, holding her hands up in a gesture of surrender, "so what brings you in today? It's not time for your annual yet."

"No. I seem to have a little discharge. And some kind of a rash down there."

"Uh-huh," The doctor replied, "And how long has this been going on?"

"A few days," Jodi answered.

"Any fever?"

"I don't think so."

Dr. Rosen reached a hand up to Jodi's neck and gently probed both sides under the jaw line with her fingers. "You have a little swelling in the glands."

"So?"

"Well, let's do an examination before we jump to any conclusions."

"What kind of conclusions?"

"Any conclusions," the doctor repeated.

"Like what?" Jodi asked again.

"Like if you may have contracted an STD, for instance" the doctor replied, matter-of-factly.

Jodi froze, momentarily paralyzed by a powerful combination of fear and anger. The muscles in her chest and back contracted, and a hollow feeling took root in her stomach. She wanted to reach for her cell phone. She wanted to run out of the room.

"What?"

"The symptoms you describe are consistent with herpes, among other things."

"*Herpes!?*"

"Like I said, let's not jump to any conclusions until we've done an exam."

Wendy was very professional. Concluding that Jodi had, in fact, contracted herpes, she explained—in a voice almost entirely devoid of judgment—the day-to-day reality of living with the disease.

"Herpes is very common, Jodi," she said, "and most people with herpes live completely normal and satisfactory lives."

Jodi nodded her head, and wished more than anything that Wendy would stop saying the word herpes.

"If you're careful, you can even have sex with an uninfected partner without placing them at much risk," she said, adding "but you would be well-advised to tell them first. And of course we'll want to do an HIV test, just to be on the safe side."

Shellshocked, Jodi sat quietly thinking. She assumed that behind Wendy's veneer of professionalism, she was judging and classifying her as either a whore or the pathetic victim of a philandering husband. It was humiliating. After the diagnosis and the withdrawal of a large vial of blood, and after enduring the speech about how to spot an outbreak, and after being handed a pharmaceutical company-sponsored brochure with bad illustrations of people involved in difficult conversations, Jodi was spent. Exhausted, and filled with an emotional stew whose component parts were hurt, rage, disappointment, and embarrassment, she then had to go in search of a previously unvisited pharmacy to fill her prescription. She chose a Duane Reade at the corner of 49th and 9th.

"Have you been here before?" the pharmacist asked.

"No," Jodi replied, watching the pharmacist peer at the prescription, then back at her.

"I see."

Prescription in hand, Jodi headed home. By the time she pulled into the driveway of the home she shared with Dave she had decided what she would do. The anger that had flashed then faded to fill her with a depressed lethargy in the city had rekindled. It sparked a firestorm of manic energy that quickened her breath and sent electric jolts through her nerves and muscles.

Jodi was able to locate several large, empty cardboard boxes in the garage. She was surprised to discover that it took only a little over an hour to pack each and every single article of Dave's clothing. He had an abundance of suits, slacks, ties, shirts, and so on, but the act of ripping the items from hangars and throwing them helter-skelter into boxes was much less time consuming than packing in any organized way. When she had sealed the boxes, Jodi called several Salvation Army offices to locate a group that was willing to make a pickup that day. Within a few minutes, she had. They would have to come from Essex county—Newark, in fact—but perhaps due to the wretched state of the economy and the depth of need in the community, they were only too willing to oblige.

"I can have a truck in your driveway by the end of the day," the woman on the phone had said.

"Not sooner?" Jodi had asked.

"Not today," the woman replied.

"But what if I were to make a contribution?"

"What kind of a contribution?"

"Five hundred."

"Cash?"

"I could run to the ATM."

"We'll be right there."

Later that afternoon, after the Salvation Army people had come and gone, after the locksmith had finished changing each of the locks in the house, and after she had contacted the security company to apprise them of the changes in her household and the need for extra vigilance, Jodi was overcome by a steely calm. Granted, a portion of that calm was made of vodka; but she had decided on a path of action, and she would take the necessary steps to see it through.

She called Dave's assistant.

"Shelly?"

"Hi Jodi. He's not in."

"That's fine, I'll leave a message."

"Do you want voicemail?"

"No, I'll leave it with you."

"Go ahead."

"Make sure you write it down. It's specific, and kind of long."

"My hands are on the keyboard."

"Okay, here it is: You gave me herpes, you fucking prick. I've given all your clothes away, and changed the locks on the house. I never want to speak to you again. The next time you hear my voice will be in court. Rot in hell."

"Uh, okay. Is that all?"

"I think so."

"Okay."

"Okay."

"Bye."

"Bye."

With that, Jodi wrote off her marriage. Strangely, she felt no need for a direct confrontation. Not immediately, at least. She would ask her father for the name of the most vicious divorce lawyer in New York, and then systematically destroy Dave. Like a vulture on a fresh piece of roadkill, she would strip away all that he held dear. And she would make certain that her father fired him from the agency. With those objectives in mind, she picked up the phone to call her father, the great and powerful Mitch Sanders.

THIRTY-TWO

Dave stepped out of the elevator car and walked slowly toward Mitch Sanders's office, his apprehension growing with each step. The agency had six floors in the building, each offering approximately 10,000 square feet of office space. The lower few of the contiguous floors housed the mailroom, security, the IT department, and the rowed cubes of administrative functionaries who ensured that the nuts-and-bolts elements of the business were accomplished in a timely fashion. The endless paperwork that is the sturdy foundation of every great organization. Each year, at an appointed time, a line of trucks would appear to haul the accumulated harvest of this cube farm away to a secure, water- and fire-proof storage facility upstate, never to be seen again. At least until the next lawsuit or audit, at which time the documents would either easily appear—or magically disappear—depending on which suited the needs of the day.

Dave's office, while fairly large and in possession of a spectacular view of midtown, Brooklyn and Queens, was itself a cube compared to the offices on the executive floor. The uppermost of the agency's floors housed Mitch Sanders's office, the state-of-the-art conference room with the latest electronic gadgetry, the vast offices of the CFO and the heaviest money guys, and four or five of the top-producing agents. To work on the floor was to know true power. At least the kind that mattered in the entertainment business. It meant that you were able to secure reservations at the right restaurants (and perhaps equally important, be seated at the right tables in those restaurants), and that you were acknowledged and respected in New York, Los Angeles, Aspen, Sundance, Cannes, the Hamptons, and St. Barts. Outside of those places nobody would know who you were, but that was immaterial, because the people who worked on the executive floor only ever traveled to those seven places. To travel elsewhere would mean to suffer the indignity of being unrecognized and, further, to have only the basic set of rights and privileges that come with having been born human.

Dave had hoped to move up to the executive floor after the DuVal deal was signed, but as he walked the quiet halls toward his father-in-law's office, he could feel the likelihood of that event shrinking like the penis in his pants. A profound and deep fear had taken root within him. He was unsure of what was going to happen in the meeting, but he was reasonably certain that it wasn't going to be good.

"Good morning, David," a gravelly female voice said as Dave entered Sanders's suite of offices.

The voice was that of Eleanor, Sanders's loyal assistant of thirty-seven years.

"Hello, Eleanor," Dave replied, his reply met with a sweep of a bony finger pointing him toward a couch.

It was a chilly reception. After all their years together, Eleanor had what amounted to a psychic connection with Sanders. She was also, for all intents and purposes, a surrogate mother to Jodi. From her withering gaze, Dave realized that he might as well have given Eleanor herpes. It was a sobering thought, because Eleanor was approaching retirement age, and she had smoked three packs of Winstons a day since age 11. Not that she would ever retire. Dave figured she was like the Pope: she would probably go down in the office.

Dave was extremely uncomfortable. And that discomfort grew with each of the twenty-five minutes that passed before finally being summoned to the inner sanctum. It was a long and lonely time. He first tried reading the trades that were assembled on the low table in front of him, but found he was unable to concentrate. Next, he feigned interest in something imaginary on his shoe, carefully examining and picking at it. Finally, he just sat, like a ten year-old waiting to be called into the principal's office. Then, suddenly, without receipt of a call or any other sound or movement that would indicate that something had changed, Eleanor spoke.

"Mr. Sanders will see you now."

Dave stood from the couch and walked toward the double wooden doors that shielded his father in-law from the outside world. As he turned the knob and gently pulled the right-hand door open, Dave marveled at the solidity and weight of the object, and also at the ease with which it swung on its hinges. Quality. Nothing was too good for Mitch Sanders.

"Sit down, Dave," the president and founder of the agency intoned.

"Thank you."

Mitch Sanders was seated behind an ash-colored, modern wood desk that had nothing on its surface save a burnished titanium Mac PowerBook and a telephone. Neither paper nor pen was in evidence. If the man had files it was anyone's guess where he kept them.

Tall, thin, and with a full head of grey hair that was the envy of many a man over sixty, Sanders, among other things, had the memory of an elephant. He was able to recall, in the most minute detail, pretty much every element of every deal he had ever done. It was an amazing and intimidating faculty, and one that had stood him in good stead over nearly fifty years in the business.

Dave sat in a chair across from his father in-law. There were two chairs side by side, and he had stumbled for a moment making a decision about which to occupy. Had he known how short the meeting would be Dave might not have wasted any time making his choice. Because Sanders got right to the point.

"I can see by your clothes that you haven't been home."

This was, in fact, an accurate observation. Having received Jodi's message the previous evening, Dave had driven to New Jersey to make a half-hearted attempt at explanation or apology. There, he had learned that Jodi would answer neither the door nor the telephone, so he'd returned to Manhattan and rented a room.

It had been a strangely disquieting night. While Dave had been considering ending his marriage for several years, when circumstances had forced the matter he was left feeling alone, frightened, guilty, and uncertain.

Sleep had not come easily. Even after a few drinks in the hotel lobby bar. Or perhaps because of the few drinks he had had in the hotel lobby bar. There, surrounded by young, cosmopolitan singles, he had felt like the old, slightly overweight guy who couldn't quit staring. With herpes. He hoped to speak with Jodi later in the day, if only to arrange a time to pick up some clothes. Then, there was much to be done. He needed to find a place to live (an apartment in the city, he thought) pronto. And he would need the services of a lawyer to navigate the intricacies of a divorce. He also needed to finalize the DuVal deal, of course. With regard to the final item, the previous two couldn't be happening at a worse time. He needed his full powers of concentration to bring the DuVal deal across the line. DuVal was taking his sweet time making a decision, and in Dave's experience, every day that a deal was sitting on the table it accumulated risk.

Dave was troubled by the look on Sanders's face. He looked like he had just stepped in a pile of noxious dog shit.

"I never liked you, Dave," Sanders said, "I always thought you were a nothing."

Dave moved his mouth almost imperceptibly, trying to summon a rejoinder. Sanders held up his hand like a traffic cop stopping a line a cars while a funeral passed through an intersection.

"Don't bother," he said, indicating, on no uncertain terms, that he would entertain no banter, "I suspected you had been fucking around on my daughter, you prick. I figured the two of you would sort it out. But giving her herpes? Are you fucking *kidding* me?"

Sanders paused to let the full weight of the accusation sink in.

"They're packing your office up right now, you piece of shit," he added, "If you run down there fast enough you might be able to meet them on the sidewalk."

"You're firing me?" Dave managed.

"You never worked here, as far as I'm concerned," Sanders said, rising to his full height.

"But what about my clients?" Dave sputtered.

"*YOUR* CLIENTS?" Sanders roared, raising his voice for the first time, "The ones who come to see you in MY offices? I've already contacted them. They all prefer to stay with the agency."

Sanders had come around the desk and was towering over Dave. Dave figured there was about a 40% chance that Sanders would hit him.

"What about DuVal?" Dave said, with the urgency of a drowning man in a dark sea crying out for a lifeboat that is receding into the distance.

"You can keep DuVal if he's stupid enough to work with you. I despise that guy. It makes me feel dirty to have him on the agency's roster."

Sanders grabbed Dave by the shoulder of his jacket and lifted him from his chair.

"And it makes me feel sick to have you in this building," he said, "Get the fuck out of here, and don't come back."

Sanders had been true to his word. In the time it took to get fired, declared a nothing, and ride the elevator down to the lobby of the building, every single item in his office—save his client files—had been packed into boxes and placed on the sidewalk. As Dave walked through the front door he saw a group of nine boxes on the sidewalk, his name scrawled on them in magic marker. What a pain in the ass, Dave thought. He wondered what he would do with the boxes. He would have to throw them into a cab and take them back to the hotel. Of course the boxes were the least of his worries. Dave needed to do some major damage control. More than anything, he needed to speak with DuVal immediately. It was a dicey situation, and it needed to be handled gingerly. He would call DuVal's office and arrange a meeting. Dave retrieved his cell phone from his jacket pocket and flipped the device open. The LED screen read NO SERVICE.

THIRTY-THREE

"So near," she said, speaking to him for the first time since they'd left DFW.

"Yet so far," Roy replied, turning his head to one side to look out the window at the gap between the plane and the jetway, then back in the other direction to look at the passenger in the seat beside him.

He'd noticed her before. First when he took his seat, and then again as he'd asked her to stand as he got up to use the restroom. She was attractive. Pretty, even. She was perhaps thirty years old, and wearing low-cut jeans that showed several inches of smooth, hairless skin above them. She had a fresh, unlined face, and one of those vaguely tribal tattoos that spread width-wise across her lower back. Roy imagined she was a native Texan. Or as native as one could be without being a Mound Builder, a Spaniard or any of the other peoples who had occupied Texas in its long journey to its present state.

"The delays get worse every time I fly. Especially into LaGuardia."

"I was on the tarmac for an hour before we took off on the way down," Roy commiserated.

"That sucks," she said.

"Barely made my connection," he added.

"Story of my life," she said, leaning forward to look out the window, then turning to look Roy in the eye. "You live here, or there?"

"Where?" Roy asked.

"Austin," she said, "or wherever you were."

"Here," Roy said, "I live here. I was in Austin for work."

"I live there," she said. Then added, "I wonder what's taking so fucking long?

"Everything's stacked up," Roy said, "Planes are circling the city in layers day and night," he added, twirling his finger in the air. "And now that we're on the ground, we're probably waiting for somebody who can operate the jetway."

"They should figure out how to schedule things better," she said, "this is bullshit."

Roy started to laugh, and then noticed that she was crying. Not sure what to do, he took a napkin from the seat back in front of him and handed it to her.

"Thank you," she said, "I'm sorry."

"For what?" Roy asked.

"For crying," she answered, dabbing her eyes with the napkin, then crumpling it in her hand.

"Don't worry about it," Roy said, "I mean, I'd rather you *weren't* crying, but not because it bothers me."

"Thanks," she said, pausing as the aircraft pulled a little closer to the gate, moving ahead in fits and starts, and came to another stop. "Fuck."

"It won't be long," Roy offered. She began to cry again, then dabbed the balled-up napkin into the corner of one eye.

"I'm usually not like this. My boyfriend broke up with me a few hours ago."

"Oh," Roy replied, not knowing what else to say.

"Actually, he might've broken up with me yesterday. I got the e-mail a few hours ago at DFW."

"Ouch."

"A fucking e-mail. Can you believe it? I didn't even like him that much," she said, suddenly laughing, "we'd only been going out for a few months, so..."

"Oh," Roy said again, looking away from her for a moment to watch the sad, predictable ritual of eager people standing to retrieve their items in the overhead compartment. Sad, because the aircraft was not yet at the gate, and their behavior precipitated quick admonishment from the flight attendants, who used the public address system to curtly remind the passengers to remain seated until the aircraft was safely stopped there.

"Dumbasses," she said, "it happens every time. They never learn."

Roy wondered, for a second, if it was possible that these people didn't know that they were not yet at the gate. Perhaps they had never flown before. Or, he thought, maybe they do know that the aircraft is not yet at the gate, but they are somehow compelled to do the wrong thing.

"It's a puzzle," he said.

"I don't know why it bothers me so much," she said.

"I know. It bugs me too," Roy answered.

She looked at him and smiled. Roy nodded his head.

Suddenly, the aircraft moved forward and then came to a gentle rest. A chime, indicating the actual conclusion of the flight, sounded over the PA system. The passengers (except for Roy and his row-mate) sprang into action. The same people who had refused to check their bags that were a little too big—then needed the assistance of a flight attendant to cram those bags into the overhead compartment—struggled to remove them. Children were gathered and organized, their precious scattered possessions (stuffed animals, plastic cars, Game Boys) found and put away. Elderly people, using the headrests of the seats in front of them as levers, struggled to rise.

Then, just as quickly, the movement stopped. The passengers seemed to gel into a solid mass. A long line of figures stood motionless in the aisle and at their seats while nothing happened.

"Here we go," his row-mate said.

"Or stay," Roy said, adding, "for a few more minutes, at least."

Roy was as eager to disembark the aircraft as anyone on board. He just knew that standing up at that moment wasn't going to get him into the jetway any sooner.

He'd called Diane that morning, and it had been agreed that she would meet him at the airport. With the increased security that had recently been put in place it was, of course, impossible to be met at the gate. She would instead be standing in the baggage-claim area near the multitudes of car service drivers holding cardboard signs displaying the misspelled names of arriving passengers.

The time Roy had spent away in Texas—along with the lengthy, ranging telephone conversations that he and Diane had carried on for several nights running—had made him eager to see her as soon as possible upon his return. And now that the plane was on the ground, an entirely new level of excitement was beginning to well within him. He was overwhelmed with a desire to see her, and he couldn't remember the last time he had felt this way about someone.

"Hey," she said, interrupting Roy's silent reverie, "my name is Sandy, by the way."

"Oh, I'm Roy," Roy answered.

"It was nice talking to you."

"You too," Roy answered.

She scribbled a name and a number on a small strip of paper and handed it to Roy. He took the paper in his hand. It was a fortune from a fortune cookie. On one side, it read: Sandy Furlong 512-555-1212. On the other, it read: LOVE HAS A WAY OF FINDING YOU.

"It's the only paper I could find. Call me the next time you're in Austin," she said, standing.

Roy slipped the paper into his pocket.

"Good luck, Sandy," he said, uncertain of what else to say.

The rows of seats in front of them began to clear, and Sandy stepped into the aisle. He felt a pleasant flutter in his stomach, and an involuntary smile stretched across his face. He wondered what he and Diane would do. They hadn't discussed specific plans. Roy wanted to hold her in his arms and smell the light scent that she wore. He wanted to believe that she was as glad to see him as he was to see her. He stood, took his bag from the overhead compartment, and began walking toward the exit, looking at Sandy's back, at her tattoo, and thinking about Diane.

THIRTY-FOUR

"Hello, Mr. DuVal?"

"Yes," DuVal said.

"I'm calling from Dr. Meltzer's office."

"Okay," DuVal said, his body stiffening with fear.

"Dr. Meltzer wanted me to tell you that the results of your biopsy were negative."

"Oh," DuVal said, suddenly speechless.

"He did want to schedule a follow-up appointment, though."

"Okay," DuVal said, "I'll have my assistant call later."

DuVal placed the phone in its cradle and fell back into his chair. He didn't have cancer. For the better part of a week, he'd obsessively constructed scenarios in his mind about what he would do when he was told that he did, in fact, have cancer. Now, it felt like only tension and dread had been holding him together, because along with a tremendous feeling of relief, a wave of fatigue and sadness suddenly washed over DuVal. The fatigue he could understand: he had been sleeping poorly and drinking even more than usual to knock himself out at night. Of course, going to sleep drunk precipitated a fitful night of dreamless sleep, punctuated by piss breaks and trips to the kitchen to refill his bedside water glass. Still, in DuVal's mind, it beat lying awake taking a trip into the spiral of death, where he was told he had cancer, the treatment caused him to lose his voice, his voice loss caused him to lose his job, and his job loss caused him to lose his purpose for being, and ultimately, his will to live.

The sadness that now gripped DuVal was a different issue. Slumped in his chair and staring out the high-floor window of his office, he considered its roots and implications. His career trajectory, with the frequent moves, increasing levels of success and single-minded focus on work, he now realized, had exacerbated what were some not-so-wonderful qualities of his personality and character. He could be a bit of a dick, sometimes. And he hadn't properly understood the value of interpersonal relationships, or, when he thought about it, other people at all. As a result, when the cancer scare came and chips were down, he had nobody to turn to. It was a watershed moment. And one that DuVal hated himself for. Because there was little that Jack DuVal despised more than the Dr. Phils of the world: those therapists, people, or pundits who reduced every situation and person to the predictable, insistent, and undeniable human need for social intercourse and love. But in this moment of self-loathing and clarity, DuVal realized that if he was going to have a satisfactory life, if he was to get any enjoyment out of his ever-increasing wealth and success—true, lasting, and meaningful enjoyment—he was going to have to change. He would need to find a way to connect with people. To give a shit. He had no idea where to start. He didn't know if it was even possible to change such a fundamental element of one's character. First of all, he'd always been a loner. He was an only child, and one who didn't particularly care for his parents. He had spent the bulk of his adult life alone in a dim room talking at people. Not with them, or to them, but at them. True, he had guests on his show and took calls from listeners, but the fact of the matter was that he was a monologist. His programs were much more like to lectures than conversations. So change, if there was to be any, was going to be difficult. But the cancer scare was exactly the type of thing that might foster change. And in spite of himself, he thought he just might be ready for some.

DuVal shook a cigarette loose from his pack and lit up. He inhaled deeply and then exhaled a long plume of delicious smoke into the dry air of his office. It was the first lungful that he had been able to enjoy since Dr. Meltzer has seen the polyp. And enjoy it he did. Deeply, and fully. He savored the expansive sensation, and took another long drag to prolong the moment. I will change, DuVal thought. He didn't know how he was going to do it, and he knew it would take time, but with the fear of cancer vanquished, DuVal felt he had the courage to dip his toe in the chilly waters of the human race.

First, though, he needed to get his business affairs in order. He needed to call Dave Miller. He had spoken to the accountants and the lawyers and it was time to nail things down. Everyone was telling him the same thing: that the difference between the deals on the table was negligible; he should work where he wanted to work. Where he thought he would be the happiest. And now, for the first time, DuVal actually considered that advice. Throughout his career, most of these types of decisions had been made for him. He was either asked to leave a station or, more often, offered a much better salary in a larger market. It was odd to be making a career decision based on solely on, for lack of a better word, his comfort.

DuVal was leaning toward staying put at the Syndicate. The CEO had called and personally asked him to stay.

"Jack, we really think of you as part of the family here," he'd said.

"That's nice of you to say," Jack had replied, realizing that he must be a particularly estranged member of the family, since the last time he had seen or spoken with the CEO was the day he had signed his original contract a few years previously.

"I'm flying down to St. Barts this weekend; why don't you come? We can relax a bit."

DuVal, initially suspicious, had been touched. He knew deep down that he was nothing but a dollar sign to the guy, but it was a fairly meaningful gesture for the CEO to offer to give up a weekend with his wife or mistress to try to keep him on board. In the end DuVal had passed on the trip, but sent his profound thanks for the offer. Truth be told, DuVal hated to fly. He also didn't golf, and the sun was unkind to his fair skin. Perhaps they could have dinner one night in New York, he suggested. They had scheduled something for the following week.

There was a chance, of course, that his agent might not be happy with this decision. Dave had urged DuVal to take whichever deal he wanted, but after all, there was less money up front with the Syndicate deal. Of course, in the long run there would be more for everyone, Dave and his agency included. An extra 15% of $5 million for them, in fact. That's how DuVal would spin it. And fuck 'em anyway, the agency is supposed to be working for me, he thought. Christ, he reflected, catching himself; I've got a hair-trigger asshole response. How am I supposed to rein that in? He decided to devote some serious thought to the matter later, perhaps when he got home after the show. A period of quiet contemplation in the spa on his terrace.

He refocused his mind on the deal. Staying at the Syndicate would have considerable advantages. First of all, he wouldn't have to pack up all the crap in his office. Secondly, they had really done right by him when they put his room together. The studio was his, and his alone, to use; it had been built to his specifications. It was comfortable and functional, and more important, done. And that was a big deal. Because DuVal had learned that getting things done with contractors in New York was an incredibly difficult process and money was no guarantee of success. Regardless of the scope of the project, it was a given that the timeline and the budget was going to balloon uncontrollably. And any mention of the ballooning budget or timeline would be met with complaint, or worse, by the contractor. He would moan about the unions, permits, the parking situation on the street, and finally offer—in tones that were more suggestive of a threat—to walk off the job. And though technically it wasn't DuVal's role to deal with that kind of crap, in the end, it affected him. Yes, staying put, he realized, would have its advantages; particularly if he was going to continue broadcasting from New York.

DuVal reached for his phone. He would call Dave, tell him his decision, and move on to the next order of business. He dialed Dave's office number and reached voicemail. The voicemail message was spoken by a voice that was unfamiliar to DuVal. It indicated that the voice mailbox had been closed. Odd, DuVal thought. He checked the number against the one in his address book and redialed, producing the same result. Some fuckup with the phone system, DuVal surmised, thinking *this stuff is supposed to make our lives easier, for Christ's sake.* He dialed Dave's cell. After three rings, DuVal received another prerecorded message; this one indicating that the cell account was no longer active. DuVal redialed the cell number and again received the same message. Confused, and edging over into the area of pissed, DuVal hung up the phone. What the hell is going on, he wondered? The thought was punctuated by the ringing of his telephone. Answering, DuVal listened as Jeffrey announced that he had Dave Miller on another line, and asked if DuVal would like to take his call. DuVal indicated he would.

"What the fuck's going on, Dave? I called both your numbers, and nothing."

"Something's happened, Jack," Dave said, "Jodi kicked me out."

"Well, there's a surprise," DuVal deadpanned.

"It came completely out of the blue."

"Fuck anything that walks upright behind your wife's back and that kind of thing'll sneak up on you," DuVal said.

"Ouch."

"So what's the deal with the phones?"

"That's what I called to talk to you about. I'm out, Jack."

"Out? What do you mean out?"

"Out of a job, Jack," Dave explained, "and out of my house. Locked out."

DuVal thought he heard Dave's voice break as he said the word house. He didn't know what would happen if Dave started to cry. It would be extremely uncomfortable.

"Well, Dave," DuVal said, "I'm sorry to hear that."

Dave started to sob. DuVal's head fell forward, his chin resting on his chest as he pulled the phone receiver an inch away from his ear.

"Jack, I don't know what I'm going to do," Dave said, choking back heaving sobs. The sobs sounded unnatural and animal-like, coming, as they were, from an adult man who was utterly unaccustomed to crying. "They've cut off my cell phone, my credit cards, everything. I'm out on the fucking street."

DuVal could, in fact, hear street noise in the background. He wondered if Dave was on a payphone, and if anyone could see him crying. He wondered if someone was standing a few feet away, impatiently waiting for Dave to finish his call. DuVal's mind wandered. He thought about how few pay phones there were on the street nowadays, and how few of those worked. You never see a phone booth anymore, he thought, they're just gone. He forced his attention back to the conversation.

"Where are you now, Dave," DuVal asked.

"Fifty-third and Madison," Dave replied.

"Listen, why don't you come up to the office and pull yourself together," DuVal suggested.

A loud sob burst through DuVal's earpiece.

"Thanks, Jack," Dave blubbered, hanging up.

THIRTY-FIVE

Diane and Roy sat side by side on the banquette, the fingers of her right hand entwined in his left. She'd met him at the airport, waiting alone for over an hour in the baggage claim area for the arrival of his plane, then together for another forty-five minutes for his luggage to appear. Finally released from the bondage of modern air travel, they had sped by cab to Manhattan.

"Want to know something?" Diane asked.

"I want to know everything," Roy replied.

"I was on pins and needles waiting for you at the airport," Diane said.

"Really?" Roy asked.

"It's true," she said, "Every time a group of people came down the escalator toward the baggage claim, this feeling would well up in my stomach," Diane continued, pausing to kiss Roy on the cheek, "then I'd scan every face in the crowd looking for you. When the stream of people would slow to a trickle and you weren't among them, I'd have to accept that it wasn't your flight. And a few minutes later it would start all over again."

"I was going through something similar on the plane," Roy admitted.

"Tell me."

"Well," Roy said, "I was really eager to see you, but the plane kept circling the city. Then when we finally landed, we just sat."

Roy abandoned his thought in mid-sentence. He wrapped his arms around Diane, enveloping her in a close embrace that summarized the unexpectedly deep longing he'd felt while he was gone. He then slid his cheek along Diane's, finding her mouth with his own and beginning a long, impassioned kiss. It was a kiss like neither had experienced since their early teenaged years of making out in car seats.

"I sure am glad to be home," he said.

"Ummm," Diane agreed, leaning in to kiss him again, then pulling their lips apart for a moment, she murmured, "I love you."

Roy's body jerked back a fraction of an inch, tightening just enough to announce that it had done so. His eyes widened a sliver. It was involuntary movement, like the convulsive spasms associated with sneezing, or nausea. Not knowing what to say, shocked by Diane's words, and embarrassed by his reaction, he leaned in to kiss her again. She placed her thumb on his chin to keep their lips apart.

"Oh no," she said, "I didn't mean to say that."

Roy's shoulders relaxed a bit. "I don't mind," he offered, knowing, as he said them, that those too were the wrong words at the wrong time.

"Look," Diane said—horrified that she had let slip the three words most likely, when spoken too soon, to send almost any man running—but also somehow unwilling to issue a retraction, "there's no explaining it. And at this point, there's no denying it. I think I may be falling in love with you. Or maybe I already have. So if that freaks you out, I'm sorry."

"No," Roy said, as a flurry of thoughts rushed through his head. Truth be told (even if he couldn't manage to tell it at this particular moment), he was having similar thoughts. It did feel as if their relationship had rapidly progressed from a nice-to-meet-you kind of thing to an I-can't-live-without-you kind of thing. It was crazy. They barely knew each other, and he had spent the bulk of the time since their first meeting out of town. But conversation with Diane came so easily. She was fun to talk to, extremely smart, quick to laugh, and they shared many interests. She was altogether alluring. It was also nice to meet someone who, in this day and age, still liked to read, and who made time to do it. She read everything, and he loved that she could talk as easily and knowledgeably about Publilius Syrus as she could about Paris Hilton. But it was moving too fast. What if he got in over his head? On the other hand, what did he have to lose? Why not just take the ride, and see where it might go? She was a great kisser. And when they kissed, he felt that thing. That excited thing that radiated from deep in his stomach and stayed with him for hours after they parted. The one that kept him lying awake at night, wondering what she was like in bed. But what about that? They hadn't even slept together yet. What if it was really bad?

"No what?" Diane said, interrupting Roy's runaway-train of thought.

"No it doesn't freak me out," he said.

Diane eyed him questioningly.

"Okay, that's a lie. It freaks me out a little."

"I understand."

"But just a little."

"Say something good now."

"All right. I like that you're 36."

"Jesus. I hope this gets better. Fast. Because reminding me that I'm 36 isn't helping to bring me back from the dark abyss of vulnerability I'm falling into right now.

"No, 36 is good," Roy said.

"I'm all ears."

"It's good because you don't say 'Oh my god' all the time, as if every observation were actually a revelation. Which I suppose it may be to girls who say 'Oh my god' all the time. I like that you don't upspeak, so that every sentence sounds like a question. That drives me nuts. And I like that you know that there was another George Bush before this one, and that the first one wasn't as dumb as a bag of hammers. In short, you're a woman and not a girl. Should I go on?"

"Been dating some young ones, have you?"

"A few," Roy admitted.

"Poor boy."

"If you only knew," Roy said. "You may find this hard to believe, but most of the good ones my age are taken; or at least it seems like they are. But my friends have been able to provide a seemingly endless supply of thought-free, reading-impaired, 25-year-old friends-of-their-wives-or-girlfriends to fix me up with. Which explains why I had pretty much stopped dating altogether."

"Well I hope you got some enjoyment out of it before you quit," Diane said.

"I did my part."

"Tell me more about Bingo," Diane said. And with those words they seized the opportunity to move away from the uncomfortable task of trying to define their budding relationship.

They lingered over dinner, decided against coffee, and shared a crème brûlée. When it came time to settle the bill, Diane, over Roy's strenuous objections, insisted on paying.

"Please, let me get it. I asked you out."

"I don't remember that," Roy said.

"Well, I offered to meet you at the airport, and we wound up having dinner," she added.

"That's a bit of a stretch," Roy countered, wallet in hand.

"You go get the coats and bags, I'll settle up here."

He gave in.

"I'm going to expense it, anyway," Diane added, as Roy stood.

"Fine, then."

Crossing the floor to the coat check, Roy gazed up at the mirrors that circled the room just below ceiling level. They were angled to allow diners to scan the room from wherever they might be seated. He found Diane's reflection, and watched as she quickly reviewed the bill. Her hair was a deep shade of brown, and cut blunt to a length that was between the bottom of her ears and the top of her shoulders. It fell forward as she bent, and she tucked one side of it behind an ear. This movement allowed Roy to consider her glasses, which framed and drew attention to her eyes. Though he couldn't see them at that moment, Diane's eyes, Roy thought (having stared into them for most of the last few hours) were lovely not just for their shape and the richness of their brown color, but also for the twinkle of life that lived within. It was a characteristic that Roy had seen and tried to define before. Some women—and men for that matter—seemed to have a light in their eyes that was not present in others. And in Diane's eyes, the twinkle became even more pronounced when she smiled or laughed. Which is exactly what she did when she looked up at the mirror across the room to see Roy looking back at her. They both laughed, then broke eye contact as Roy bumped into the back of another diner's chair and took a moment to express his apologies.

Diane gave her credit card to the waiter, and the thought of having told Roy that she loved him suddenly rushed back over her. She cringed. What was she thinking? And what was going to happen? He probably wouldn't run out of the restaurant right now, but she figured there was only a 50/50 chance he would call her again after they parted tonight or in the morning. She looked up and followed him with her eyes as he approached the coat check. He walked with self-assurance, and Diane imagined that he was comfortable wherever he went. She wondered if he was considering if they would sleep together that night. She had devoted a good amount of thought to the topic while he was gone, building various mental scenarios around when the first time would be, what it would be like, and so on. She had gotten a bikini wax that morning just in case. She wondered if she should feel weird about having sex so soon after the abortion. As far as the information she had received from the gynecologist was concerned, she knew it would probably be okay to have sex from a physical point of view, but she wondered if she should be feeling some weirdness on an emotional level. But at that moment all she could think about was Roy, and how she wished she hadn't said that she loved him, and that she wanted to get him into her bed.

After signing the credit card slip, she gathered her things and met Roy at the inside front door of the restaurant. Feeling she had little left to lose, Diane ventured a direct question.

"Would you like to come back to my apartment?"

"Yes," Roy said, "I would."

"Good," Diane said, "because I really want you to."

After, as they lay in Diane's bed, Roy felt a range of emotions. He was excited by this new thing, by the feeling of unlimited possibility, by love, and lust, and the unknown. The physical root of this feeling extended down into his lower abdomen, where he felt a kind of low-level vibration, a gentle tingling. It was similar to the feeling he had after they kissed, but deeper somehow. In addition to this sensation, he also felt a sense of peace. As if he were exactly where he was supposed to be, perhaps, in this sense, for the first time in his life. He lay with his left arm and left leg across Diane's body, she on her back, now sleeping, her breath rising and falling gently with a constant, predictable rhythm. Roy stared sideways at Diane's profile, remembering how, before she had fallen asleep, she had asked him if he would stay the night. And how, despite his concern about her revelation at dinner, he had said yes without a moment's hesitation.

THIRTY-SIX

Marie Lerman scrambled out of the passenger-side front door of the unmarked police car and ran toward the Emergency Room entrance to Kings County Hospital. She extended her hand toward the door handle, pausing for a half-second to consider a smudge on her still-wet thumbnail. The plain-clothes officer, following closely behind, opened the door for Marie and ushered her inside.

"WHERE IS HE?" she yelled, to no one in particular, although a passing nurse, dressed head-to-toe in white, offered a reply.

"Calm down, ma'am. Who you looking for?"

"MY HUSBAND! HE'S BEEN SHOT!"

"Uh-huh," the nurse replied.

Two uniformed officers, standing in the corner of the busy waiting room, overheard the conversation and walked quickly and purposefully toward Marie. One, a paunchy middle-aged man with gin blossoms on his nose, stood a step behind the other, a younger woman with a thick, powerful build. The plain-clothes officer stood silently behind Marie as the female officer addressed her.

"Mrs. Lerman?" she enquired, "I'm Officer Wright."

"Where's Mike?" she replied.

"Detective Lerman is in surgery," she went on, her hands nervously at her belt, unsure of whether to reach out to the other woman or not.

"How is he?"

"That's really all we know," she replied.

The plain-clothed officer, clearly above the uniformed officers in rank, now stepped forward to reassure.

"I'll try to get an update. Find out what they know," he said.

"Where's Paul?" Marie asked.

"Who's Paul?" the other uniformed officer asked, his breath redolent with the aroma of stale beer.

"Ossola. His partner," the plain-clothes officer replied, flashing a look of disapproval.

"He went in with him. He's back there somewhere," the officer added, pointing toward the inner sanctum of the hospital, beyond the registration desk and the triage station.

Hours later, after the precinct brass had arrived, after Marie had felt the sweat from Detective Paul Ossola's shirt soak through her own as he comforted her, after the surgeons who had worked diligently to repair the damage done by two bullets bouncing and tearing through his heart and lungs had come to her with serious faces and apologies, Marie came to the realization that Mike was dead. Really and truly. She had known from the moment she arrived at the hospital that the situation was grim. Every person she had spoken with had offered comforting words, but those words had an undercurrent. *"He's a fighter." "They've got two of the top surgeons in there, doing their best." "He can still pull through."* And all the while, she had honestly believed that there was no other possible outcome than Mike's survival. It was simply an article of faith for Marie.

Before Mike's body was even cold, the circus of the well intentioned and the politically motivated began. Wave after wave of police and city officials came, their elevation in rank mostly matched, in Marie's mind, by increasing levels of disingenuousness. The precinct captain, trembling and red-faced, was genuinely bereft. He had known Mike for over a decade, and, fighting back tears, was so grief-stricken and apologetic that he almost unable to speak. The commissioner, on the other hand—in grave tones— recited a twenty-word sympathy speech so rote that Marie could imagine it under cloudy, scratched plastic on a photocopied piece of paper, taped to a beige wall in an office in downtown Manhattan.

The Brooklyn Borough President arrived, and after having quickly dispensed with his sad chore, devoted his energies to finding something to eat and imploring his aides to prepare for the Mayor's arrival; this, apparently, being some kind of code for ensuring that he would be able to share the stage with the Mayor during the statements to the press.

The Mayor asked to speak to Marie alone. In a quiet room, devoid of cameras and flacks, the billionaire expressed his sympathy and the gratitude of the city for her husband's sacrifice.

"I didn't know your husband," he admitted, "but the captain tells me he was one of the good guys."

Marie nodded.

"As Mayor, it's my duty to show up at terrible times like these," he told Marie, taking her hand in his, "and it's probably the hardest part of my job. But I'm also a life-long New Yorker," he went on, "so I feel that it's my responsibility, as a citizen, to be here. To tell you how very sorry I am for your loss. And to say that I know that a police officer gave his life today so that I, and other citizens like me, could be safer."

"Thank you for coming," Marie said, not knowing what else to say.

The Mayor pulled a small notebook from the inner pocket of his suit jacket. He scribbled a phone number on a piece of paper, tore the page from the notebook, and handed it to Marie.

"If there is anything you need, call this number."

Marie folded the paper and clutched it in her hand.

Then, as quickly as he had arrived, the diminutive man was out the door to confront the barrage of cameras, lights and inquisitive reporters who had appeared at the hospital and stood waiting like sidewalk umbrella salesmen on a cloudy day.

The press focused on the Mayor as he solemnly expressed his outrage and sadness at the loss of a police officer's life. They barely seemed to notice Marie as Paul guided her shrouded figure toward his unmarked car.

"Cover your head with this," he'd said, as he removed his overcoat and draped it over her.

"Why?" she had asked.

"The pictures," her sister Helen (who by then had been notified, and had come, as quickly as a cab could carry her) answered.

As it turned out, the press had already secured their shots of the shocked widow, her face contorted with grief, confusion, shock and anger, as she arrived at the Emergency Room. The images would run, depending on the progress toward war, on page one or page three of the tabloids, but certainly toward the top of the hour on NY1. Violence and its aftermath—the cornerstone of the local television news business—and the sturdy platform on which ratings and ad sales are built.

For Marie, it was all like a dream sequence; one of those vexing dreams where everything that is happening seems to have happened before, but nothing is as it was, or as you know it. Perhaps because she had seen this scene, or subtle variations of it, played out on the nightly news so many times before. All those times she had watched with special attention, thinking, *the poor wife, husband gone*, then with a sort of guilty relief, *thank God that's not me.*

They pulled slowly away from the hospital in Paul's unmarked car, a blaze of light reflected in the windows. He drove the pair of widows to Marie's apartment building, where she had requested that they go.

"Come up for a cup of coffee," Marie said to Paul, not knowing what else to do, or say, and not wanting to end this terrible day for fear that the next one could possibly be even worse.

"Are you sure?" Paul asked.

"Please."

And as Marie made coffee, and Helen worked to find the makings of a presentable snack, Paul began to cry. He wept for the loss of his partner and friend, and apologized for not offering more strength during Marie's time of need.

Late that night, as Marie lay awake in bed beside her sleeping sister, her mind began to rehash the events of the previous week. Her brother in-law's death and funeral. The attention her sister had received. The familiar jealousy that had risen in her heart. The wish—fleeting as it was—that it had been her, and not her sister, who was the object of all that attention. Did it mean she had wished her husband to die? Had there been a moment, or moments, where she had thought, if only Mike had died—instead of Earl—I could begin my life anew. There had, she knew. With that acknowledged, a monstrous wave of guilt came washing over her. It gripped her chest, and made her body stiff with the recognition of its weight and implications. She lay flat on her back staring at the ceiling, listening to her good sister's breath rising and falling with calm dependability, facing upward to a God who she was sure looked down in harsh judgment.

THIRTY-SEVEN

Dave's mouth was dry and he needed to pee. Where was the bathroom? He pulled the blanket down from around his head to examine his surroundings. He scanned the room, looking for visual clues to establish his location. He was on a couch. Early-morning sun was streaming through a wall of floor-to-ceiling windows, causing a wretched headache to bloom like a tiger lily at first light. The coffee table before him was full of empty and half-full beer bottles, an over-flowing ashtray, and two glasses that held what looked like unfinished snorts of whiskey. DuVal. He was at DuVal's apartment. But why?

He had gone to DuVal's office the previous afternoon; that he remembered without a great deal of difficulty. It had been a humbling experience. Confronted by DuVal about his unavailability by telephone, he'd been forced to admit his circumstances: he had lost his job and been locked out of his house because of his ongoing sexual indiscretions. He had withheld the tidbit about having given his wife a case of herpes, as far as he remembered. But with the realization that he had drunk to blackout the evening before, he couldn't be certain. He wondered for a moment. Was this concern indicative of his morality, or lack thereof? That it was somehow acceptable to have whored around on his wife, and been fired from his job, but not to have contracted—and have passed on—a fairly common sexually-transmitted disease? Was it vanity? Shame? An uneasy feeling expanded in his stomach and rose through his chest. Fear. He had pissed away everything he had, and now he had nothing. Without his job, without his home, without his wife, and without his money (and all the things that came with that money), he realized that he didn't know who he was. Or, in fact, how to be himself. He had no identity. He was a nothing, just like Mitch Sanders had said. The blue-sky feeling of liberation that he had expected and fantasized about for the past several years while imagining his exit from his marriage had not materialized. Instead, he was confronted with a feeling that was more akin to being alone in an under-inflated rubber dingy, tossed from wave to wave by an unfeeling ocean, beneath the shroud of a starless autumn sky.

How much of this had he confessed to DuVal? And what damage had been done?

He remembered jagged pieces of conversation.

"Jack, you don't understand," he remembered saying, reaching for a beer and knocking the bottle to the floor, "I love women and women love me, what am I supposed to do?"

"Dave, I hate to tell you, but if you have to pay for it, it's not love. It's not even lust, for her. It's business."

"But I don't always pay for it."

"Okay, Dave."

The balance of power, or the illusion of the balance of power, had surely shifted. There is a natural arc to any relationship, and the relationship between an agent and the talent is no different. In the beginning, the talent needs the agent more than the agent needs the talent. The relationship exists according to the agent's whim. Phone calls are returned in direct proportion to commissions received. If and when success arrives—and especially phenomenal success—the balance of power shifts dramatically. The agent is suddenly more accommodating, ever aware that the talent may harbor resentment over any previous lack of attention. A good agent knows that there are only delicate threads holding the relationship intact, inertia being one. At this stage the talent may demand a reduced-percentage commission, or bolt to a new agency for undefined or capricious reasons. A perceived slight. Flagging ratings. A negative news item. Boredom. Dave's new circumstances made things precarious. There was no question that DuVal had legitimate reason to leave Dave. And little reason to stay. And without DuVal, Dave really was, at this point, nothing. A bum in the street. The fear that had gripped Dave quickly spread south. He needed to take a shit. Fast. Where was the bathroom again?

DuVal appeared in the doorway of the living room. He was clean-shaven, showered, and dressed. "Morning Dave."

"Good morning, Jack," Dave managed, standing to ask, "Where…"

"I just threw a blanket over you last night after you passed out. You were in sad shape. Blubbering."

"Thanks, Jack. I…"

Dave pressed his legs together as a cramp shot from his abdomen down through his rectum. Sweat beaded at his temples. The situation was suddenly becoming urgent. Critical. Pressurized.

"Don't worry about it. Listen, let's just get this deal done and go from there. Make the adjustments we talked about last night, and finalize the thing. I'm sick of thinking about it."

Clinging to a last bit of hope that good fortune could still smile upon him, Dave thought he might be able to cheat a fart out. He relaxed his grip. It was misguided. He was not entirely wrong about the fart, for as the shit came forth—putrid, hot, and largely liquid—it was introduced by a loud, loose, sputtering sound. And that sound (along with the acrid smell that accompanied the product as it slid through the crack of his ass and mostly down his left rear thigh, finally dammed by the reinforced band at the base of the leg of his boxer briefs), introduced a look of bewilderment to DuVal's face.

"What the hell? Did you just shit yourself?" DuVal asked.

"I think so." Dave replied.

"Christ."

"Where's the bathroom?" Dave asked.

"Down the hall. First door on the right." DuVal replied.

"I'm going to get cleaned up."

"Please do. Then let yourself out and come by the office. The door will lock itself when you leave," Duval said, shaking his head, and adding, "you poor, dirty bastard."

Dave squeezed his ass cheeks together and did a stiff-legged duck walk toward the bathroom.

By 1 P.M. Dave had appeared at DuVal's office. He was showered and clean-shaven, and looked only somewhat worse for wear. He had dipped into some hidden funds on the way uptown in order to finance a quick trip to Barney's. The suit he had worn the previous day and night (apparently his only remaining) had, with its fairly detectable odors of smoke and alcohol, carried not only the painful memories of the previous 24-hour's humiliations, but kindling for the fires of his hangover as well. He realized that he wouldn't be able to contend with the smells and keep his headache, fatigue, and unsettled stomach at bay. Not on this day. So as he rode the elevator to DuVal's floor, he wore new slacks (light grey, tropical wool), new furnishings (socks, underwear, t-shirt), a new sweater (charcoal grey, merino wool, 3-button from the collar), and a new brown suede car coat. $2350, all in. The coat, at $1300, had been a splurge, but it would stand him in good stead for the season.

He had come to the office with two objectives. First, to finalize DuVal's understanding of the deal in order to move it along to the next stage of the process; specifically, to get an informal acceptance in front of the decision-makers on the Syndicate side. Dave realized that the process was going to move more slowly than might be ideal given his circumstances. He had received an offer memo from the Syndicate, but he knew all too well that elements of a deal could easily change if left on the table too long. And they could change again when the lawyers entered the picture in earnest. The process would be very delicate, and would require patience. And patience would be difficult to muster. Dave needed money, and he needed it in a right-now kind of way.

Renting an apartment was probably out of the question. Technically, he was unemployed. And Manhattan landlords were largely unsympathetic to personal tales of woe. That left him few choices. He could stay at a hotel, assuming he could locate one that accepted cash. That, in and of itself, was a colossal assumption. And even if he were allowed to pay cash, it would only accelerate the depletion of his slush fund. A second—and equally unpalatable—option would be to rely on the hospitality of a friend. This choice was complicated by the fact that he had few friends. He had acquaintances; there were couples that he and Jodi had socialized with, but those were mainly either her friends from childhood or his business associates. Neither of these camps would be dependable, or desirable, sources of accommodation. And truth be told, the entire situation was embarrassing. Even (and especially) in this dire time of need, Dave had no inclination to show his ass to the world. It would be much better if he could stay with someone who lived outside the stream of his former life. He decided to find Diane.

THIRTY-EIGHT

Diane opened her eyes to see the back of Roy's head on the pillow next to hers, his dark, wavy hair matted and showing the odd gray strand. She could hear his breath rise and fall with the ease and predictability of someone deeply and comfortably asleep, and watched as the musculature in his back expanded and contracted with his breathing. She had slept through the night without interruption, and felt luxuriously rested. It was a singular event for Diane, this unbroken night of sleep, especially coming, as it did, with an inaugural sleepover with a new man. She thought it was auspicious.

It would be her first full day back at work since the abortion. Diane came to this realization as she gently laid a hand on Roy's hip. He stirred, turning his head to the side to look back at her.

"Good morning."

"Good morning."

"What time is it?"

"Time for me to get up and ready for work," Diane said.

"Right now? Do you have to?"

Diane's recognition of the need to get underway ran headlong into an equally powerful desire to stay in bed with Roy. The night before, other than blurting out that she loved him, had been as close to a perfect evening as Diane had ever experienced. Every element, from their first lingering kiss to the way he had held her after they had sex exceeded any expectations that Diane had allowed herself. It just felt right. And that came as a surprise. Because it was a sad fact that at this stage of her life, Diane was—until recently—unwilling or unable to muster the emotional resources to actually look forward to any given dating scenario with much more than the belief that it would end poorly. Or, worse yet, simply die from neglect or disinterest. Was it a lack of faith? Despair? Or just acceptance of the conventional wisdom that a woman in her mid-thirties in Manhattan had a fart-in-a-windstorm's chance of finding a man who wasn't married, gay, or deeply flawed in ways both too numerous and predictable to merit elaboration. Now, it seemed that Diane's point of view on romance had shifted a full 180°. She was brimming with hope, she dared to have expectations, and she was apparently unafraid to admit that she was falling in love—or more deeply in love (for she had realized she felt this way even before he had returned from Texas)—with Roy Eldridge, the man who lay sleeping in her bed.

She knew there were inherent risks in this reckless feeling of abandon. Not the least of which would be judgment in the court of public (well, Sarah's) opinion. Sarah would caution her to go slowly, perhaps hire a private investigator (after all, you don't really know who this guy is, do you?), and to practice a little emotional restraint. To build the equivalent of a system of airbags and nets around her heart to prepare for what could only be an inevitable, grizzly, oncoming crash and burn. What was that? That thing that women did to each other? Was it borne from genuine concern? Or was it borne from envy? Some combination of the two? The joy she felt at this moment begged expression. Specifically, expression to another woman. Someone who understood the dangers of making oneself vulnerable to a man, and the pure happiness that could come when that vulnerability was met with tenderness and even, dare she think it, love. Diane realized that she was reluctant to even call Sarah. Maybe later in the day. She couldn't call her mother, because her mother had died when she was 12, when she had truly been vulnerable and full of hope. Hope that 7th grade would be more fun than 6th (it wasn't), hope that she would get boobs that year (she didn't), and hope that her mother would survive the cancer that had started in one of her breasts and had metastasized throughout her lymph system with quiet persistence. Was that the last time she had allowed herself to be vulnerable? It was a question for the shrink. Perhaps she would call Dr.

Sammuels later that day instead of Sarah. Kill two birds with one stone. For now, she would enjoy this time with this man.

"I could be convinced to stay in bed," she answered.

Later, after the coffee had been made and poured and lingered over, they showered together. As Roy lay seductively across her bed, draped only in a towel, Diane hurried to dress for work. She made quick, deliberate choices: a black fitted Prada skirt that fell mid-calf; a sleeveless black sweater; a pair of Manolo Blahnik mules.

"Very nice," Roy offered, as Diane looked over her shoulder to catch him admiring her ass. Bingo, she thought, money well spent.

"Is my skirt too tight?" she asked, courting an expanded opinion.

"I guess that depends on what you're going to be doing."

"Trying to avoid the shit-eye, mainly," Diane said, stepping out of her closet and toward Roy. He stood, his towel falling to the floor, and gave her a kiss.

"The shit-eye?"

"That look women give you on the sidewalk when they don't like your outfit."

"That's a great outfit."

"I know, but it veers toward trying too hard."

"Women are rough."

"Yes they are," Diane said, briefly cupping Roy's balls in her hand before stepping to her dresser to select a pair of earrings.

"Why don't you get back in bed and relax for a while?" she asked, losing herself to a brief fantasy about him waiting for her when she came home from the station. She turned to see him pulling on his jeans.

"I should get back to Brooklyn and unpack. Check my messages," he said, adding, "what about dinner again tonight?"

"That sounds good," Diane said.

A few minutes later on the sidewalk in front of Diane's building they kissed, neither wanting to part.

"Roy," Diane said.

"I know. Me too," he replied.

Diane hailed a cab, and when it slowed to a stop Roy opened the door for her, careful to check that the hem of her skirt had cleared the frame of the door before he shut her in. As the cab pulled away, Diane looked back through the rear window to see him smile, then turn to walk toward the subway. She felt happy and alive, and wished for the day to pass without incident or delay so she could see him again. Her heart was full, and she was happy.

Diane had devoted an hour or more over each of the previous several days to going through her work e-mail, hoping against hope that when she returned to the office she would be able to hit the ground running and get back to the business of producing a hit radio show. Despite all of this preparation, she still had a hint of that first-day-of-school feeling in the pit of her stomach as she rode the elevator up to her floor. She was nervous. Nervous about the number of phone calls she would have to return. Nervous about seeing DuVal. Nervous about whether the show had experienced any problems in her absence, or, perhaps an even more unsettling possibility, if it had run smoothly. What if they realized they didn't need her? It was stupid stuff, and deep down Diane knew it. But she took pride in her work, and had a proprietary feeling about the show.

"Welcome back," Kerri said, as Diane approached her desk. The tell-tale sound of an IM prompt punctuated her greeting.

"Thank you. How've things been?"

"Fine. No fires."

"Good."

"How're you feeling?"

"Fine."

"Good."

"Okay, then."

"I printed out your calls, and put the list on your desk."

"Thank you."

Once in her office, Diane discovered that Kerri had done her best to prioritize the calls that had come in. Some urgent, some less so, others that didn't need to be returned at all. Using the list as her guide, but also using her own judgment on a call-by-call basis, Diane spent the first two hours in the office with her door closed, solidly and diligently on the telephone.

There were the usual calls from agents whose clients had new books or new movies that needed to be shilled. There were also calls from Washington. Those came from elected officials and their minions. The push toward war was becoming more urgent, and the case for war needed selling. It was understood, or believed, that DuVal could help with the effort. Not that his audience needed much convincing. Diane figured a good percentage of them already had their own weapons loaded, just in case.

There were also a number of calls from various Muslim groups concerning comments DuVal had made on the air in a show broadcast a few nights before. Diane had missed the broadcast, but apparently DuVal had questioned the value of the *Koran* as a religious document and, worse yet, implied that the beliefs of Muslims—in aggregate—amounted to a load of horse shit. As she spoke with representatives of these groups, Diane realized that they might have a situation on their hands. The outrage was palpable, and there were veiled threats. Not the we're-going-to-hurt-DuVal type of threats, but more along the lines of we're-worried-that-somebody-might-hurt-DuVal type of threats, which somehow seemed even more threatening.

Plenty of nutcases had threatened DuVal over the years. It came with being celebrated and outspoken. It was generally accepted that if you saw a name in bold-face type on Page Six of *The New York Post*, it was likely they had, at a minimum, a stalker. But the threat posed by some lone nut, who may or may not simply be engaged in a prank, was very different from the threat posed by a fanatical segment of the worldwide Muslim population. Especially in the current political climate. She would need to discuss the situation with DuVal and take some action. Whether the correct action was to hire additional security, to contact somebody about a PR solution, or some combination of the two, the difficulty, Diane knew, would be getting agreement out of DuVal that something needed to be done. But first, she needed to hear the broadcast. She called Kerri.

"I thought you said no fires."

"What?"

"The calls from the Muslims."

"Oh yeah. Maybe one fire."

"Get me a tape of the show."

"Now?"

"Now."

THIRTY-NINE

Jodi Miller slowed heading into the toll plaza, the stereo system in her new Mercedes SL55 AMG automatically reducing the volume as she depressed the brake pedal. Germans, she thought, they don't miss a trick. She'd bought the car off the showroom floor the day after she locked Dave out of the house. It was an impulse buy. A pick-me-up. But despite the brilliant silver metallic paint, the supple ash-colored leather seats, the burled walnut trim, the 18" mono block alloy wheels, and the $113,970 pre-tax price tag, she had found herself—after an initial burst of feeling liberated and even somewhat empowered—vacillating between feelings of anger, sorrow, and despair. The house, at 6,500 square feet, was, by any definition, mostly empty when they both occupied it. Now it seemed even more so. Though she and Dave had enjoyed nothing like an ideal marriage for the last several years (if ever), there was a familiarity and a rhythm to their life together. With that rhythm disrupted, she felt listless and, of course, alone.

After a few days of shopping and spa treatments, she had exhausted the ability of spending and personal care to take her mind off her split with Dave. Nor would these pursuits allow her to avoid thinking about the herpes diagnosis, the humiliation of having been cheated on repeatedly, or the likelihood, as a 40 year-old divorcee, of spending the rest of her life solo. So it was in the spirit of putting one foot in front of the other that she drove toward Manhattan, dressed head-to-toe in new garments, recently massaged and manicured, to meet with her divorce lawyer and check in on a few of her rental properties.

Waiting in the EZ-Pass lane, Jodi folded her visor down to check her hair in the mirror. She'd gone, only the day before, to a deeper shade of red. Another impulse. Having always, in adult life, leaned toward strawberry blonde, the actual color of her hair in childhood, it was a little disconcerting to see the reflection of her face framed by fiery wisps of auburn.

"It's fabulous, honey," Andre, her hairdresser had opined.

"It's not too dark?"

"For what, baby?"

"I don't know, my skin?"

"Honey, it's gorgeous."

"Really?"

"Really. Now get out of my chair and go get some men."

The color was a substantial change, but Jodi felt she was going to have to make many substantial changes if she was going to live a different life. But hair aside, she wasn't sure what kind of changes she was going to make, or how she might go about making them. The first thing that had come to mind was moving back to the city.

The move to New Jersey had been to accommodate a baby that had never come, and a dream of an idyllic suburban marriage fantasy that had simply not materialized. Pool, hot tub, and fairly unlimited space aside, there wasn't really any reason for her to live there anymore.

She had taken up the subject with her father on the phone. "I'm thinking of moving back in to the city, Daddy."

"Good idea," Mitch Sanders had replied.

"I mean, it's not like Dave and I made any friends out here."

"I'm not surprised."

"What do you mean by that?"

"Nothing. I mean, what do you have in common with those people."

"Exactly."

"Do it, then."

"You think I should?"

"Yes. But I have to go now. Call me tomorrow if you want to. Love you."

It was true. She and Dave had mainly socialized in the city, and treated the house in New Jersey like a weekend place that they just happened to go to every night. She wondered if other people in the suburbs made friends there. And if so, how they did it. Presumably, some people had grown up in those towns and had childhood friendships that carried over into adulthood. But for the newcomers, was it all related to parenting functions? Business associations? Did people ever actually bake a cake and drop it by a new neighbor's house as a means of introduction? Jodi wondered. However it happened, it hadn't happened for the Millers. They had remained as isolated from their neighbors as their neighbors were from them. She remembered attending a holiday party at a neighbor's house a few years before. Men in blazers and turtleneck sweaters drinking too much scotch, while the women flitted around sharing diet tips and complaining about the lack of trustworthy, affordable domestic help. It was mind-numbingly boring. She had tried to start a conversation with the hostess, a reed-thin bottle-blonde named Happy Hunter.

"How long have you lived in this neighborhood?" she'd asked.

"Oh, forever. Since Bill took the job with Credit Suisse. That was back in '85."

"Wow."

"Long time. The schools, you know. We've got three. I'd love to live in the city, but…"

"Get in much?"

"Not really. Too much to do. And too much traffic; drives me crazy. No pun intended. Shopping, now and then, you know."

"Danielle!" the hostess exclaimed, touching Jodi's arm as she walked away to greet another guest.

Jodi had gone to find Dave, and they had left a few minutes later. On the walk home they'd mocked the other guests, and laughed as they theorized that they had only been invited so they wouldn't grouse about cars parking in front of their house. Her eyes began to tear a bit with the memory.

On the Manhattan end of the Lincoln Tunnel, the river of traffic that flowed from the west split into two branches, one heading north and the other heading south. On a whim, Jodi headed south. She dialed Raoul Felder's office on her cell.

"This is Jodi Miller," she said to the woman on the other end of the line.

"Yes."

"Tell Raoul I'm not going to be able to make it in today."

"You're aware that we have a 48-hour cancellation policy, Mrs. Miller?"

"Whatever," Jodi said, "I'll call later to reschedule."

"Please make sure you do."

Jodi flipped her phone shut without saying goodbye. She had lost all interest in speaking with her divorce lawyer. She had also, she realized, lost interest in visiting her rental buildings. It could wait. All of it. Her wretched marriage, and the equally wretched process of ending it, would not be affected by pushing this meeting with the lawyer back by a day or two. And barring some unforeseen terrorist act, fire, or natural disaster, her rental properties would still be standing (and generating considerable income) tomorrow, weeks and months hence. Nothing was urgent, and nothing had to be done today. She would drive downtown and visit some real estate brokers. She could start thinking about where she might move, and maybe even see some listings. If she moved back to Manhattan she could make a new start. It might, she rationalized, be easier to meet men (provided there were any available in her age and income range), and it would definitely afford her better day-to-day management of her business interests. And if she was going to move back to Manhattan, it followed that she would need a place to live.

The market was heating back up, but Jodi was hopeful that the brokers she visited would have some inventory. Nothing is worse, she thought, than wanting to buy something—anything—and it not being available for sale. It was a lifelong frustration for her, which typically cropped up whenever a new article of clothing or accessory achieved must-have status. Most recently, this frustration been visited upon Jodi when she had made her way to the Hermès store on Madison Avenue in search of a Berkin bag.

Credit card in hand, and prepared to pay the $8000 list price for the hand-tooled leather bag, Jodi had audibly gasped when the salesperson told her there was a four-year wait.

"Could you check for inventory in your other stores?" she had asked.

"The wait is four years," the salesperson had curtly responded.

"There's nothing in Atlanta, or Dallas?"

"The wait is four years."

"I'll pay a premium."

"Four years."

It was humiliating. I bet if I was Gweneth-fucking-Paltrow you would pull one out of your ass somehow, Jodi had thought. But that thought had remained unexpressed. Instead, she had gone home empty handed, unsatisfied, and obsessed with finding this rare and precious object. She had called the stores in Dallas and Atlanta herself. New Orleans as well. Each store reported the same wait, albeit with variations in accent and degree of sympathy. On a final desperate call to the Memphis store a salesperson had reluctantly disclosed that Birkins occasionally turned up on eBay. Jodi had hung up the phone an immediately typed http://www.ebay.com into the address bar of her browser window. There, she entered into a four-day bidding frenzy on a brand-new, 35 cm, orange Clemence leather Birkin. And her dogged persistence paid off. Two days after placing the $14,536 winning bid, the bag arrived via FedEx. Of course, the unfortunate thing about fashion is that it is, well, fashion; things come in and go out of it. It is a cruel master, with pleasures that are fleeting. But for a week she was walking on air.

And now, as she steered her new car down Ninth Avenue heading toward Tribeca, Jodi was again walking on air. Or riding on a soft cushion of the stuff, compressed into the suspension of an expensive German roadster. But she had purpose. Clear purpose. An attainable goal. It would be difficult, that was certain. She would see properties that were out of her price range that she desperately wanted. And she would undoubtedly visit places with the right attributes in bad locations, and vice versa. But she was certain she could find a charming place to live. A new home.

FORTY

Walking through the long corridor toward her office, Dave wondered how he might best approach Diane. Or, more accurately, her office. If her assistant, Cherry or Kerri, or whatever her name was, was at her desk he could face some mild resistance. First of all, he didn't have an appointment. Two weeks earlier that wouldn't have been a problem; he would have simply waltzed past, opened Diane's door, and received a warm welcome. But in light of the severing of their sexual relationship, and especially in light of the fact that it was initiated by her, that assurance was no longer something he could depend on. To complicate matters he had no inkling of the amount of confidence that was shared between the two women. It was as probable as not that she knew every detail of their relationship, such as it was. She could have a completely accurate description of his dick, for all he knew. Women were like that: quick to tell, and in lurid detail. It was a toss of the coin; anything could happen. He would just have to move in with his eyes open, and be ready to roll with whatever came his way. He was good at reading situations, he told himself by way of a pep talk, good with people.

Kerri sat at her desk outside Diane's office. She was alternating her attention between a new tattoo on her arm and an IM conversation about the tattoo with her friend Kristen. She had removed the bandages that morning in order to give the wound some air. The inked image was a vivid tableau: a glistening silver dolphin jumping out of a shimmering sea with a perfectly round yellow sun glowing in the background. This permanent addition, Kerri believed, would not only demonstrate one of the sterling qualities of her character—a love of animals—but it would also provide perfect relief for her delicate features and fair skin.

KerriRules: looks wet

SexyK79: bloody?

KerriRules: no like the inks wet

SexyK79: hurt?

KerriRules: some, not bad

SexyK79: Ew

Kerri looked up to see Dave approaching her desk. She had been given explicit instructions to not bother Diane under any circumstances, unless, of course, it was DuVal. And even then, Diane had said, get a good reason.

KerriRules: ew ew! Dianes gross ex-boyfrnds here

SexyK79: the agent one?

KerriRules: Y

SexyK79: Ew

"Can I help you?" Kerri asked, in a way that she hoped gave the impression that she was trying to give the impression that she had purposely forgotten who he was.

"I was hoping to see Diane." Dave replied, making a great effort to not betray any reaction to the negative attitude that was oozing from the young woman before him. He decided on another way in.

"Nice ink," he said, pointing to the tattoo.

"Do you have an appointment?" she asked, closing off that avenue.

"No, I'm here with DuVal. Just stopping by to say hello. Informal."

"I'll tell her you came. She's asked not to be disturbed by *anyone*," Kerri added.

"Why don't you call her and tell her it's me," Dave asked, his fatigue allowing a little bit of annoyance to creep out from around the edges of his hangover.

"I can't do that. She really did ask not to be disturbed by anyone," Kerri said.

"Can't, or *won't*? Dave asked, with a slight increase in volume that was not lost on Kerri. Feeling challenged, she stood from her chair.

"Both. Either. Does it *matter*?"

"Come on. Do you really want to fuck with *me*?" Dave asked, pointedly.

"No, I don't. And apparently Diane doesn't either," Kerri added, trying to remain calm. She was starting to be concerned about where the conversation/confrontation was headed. Knowing that Diane had broken things off with this asshole agent, and that she had asked to not be disturbed under any circumstances, suggested to Kerri that she was taking the right tack. On the other hand, that the asshole agent was DuVal's agent, and that Diane, like any woman, might actually want to see the guy—for whatever reason—to tweak him a little about the fact that she was seeing someone else, or to revisit the cause of the breakup, complicated matters significantly. It was a dilemma. But she would not have to suffer on its horns for long, because at that moment, Diane's office door opened and she appeared in the doorway.

"Oh. Dave."

"Hello, Diane," he replied, shooting a smug glance toward Kerri.

"What are you doing here?" she asked, with enough emphasis on the personal pronoun to convey that it wasn't an entirely pleasant surprise.

"DuVal business. Just thought I'd stop by to say hello. Have a chat."

"Oh. Bad time. Really busy," she said, backing into her office and closing the door.

"Well, then," Kerri said, "maybe another time."

"Okay," Dave said, nodding his head. Turning to walk away, he added under his breath, "Dolphin arm."

"Whatever," Kerri replied, somewhat louder, as she sat, triumphant.

KerriRules: drama

SexyK79: tell

KerriRules: wouldnt see him

SexyK79: ouch

KerriRules: called me dolphin arm

SexyK79:?????

KerriRules: my new tat

KerriRules: ur new name

SexyK79: F U

Entering the building—before the Diane debacle—Dave had called up to DuVal and been told it would be late afternoon, and perhaps after the broadcast, before they could meet. As often happened, DuVal hadn't looked at his research and was now scrambling to bone up on the topic for that evening's show. On the slate was another examination of the march toward war; the guest, a retired general and rumored Democratic presidential candidate named Wesley K. Clark. DuVal, for his part, was in the process of taking a crash course in the history of Iraq, undoubtedly trying to absorb the entire span—from the Sumerians to Saddam—within a few hours of nicotine-fueled study. But DuVal had an excellent memory for facts, and could make much hay out of a few well-chosen straws.

DuVal's schedule and Diane's rebuff had left Dave with several hours to kill. Hours that he might otherwise have spent in his office, juggling phone calls and e-mails while browsing online porn. But his office was no more. Or rather, it was his no more. He'd managed to slip out with his laptop, at least, but he had no Internet connectivity. For the time being, he would need to get a wireless card and do business out of Starbucks. It would be hard to look at porn there, however. Unseemly. He was still without a cell phone as well. Another expense. And without an assistant, he realized he would have to navigate the waters of technology acquisition by himself. It was daunting. But the sooner he got started, the sooner he would be back in the swing of things, doing what he did best: talking shit and doing deals. He would spend the afternoon on the streets of midtown Manhattan, locating a wireless card and a cell phone, and signing up for whatever wireless Internet service Starbucks had to offer. He would then circle back to meet with DuVal. It was a plan.

FORTY-ONE

After several hours of returning phone calls and e-mails, Diane had formulated a course of action. DuVal, she knew, was unlikely to ever dig himself out of a hole unless she, or someone, threw him down a shovel and managed to somehow convince him that it was his idea to use it. Her first thought had been to try and get General Clark to talk some sense into him. Arrange a brief pre-show conversation between the two in which the general could offer an unsolicited opinion about the credibility of the threats that had been made, and suggest a few options for how to mitigate those threats. Of course, Diane knew that DuVal would never, under any circumstances, extend a formal apology to anyone. The best she could hope for was that he might agree to a somewhat flip mea culpa in the context of the show. Something along the lines of, hey-you-know-the-other-night-when-I-said-Muslims-were-a-bunch-of-nut-case-religious-fanatics-whose-entire-belief-system-is-a-load-of-horse shit? *I was only kidding*. Deep down, even as she was thinking it, Diane knew that the General Clark idea was a fantasy. First of all, DuVal never liked to speak with his guests before a show. Secondly, why would the general agree to such a thing? They didn't have a relationship, and his schedule was undoubtedly extremely busy. Since retiring from the military he had embarked on an investment-banking career and, with war approaching, he was in great demand as a pundit. She had been lucky to book him at all. That meant it was up to her.

But why did she even give a shit? If DuVal didn't care about offending people, and if he wasn't concerned about his physical safety, why should she be? His audience certainly ate it up. They didn't look to DuVal for equivocation or apologies. They wanted strong opinions, something they could repeat to their friends or in conversation with like-minded strangers at the bar. They wanted a guy who would say the things they felt but were too stupid, too timid, or too weak to express. And that, perhaps, was DuVal's Faustian bargain: in order to remain relevant to his audience he had to continually place himself out on a limb. And the more powerless his audience felt, the further out he had to go. At the moment, this situation was a tempest in a teapot. They had received calls of protest, and non-specific threats had been made. A few organizations and religious leaders had demanded a public apology. These demands had been reported in the newspapers, but so far it was either below the fold or off the front page altogether. How DuVal handled the topic this evening—particularly during the call-in segment of the show—would determine whether the storm would blow up or over.

On reflection, Diane knew she cared because she cared about DuVal. Not that she loved him, or ever had. She had flirted with the idea of being in love with him a few times over the previous decade, but each time she knew it was just convenience, and the desire to be in love with someone. Or anyone. And now that she was in love with Roy, she knew the vast gulf that separated being in love and being in love with the idea of being in love. But DuVal did mean something to her. Professionally and personally. He had recognized her talents early, and nurtured her career as she moved from production assistant to assistant producer; then from producer to executive producer of his now-extremely-popular nationally-syndicated show. He had also always listened to her ideas, and backed her in every instance she could think of with their various employers, even in salary disputes. In short, he had treated her like a partner in the enterprise. That their relationship had become complicated by sex was a shared responsibility. And Diane knew that it was an issue they would have to work through going forward if they were going to continue their professional association. Especially if her relationship with Roy became as serious as she hoped it would. Granted, the abortion and his callousness—or rather, his ineptitude—at dealing with anything of emotional consequence had been a particularly unpleasant wrinkle. Still, she was reasonably confident they could salvage their friendship and continue to produce great radio together, if that was what she wanted to do with the rest of her life. But those issues, the personal and the professional, the large and the small, would all need to wait until she dealt with the crisis at hand.

Was it a crisis? If she ignored it, would it go away? Was there time to figure that out, or was it imperative that she act now, and act decisively? After careful consideration, Diane had come to the conclusion that it actually was a crisis. Or at least it had the potential to develop into a crisis if she didn't convince DuVal to do the right thing. Somehow, she felt, this wasn't like pissing off Jessie Jackson and having him call for a boycott of your sponsors. If only. That kind of situation could be sorted out very quickly with a check. These people, or at least some of them, seemed to want blood. And while DuVal's blood arguably ran a little chilly, he did have a finite amount of the stuff. She dialed his number.

"DuVal," he answered.

"Got a minute?" Diane asked.

"A minute. I'm trying to catch up on my reading. Wesley Clark, Iraq, got my hands full."

"Glad to hear it. Can I drop by?"

"Everything all right? The general still coming?"

"The general's still coming," Diane assured him. "I'll be right over."

As Diane hung up the phone, DuVal was gripped with a minor surge of panic. Fuck, he thought, is she going to bring up the abortion? Do we have to talk about that now? He knew, deep down, they would probably have to discuss the events leading up to the abortion, the abortion itself, and the effect it was going to have on their working and personal relationships at some point. But he hoped that point hadn't arrived. What he really hoped was that the time would never come; that the swirl of daily events, the passing of time, and inertia would conspire to sweep the issue steadily toward that far-away place where unpleasant things are never discussed. That was, of course, unlikely at best.

Diane could smell cigarette smoke twenty feet from DuVal's office door, and the door was closed. From experience, she knew that the more deeply DuVal was concentrating—on research, worry, or whatever might be at hand—the more aggressively he smoked. He could smoke upwards of ten cigarettes an hour, given the right circumstances. It was repugnant, but also strangely impressive. And it served as a kind of force field of people repellent around his person. Diane suspected that the wave of anti-smoking law and sentiment would only strengthen DuVal's resolve to smoke where and when he wanted. And despite laws forbidding it, DuVal had found many restaurants around the city that let smokers practice their deadly vice unmolested, and the Syndicate seemed to be willing to look the other way for the time being. There hadn't been any complaints from upstairs recently, and she figured that as long as their numbers were strong, there would be a tacit agreement that it was okay for DuVal, and only DuVal, to smoke in the building. At least until the conclusion of the current contract negotiations.

Diane used the knuckle of her index finger to rap lightly on DuVal's door.

"COME IN," he bellowed from within.

Diane eased the door open, and saw DuVal standing behind his desk. He set his cigarette in a brimming ashtray as she entered the room, and moved somewhat haltingly in her direction. At the center-point between DuVal's desk and the office door, they met. There was a moment of silent recognition; of the many days that had passed since they had last seen each other, of the irrevocable action that had taken place during that time, and of the incalculable ways it would influence their every interaction going forward. Then DuVal embraced Diane, fully, awkwardly, and maybe, she felt, longingly.

For her part, as close as they were at that moment physically, Diane had never, in the time that she could remember, felt further away from DuVal. Was it the contrast between the acrid smell of smoke that clung to DuVal's clothing and the smell of Roy's skin? In the few weeks that she had known Roy, she had come to know his smell, committed it to memory, and found herself invoking that memory when she wanted to conjure or heighten the intoxicating feeling of falling in love. She closed her eyes and summoned that memory in an effort to take her mind away from this moment.

DuVal pushed back from Diane, letting his hands rest on her shoulders.

"God, it's good to see you," he said, and squeezing her shoulders for emphasis, added, "it hasn't been the same without you here."

"Well, I'm glad to be back," Diane said, lying.

DuVal released Diane from his grip, walked back behind his desk and settled into his chair. He retrieved his cigarette from the ashtray and took a long drag.

"Everything set for the show tonight?" he asked.

"Yes. Any train wrecks while I was gone?"

"None worth mentioning," DuVal answered, hoping to steer clear of any topic that might lead to a conversation about the abortion.

"Hmmm." Diane said, feeling suddenly awkward standing, but knowing she would feel equally awkward sitting. In the interest of keeping the conversation brief, and maintaining whatever psychological edge she gained from looking down at DuVal, she decided to stay on her feet.

"I spent the morning answering a lot of e-mails and phone calls," Diane began.

"You usually do." DuVal replied; relieved at the turn the conversation seemed to be taking.

"Yeah, these were a little different."

"The Muslim thing?" DuVal asked.

"You've pissed some people off before, Jack, but—"

"It'll blow over."

"I'm not so certain this one will," Diane offered, "it's in the papers, and they're starting to fan the flames."

"You're not here to suggest that I apologize, I hope. Because I'm *not* sorry—that's for *god*damn sure."

"Not a formal apology. I'm suggesting that maybe you should think about tempering what you said a bit. Do it in tonight's show."

"Goddamit Diane, we've been through this kind of thing before— you know how I feel about that. I don't apologize, full stop."

"Jack, hear me out. Do me the favor. All I'm saying is that in the context of your conversation with General Clark—as you are talking about the build-up to the war and it's rationale—you say that you might have gone a little overboard the other night. A little equivocation is all. That's what I'm proposing, not an apology."

"Forget it," DuVal said, "I'm not gonna do it. And I'm a little insulted that you even asked."

"Insulted?" I've always been 100% behind you—and I am now. I'm talking about your fucking safety here. Your *life*," Diane said, with a little more emotion than she had hoped.

"I'm sorry. I really am. I appreciate your concern. Let me give it some thought, and we'll talk before the show," he said dismissively, as he turned his attention to a stack of papers on his desk.

"Why the hell do I care?" Diane said, to the top of DuVal's head, adding, "Do whatever the fuck you want to do," as she turned and walked toward the door.

"I said I'll think about it."

As Diane closed the door behind her, DuVal lit a fresh cigarette from the burning ember at the end of the one he'd just finished. *It'll be a cold day in hell*, he thought.

FORTY-TWO

Dave had spent the afternoon acquiring gadgets. First, he'd purchased a cell phone/PDA combination—an Ericsson R380 World—which also featured a digital camera, MP3 player and Web access. He'd left the store $600 poorer and with a comically unrealistic picture of how easy it would be to set up and configure all the features offered by the device.

"What are you gonna use it for," the salesman had asked by way of an initial pitch, "business or personal?"

"A little of both," Dave answered, his mind wandering as he considered the man's appearance.

The salesman stood no more than 5'5" tall and wore relaxed fit jeans with a beeper and a cell phone attached at his belt. His shirt was of the knit variety, open at the neck, revealing a full chest of hair that provided something like a nest for a fine gold chain with a horn dangling from its lowest point. That, along with his excessively gelled, thinning hair, and sideburns trimmed all the way to the top of the ear, inspired Dave to do a little mental speculation about where he lived. Staten Island? Bensonhurst? Jersey City? He was lost in thought as the salesman went in for the kill.

"Good, 'cause this thing can do it all—voice, e-mail, spreadsheets. You can even take a picture and send it to your girlfriend," he said, pointing the device at his crotch and pressing a button that caused a small flash to go off.

"I'll take it."

Later, after visiting a few other shops and buying a wireless card and an extra battery for his laptop, Dave had headed to a Starbucks feeling once again like a full-fledged citizen of the modern, connected world. Five hours and four cups of coffee later, he felt more like his ancestors who had come through Ellis Island must have felt: he was lost, he didn't speak the language, and the new world was not so friendly. In the end, he'd managed to establish wireless Web access for the laptop, synch his address book from his laptop to his PDA, and sweat through his new t-shirt and sweater. Except for the sweating, these tasks had required the help and advice of no fewer than three 20-somethings in the coffee shop. It was less humiliating than it was an acknowledgement of his advancing years and general technical ineptitude. It was also a wake-up call to the realities of his new employment situation: no tech support, no administrative staff, no paycheck; he was on his own.

When the last vestiges of sunlight had disappeared from the sky, Dave decided to head back to the station. He wanted to try again to speak with Diane at the end of the broadcast and hook up with DuVal immediately after that, if possible.

He had good news for DuVal. The lawyers from the Syndicate were putting an updated deal memo together that would be ready for review—and possibly signature—the following day. This would allow them to lock in the basic terms of the deal while the two sides hammered out the nits of the real contract. More important, from Dave's perspective, it could potentially start the cash flowing. And cashflow was something he desperately needed, especially after having depleted his slush fund by over $3000 in the first half of one day.

"Good night, and God bless."

Diane watched DuVal sign off through the thick glass that separated the control room from the studio. Speaking with General Clark for over an hour, he had knowledgeably referenced the history of Iraq—peppering the conversation with facts about everything from the Sumerians to the 1949 coup that had overthrown the Hashimite monarchy to Saddam's rise to power in 1979. He'd then opened the phone lines up for two hours of calls. Unsurprisingly, the callers had been almost uniformly in favor of starting the war, and the sooner the better.

"You know what we need to do?" a caller had asked.

"Why don't you tell me," DuVal had answered, egging a caller on.

"We need to get in there and finish the job we started back in nineteen-ninety one."

"You think so?"

"Damn straight. Take Saddam out like we should've in the first place."

"I'm just curious, why do you think we stopped short back then?"

"I have no idea. But now that Saddam has WMDs, there's no telling what he could do."

"So you think we should—"

"I think we should nuke him!"

The call-in section of the show always amazed Diane. And not because of the venom that callers felt free to express in a national, albeit semi-anonymous, venue. That she'd grown accustomed to. Rather, because of the number of callers who would repeat, verbatim, opinions that they had heard from pundits (and sometimes other callers) thinking they were adding something to the conversation. American culture, perhaps because of the Internet and the mind-numbing proliferation of media, was becoming a vast recycling plant. People could no longer think independently, and worse, were no longer able to discern the difference between an original thought, or an original expression of a thought, and wholesale appropriation. She'd recently read that the latter was now epidemic on college campuses, with students downloading papers or copying verbatim written material as a matter of course, and seeing nothing wrong with it. In fact, they seemed to think that the act of typing a topic into a search engine was research, and the act of cutting and pasting the text was writing. That, coupled with the endless sequels released as "new" movies, whose original installments were based on previous films or bad television shows, made Diane think that the entire society was crawling up its own increasingly gigantic ass. It was a problem. Or was it? Maybe it was just her age beginning to show. After all, the Greeks had really said about everything there was to say, determined how we think about the world and the narrative structure we use to talk about it, and everyone after that had just cribbed from them. She made a note to research the topic for a future show.

DuVal had carefully avoided continuing their previous conversation before the broadcast, and had not taken the opportunity while on the air to back away from his inflammatory comments about the Muslims. Diane was livid. Yes, it was DuVal's show, and yes, he did have a responsibility to his listeners. But he also had a responsibility to the staff, especially if something he said put them at risk.

September 11, 2001 had ushered in a new era in the continental United States. Before that date the populace only had to worry about its own disgruntled nutcases unleashing massively destructive acts upon its citizenry. Now, the country had to worry about disgruntled foreigners doing so as well. Diane didn't know where this situation was headed, but she felt a personal responsibility to do everything in her power to ensure that no innocent bystanders came to harm. She would have to make another effort to bring DuVal around, and decided to do so as soon as he emerged from the studio.

Opening the control room door, Diane suddenly found herself face to face with Dave Miller. He was perhaps the last person she had hoped to see: the most unpleasant element of her recent ignominious past, a sport-fuck gone awry and, to her everlasting shame, in the person of an agent. She'd hoped that her chilly welcome in the early afternoon would have dissuaded him from seeking her out in subsequent visits to the station; but that hope, like so much unrealistic hope, was, well, unrealistic hope. She forced a greeting.

"Dave."

"Diane," he answered, with substantially more enthusiasm.

"What's up?"

"I'm here to meet with DuVal, but looks like I got lucky."

"How so?"

"Well, I was hoping to see you. To talk."

"Oh. This isn't really a good time. I have to wrap things up with DuVal, and then I have dinner plans."

"Jodi and I split up," Dave suddenly blurted out. It was a gambit. Diane was being very chilly, and he had to play the sympathy card earlier than he'd hoped. But why was she being so chilly to begin with? He wondered if she had discovered any evidence of herpes. Surely she would have called him if that were the case.

"Really?" Diane asked, looking at Dave and marveling at how she could have ever slept with him.

"She kicked me out, and her dad fired me," Dave said, painting the most pathetic picture he could. He needed to lay the groundwork for asking for a place to stay. And the foundation needed to be solid.

"That's interesting," Diane said; her curiosity, but not her sympathy, aroused. "Why?"

"The infidelity. I mean—I haven't been the ideal husband."

"She found out about us?" Diane asked, a vision of an ugly confrontation with Jodi Miller going through her head.

"No, no. She doesn't know anything about you," Dave said, seeing the concerned expression on Diane's face and wanting to reassure her.

"I'm confused," Diane said, "Was there someone else as well?" Her voice lifted in volume a bit more than she had intended.

"Look, Diane," Dave said, quickly lowering his voice as DuVal emerged from the studio door not twenty feet away, "you know who I am."

"*Do* I?" Diane said, her voice slipping out of her control, causing DuVal's head to pivot on its reed-like axis, "Who are you? Because honestly, Dave, right now you're nobody to me."

Dave reached out and placed his hands on Diane's shoulders. "Come on, Diane, don't be like that," he said.

"Please don't touch me," Diane replied, lowering her voice and pushing Dave's hands from her shoulders.

DuVal, alerted to what seemed to be an unusual exchange between his agent and his producer, was by that time upon them.

"What's going on here?" he asked, the wheels in his mind turning, trying to piece together the connections between Diane, Dave Miller, and the bits of their conversation that had caught his ear.

Forcing a smile, Dave turned to DuVal. "Nothing's going on. Diane and I had a little fling, and now it's over, and that's that. It's no big deal."

DuVal looked taken aback. Shocked. "What? You're kidding, right? Well I hope you didn't give her *herpes.*"

"*What!?*" Dave said. Diane's face was instantly drained of color. Her body stiffened.

"Last night when you were crying in your beer you told me that Jodi kicked you out because you gave her herpes. Maybe you forgot to tell Diane that part."

Dave seemed to be collapsing into himself. If he could have, he would have disappeared altogether. Events were not unfolding the way he had envisioned. All he had wanted was a place to spend the night: a refuge from the exorbitant prices of Manhattan hotels.

"You and Dave?" DuVal muttered, looking at Diane, his shoulders quickly shuddering as if he'd received a chill.

"Look, Jack," Dave said, "she *is* single. I mean, if I did give her herpes—and we don't know if I did—I certainly didn't mean to."

"Jesus, DuVal said, focusing on Diane, "so I might have herpes now too?"

Dave looked shocked.

"Gosh Jack, I don't know," Diane said, suddenly about to cry.

"Of all the goddam things," DuVal said pointedly into Diane's face, which had tensed as if to receive a blow.

"Diane?" Roy's voice suddenly interrupted.

Diane, Jack, and Dave turned to see Roy a few feet away.

"Roy!" Diane said, forcing a smile, "have you been here long?"

FORTY-THREE

Curtis Jones pulled away from the curb, and clearing the bumper of the car in front of him, eased his 1993 Nissan Maxima out on to Fort Washington Avenue. He'd parked less than an hour before, locating the coveted spot after having driven from Brooklyn to Washington Heights to visit his girl-friend Octavia.

Octavia and he had been introduced at a party thrown by Luz Marie, one of the nurses at King's County hospital, where he worked.

"Do you know my cousin Octavia?" she'd asked, taking him and a curvy Dominican woman each by an upper arm and forcibly closing the space between them.

"No," Curtis had said, struggling to make his voice heard over the blaring salsa music.

"Octavia," she'd offered, smiling to reveal a front tooth that was rimmed with silver.

"Curtis," he'd replied, extending a hand and taking hers.

"She just broke up with her boyfriend," Luz Marie had interjected, adding, "pinche cabron."

Octavia had shrugged her shoulders sheepishly as her cousin walked away.

That had been six months before. And other than an occasional run-in with her ex-boyfriend Hector—who was, as advertised, an asshole bastard—it was going okay.

When Curtis worked the 8-4 shift he could usually get from Kings County to Washington Heights in an hour. Sometimes more, sometimes less. It depended on traffic, which was pretty much always bad, but some-times worse. If he got to her apartment by 5, they could usually have sex before Octavia's son Hector Jr. came home from playing after school. If that didn't happen, they would have to wait until after he was asleep, and even then it didn't guarantee that there wouldn't be an interruption. He was only eight years old, and he slept in the living room. To get to the bathroom of Octavia's apartment, he had to walk through the bedroom. It was hit and miss. But on this day, there would be no afternoon sex.

Shortly after arriving at Octavia's, Curtis' cell phone rang, and the Caller ID told him it was King's County Hospital. He had no choice but to pick up. Curtis was trying to save for a down payment on a new car, and if an extra shift was available, he would almost always take it. Unfortunately, that wasn't the case. It was Jason Allen, the prosector he'd worked with that day.

"We're fucked."

"What?"

"Patel's on the warpath."

"Why?"

"He said we left the room a mess. Violations everywhere. He wants us to get back in there and go over the place with a fucking toothbrush."

"Now?"

"Now."

As diener, the cleanliness of the room was ultimately Curtis' responsibility. He hadn't left the place spotless, but it also wasn't trashed. What the fuck? Now he was going to have to return to Brooklyn, and that was going to be a pain in the ass.

"Where are you?"

"I'm in the Heights."

"At Octavia's?"

"Yeah."

"You better move."

It had been a fairly routine day, with an autopsy in the morning and then one in the afternoon. But the afternoon guy had come in late, and it wasn't so clear-cut. He was a 38-year-old male who'd died after flu-like symptoms that had lasted a few weeks. In the 24 hours before his death he had also apparently experienced some mild, then more serious, seizures. He'd died within a few hours of arriving at the hospital. His family, understandably distraught and confused, had requested an autopsy. The examination had been inconclusive, so the prosector had taken samples of all the major organs, placed them in plastic cassettes, and then into a jar of formalin. The pathologist would make the ultimate determination of the cause of death.

"Looks like lymphoma to me," Curtis had told Jason.

"What are you, a fucking doctor now?" Jason had asked, laughing.

"I saw one like this a couple of years ago," Curtis had said, "guy had no insurance, never went to the doctor, and the lymphoma ate him up."

"Maybe you should've gone to med school instead of me."

"I *definitely* should've gone to med school instead of you."

In the middle of the procedure Jason had become ravenously hungry. He'd skipped lunch to spend a little time in an unoccupied room with one of the residents—an intern named Wendy, or some other name that ended with a Y sound.

"Order us some Chinese," he'd said.

"Now?"

"Why not? I'll treat."

Curtis placed the call, ordering broccoli with garlic sauce for Jason, and pork-fried rice for himself. But when the order arrived, he left his food in the bag.

"Aren't you gonna eat?" Jason had asked.

"Later."

"You're not hungry?

"I wasn't balls deep in a resident at lunchtime."

"Gynecology," Jason said, raising an eyebrow conspiratorially, "She knows what to do with a pussy."

Truth be told, Curtis was hungry. He just wasn't one of those guys who could eat in the room while they were doing an autopsy. So on the drive home he'd shoveled forkfuls of rice toward his mouth as he lurched between stoplights on Flatbush, then weaved through traffic on the Brooklyn Queens Expressway heading north. In the end, frustrated by the difficulty of eating rice from a cardboard container with a plastic fork, he'd thrown the entire mess out the window of his car, watching it skid along the shoulder in his driver's side mirror. The car behind him had signaled its disapproval with a honk, and Curtis had raised a middle finger in reply, screaming "FUCK YOU" to its driver. That, in turn, had spawned a brief road rage episode, where the driver of the car, a late-model Cadillac Escalade, careened around Curtis and cut him off, forcing him to slam on his brakes and narrowly avoid getting rear-ended.

Curtis could've avoided the incident by throwing his trash on the backseat floor of his car. The area was already covered with old issues of the Daily News, Dunkin Donuts bags, crumpled napkins and paper coffee cups. But he'd feared that the smell of the Chinese food might linger. Now, as he drove east across 181st Street, he felt along the passenger seat for the fortune cookie he'd set aside, and shook his head thinking about the close call. Waiting for the stoplight at Broadway to turn green, he removed the cookie from its glassine package, broke it in half, and read his fortune. CLEANLINESS IS NEXT TO GODLINESS.

"Shit," Curtis said, thinking about the hospital and the earful he was likely to receive from the pathologist.

Some dieners scrubbed their rooms until they shined like a full moon on a cloudless winter night. Curtis was not among their number. It wasn't that he had a bad attitude about work: he worked hard, and generally did what he was told. It was a matter of philosophy. Other than protecting his own health, and that of the prosector and the pathologist, he couldn't be concerned with the appearance of cleanliness. His apartment, or more accurately, his room in his mother's apartment, was—to the untrained eye—a mess. But Curtis knew where everything was, or at least where to start looking for it, should he need it, whatever it happened to be. He was on an economy-of-motion tip. He had other more important things to be concerned with. Like Octavia, for instance. And getting more shifts so he could get a new Maxima, or maybe the latest model-year Altima, with those fucked-up clear taillights.

Unfortunately the pressure was on at the hospital, and in the pathology department especially. They'd done an autopsy the day before on a cop who got shot in the line of duty, and that kind of a job always brought scrutiny from above. Plus, there had been a lawsuit filed the previous week by the family of a woman whose body had been gnawed by rats at a funeral home in the Bronx, and now every link in the death business chain was under the microscope. The area hospitals were especially nervous, because they were perceived to have deep pockets and an aversion to bad publicity, which made them fertile grounds for hungry lawyers and litigious New Yorkers looking for quick and lucrative settlements. All it meant to Curtis was that he had to work more, watch his ass, and now probably get yelled at or fired for having not done either one of those two things especially well.

Curtis turned on the radio and switched from the FM to the AM band, looking for 1010 WINS.

"Why you always listen to this station?" Octavia had recently asked, "I like music."

"I want to know where the trouble is."

"It's always the same," she'd replied in her cute, lilting accent, "bumper-to-bumper 24/7."

Truer words were never spoken. Curtis turned up the volume.

"*Traffic is at a standstill in the southbound lanes of the BQE following an accident involving a tractor-trailer and a 15-passenger van*," the announcer said, "*and rubberneckers are slowing the northbound lanes.*"

He made a quick decision to take the FDR to the Manhattan Bridge and shoot out across Flatbush. The FDR could run slow at any time of the day, but by the sound of things on the radio it was his best shot at not spending all night in the car.

The FDR itself was coming to bits. In that regard it was like most of the roads in and around New York City, especially the main arteries that were used to move commuters and cargo between the boroughs. Curtis had read an article in the Daily News about how there really was no way to upgrade the roads—there just wasn't any more room to expand them. The conclusion of the story was that as bad as traffic was it was only going to get worse in the future. There was simply no way around the fact that as every year passed there was going to be more people, more cars, and more traffic jams. Curtis tried not to think about it, instead focusing on avoiding all the double-parked cars along 181st Street as he made his way toward the FDR.

Once he was on the FDR, traffic moved at a brisk pace. Too brisk, for Curtis' liking. He found it especially unnerving when the tuners in their lowered and hot-rodded Hondas raced through traffic swerving across three lanes without signaling. They sounded like a swarm of bees when they came from behind. Motherfuckers on death runs, Curtis thought.

As he came toward the underpass that supported the green lawns of Sutton Place, Curtis caught a glimpse of a red car swerving in and out of traffic in his rear-view mirror. Traffic was moving at around 55 MPH, and the car was passing others as if they were standing still, darting from one impossibly tight gap between cars to another. Determined not to be rear-ended, Curtis juggled his attention between the road in front of him and the rapidly approaching red splotch in his rear-view mirror. As the vehicle progressed to within a few car lengths behind his own, Curtis diverted his gaze away from the roadway for a second too long; long enough to miss that in the darkness of the underpass ahead brake lights were ablaze and traffic was grinding to a halt.

The sound of the impact, an initial boom followed by a screeching, scraping sound, was considerably amplified in the hollow tunnel of the underpass. As Curtis' aging Maxima plowed into the rear of the New York City Sanitation truck, its front end immediately accordioned to the lower lip of the windshield, which due to the enormous pressure exerted by the impact, was transformed into an elaborate spiderweb pattern of shattered glass. Though his airbag deployed, it could do little to protect him from the encroachment of the superheated, six-cylinder engine as it was jammed, fluids spewing, toward the passenger compartment, or the subsequent force exerted from behind as the red car, a millisecond later, smashed into the rear end of Curtis' Maxima.

Curtis' last conscious thought, as he struggled to draw air into a chest cavity that had been severely compacted by a steering wheel, was that he probably wouldn't require an autopsy. The cause of his own death would be readily apparent to anyone at the scene.

FORTY-FOUR

DuVal sat alone at a small table outside a midtown restaurant, chain smoking and drinking a martini. He'd left the building hurriedly, searching for the nearest bar that would allow him to smoke, and an outside table at a bistro had been the best and closest option. Though the evening air was crisp with the breeze of an early fall Canadian air mass, DuVal was far from the only person at an outside table. Several European tourists and assorted other nicotine addicts had also chosen to sacrifice physical comfort for the right to smoke while drinking and/or eating. He and the others had exchanged knowing glances and nods, and periodically one of the disenfranchised would hold his or her cigarette aloft while glancing and nodding to one of the others in a show of solidarity.

"It's come to this," DuVal said, breaking the code of silence during one such exchange, pulling his lapels close together across his chest and thinking, who could have predicted it from a Republican mayor?

He took a deep drag from his cigarette, raised his glass and drained half an inch from the chilled 5 oz. vessel. As he carefully placed the glass back on the table, he met the eye of a tourist a few tables over. He nodded and held his cigarette up. The other man offered a wry smile and nodded back.

"Fuck 'em," DuVal said.

"Okay!" the man said in halting English.

It had been a very different day from the one DuVal had expected. He'd left his apartment that morning basking in the glow of a good deed: After spending the previous evening letting Dave bore the shit out of him pouring his heart out over the completely predictable collapse of his marriage, he'd offered the hospitality of his supple Italian leather couch. Not that he really had a choice. Dave, unable to hold his liquor and drunker than a mailman on a Friday payday had, in fact, passed out. Still, DuVal had stretched a blanket over his snoring, supine figure and not mocked him in the morning when he fouled himself. Who knew the guy had been fucking his producer? His de facto, ex-sort-of girlfriend? But could he really blame the guy? It could be argued that there was no way for Dave to know that he and Diane had been involved in anything other than a professional relationship. But the herpes stuff he could be pissed about. Again, not because Dave might have indirectly and inadvertently passed herpes on to DuVal, but because he may have *knowingly* given it to Diane. And Diane, at the end of the day, was DuVal's friend. Or was she?

DuVal took another long pull from his Martini and considered a few recent developments in his relationship with Diane: she'd pretty much been avoiding him since the abortion; she'd apparently been fucking Dave for some period of time; she also seemed to be seeing someone else, or at least until an hour or two ago. He could understand the anger about the abortion; he hadn't handled that situation as well as he might have. As for keeping the fact that she was fucking Dave from him, well, she was probably embarrassed. Or, was fucking Dave and the secrecy around it an expression of a deeper, long-term seething resentment that she held for him? It was vexing. As was the secrecy surrounding the new boyfriend.

In the past, Diane had been relatively forthcoming about who she was dating. When she was dating someone, they would stop having sex for while. Then, when she and the new boyfriend broke up—for whatever reason—she would typically seek comfort, or perhaps just a respite from loneliness, in DuVal's arms. It had been a fairly agreeable arrangement, especially from DuVal's perspective. At times he had feared that she was falling in love with him, but for the most part it had been a convenient way for him to satisfy his physical and emotional need for intimacy without being particularly intimate. Of course, he now realized—as he had many times over the previous week—he'd taken it for granted. He had been completely satisfied with their arrangement, and not especially concerned about how Diane felt about it, because it suited his needs.

After his divorce DuVal didn't really want to get close to a woman—or anyone, for that matter—again. At least not in a manner that didn't have a clearly marked exit. It was simply too painful. And too much of a hassle. It required effort. Energy that he would rather be devoting to his show, his career, and his own inner world. So what he missed about Diane, more than having sex with her, was her companionship. He missed calling her at home to talk about work and ending up talking about a movie she saw, or a book she read, or what she was eating for dinner. The fear that had been gnawing at him recently—that he had lost her friendship—was now deepening. Especially with the evening's revelations. As DuVal thought about it, turning the situation over in his mind and looking at it as closely and realistically as he was capable, he realized that he wasn't upset about the information she was keeping secret from him—although he would be lying if he said he didn't feel a pang of jealousy—it was that there were secrets at all.

DuVal lit a fresh cigarette from the glowing tip of the one he was finishing. He took another sip of his Martini and set the glass on the table. He'd been sitting for less than an hour and had consumed close to 15 oz. of vodka. And all at once, in the way that will happen when you drink a lot quickly, a shroud of drunkenness, weighty and warm, came settling over him. DuVal signaled the waitress.

"Check," he said.

"Can I get a check for ya?" she answered.

"Thas the idea," he unexpectedly slurred, handing her his credit card.

He needed to get some air. Quick. More air, even, than was available to him at the outdoor tables of this bistro. What he needed, he told himself, was to take a walk. A brisk, bracing walk through the Manhattan streets to clear his head and metabolize some of the alcohol that he'd ingested. The waitress returned with DuVal's credit card.

"Here ya go," she said.

"Thanks," he answered, scratching his signature across the printed slip, and adding a 25% tip.

Standing, DuVal had to place his hand on the table to steady himself. He looked at his fellow customers to see if anyone had noticed his drunkenness.

"So long," he said to the group.

Nods and a few cigarette-hand waves goodbye greeted his parting salutation.

DuVal had sent his car and driver off when he left the Syndicate building in search of a bar. Now, he figured he would walk as far as he felt like walking, and either hail a cab or call for his car if he got lazy. Midtown to Tribeca was about an hour walk, 45 minutes if you took strides as long as those DuVal was intending to take. He wasn't certain if he would walk the entire way, but as DuVal turned south onto Fifth Avenue his lungs were filled with cool night air and his spirit was filled with renewed vigor. He had thinking to do. How would he make things right with Diane? And was it even possible?

By the time he was in the gaze of the stone lions guarding the entrance the New York Public Library at 42nd Street, DuVal had already decided what needed to be done. What he and Diane really needed to do was to talk. To get everything out on the table. Clear the air. He would call her in the morning and ask her to set some time aside in the middle of the day. They would have a frank discussion about the abortion, DuVal's callousness, and Diane's recent secrecy. He would ask about her new boyfriend—assuming they were still together after the events of the early evening—and extend his genuine wishes for her happiness. From there, hopefully, they could begin to get back on track.

As he walked along the comparatively dark and uninhabited stretch of Fifth Avenue in the high 30s, DuVal was so deep in thought that he was completely unaware of a white panel van that suddenly crept up alongside him. So he was completely caught off guard when—as he stopped to wait for the orange hand to change to the white man and indicate that he could cross the street—the sliding door on the curb side of the van opened and three men piled out.

The men went about their work quickly and silently, initially covering DuVal's mouth to muffle any protest, then dragging him onto the cross street and into the shadow of a high-rise office building, then pinning him face-up against the sidewalk. As hard as he struggled, DuVal was unable to prevent one of the attackers from prying his mouth open long enough to expose his tongue. Once his tongue was exposed, it was a relatively simple matter for the attacker to grab a fleshy chunk of it with a set of pliers. The initial pain of having his tongue clamped between the teeth of metal pliers and stretched unnaturally far out of his mouth—tearing his frenulum, the vertical curtain of flesh that connects the tongue to the floor of the mouth—was fairly insignificant compared to the pain DuVal felt when a box cutter was used to actually sever his tongue altogether. Because it was an existential pain. A pain that moved through his body and down into his soul, establishing residence at the very foundation of his being. For DuVal knew in that moment, as he lay writhing on the sidewalk, blood dripping from his mouth and forming in a pool beneath his head, that it was not a few inches of flesh he had just lost. It was his voice. His very reason for being. And so, as one of the three men held his tongue aloft, and each of them kicked him soundly for good measure, and they prepared to flee the scene with final shouts of "Allahu Akbar," DuVal had little desire to rise or to be saved. Little desire to be found and transported to a hospital. Little desire, in fact, to go on with life at all.

FORTY-FIVE

Dave Miller sat alone at a window table in the slowly-turning bar atop the Marriott Marquis in Times Square. Nursing his second vodka soda, he stared out at a riot of blinking lights below, and at an expanse of skyscrapers that rose like uneven blades of grass in a narrow stretch of yard. He was drinking to quell the panic that was rising within and had ordered the cheapest well vodka in a small effort to staunch the rapid flow of his dwindling funds into the larger economy. From thirty-seven floors above the street Dave had a clear view of all that was hanging in the balance. He could never lay claim to having owned the town, but he could, until very recently, consider that he had actually made it in the big city. Now, the life that he had worked for twenty years to build—a job requiring that he lift nothing heavier than a phone receiver, a healthy six-figure income, the ability to secure a middling table at a hot restaurant—had evaporated as swiftly and surely as the dew on a hot summer morning. And after the events that had transpired that evening at the radio station, his relationship with DuVal—the diaphanous length of thread by which he was dangling above the abyss—was in jeopardy. The situation was worse than Dave had ever imagined possible.

He needed to take action.

At his earliest opportunity, perhaps the next morning, Dave would need to offer a mea culpa to DuVal. He would claim, accurately, that he had no idea that DuVal and Diane were involved in anything other than a professional relationship. But the fucking herpes! It complicated things beyond measure. He could rightly profess ignorance of DuVal's sexual relationship with Diane, but it would be a tougher sell to claim he hadn't known that he might infect Diane with herpes. He considered two lies that could mitigate the damage: he could say that he was up front with Diane about having herpes, but that would be fairly easy for DuVal to vet. All he would have to do is ask Diane and Dave would be instantly called out. A second (and more believable) approach would be to maintain that he didn't know he had herpes—that it was a recent infection—and thus, the exposure was unwitting, and much more likely to be excused or forgiven. This story also jibed well with the fact that Jodi had only recently discovered that she had herpes and had kicked him out for it. It would make him look like a scumbag, but that, Dave thought, was something he was just going to have to live with. He needed to do whatever it took to salvage his relationship with DuVal, if only long enough for the deal to go through and for the first commission check to arrive.

But what was causing a tide of panic to rise in Dave's midsection was the possibility, once seemingly so remote, that things might not work out the way he had planned. Or even remotely like he had planned. That DuVal, who was surprisingly understanding about his split with Jodi and subsequent dismissal from her father's firm, would not be as magnanimous about these latest revelations. Because this was a very different and emotionally complicated situation. Both DuVal's pride and his physical health were involved. Sticking with Dave after he had been fired was fairly predictable; it offered an opportunity for DuVal to show that he was his own man, and unbound by convention. But having been (albeit in a roundabout way) cuckolded, and possibly infected with a pernicious and incurable sexually transmitted disease, was another matter altogether. Dave was forced to ponder the unthinkable: that his ship—or at least this ship—actually might not be coming in. And the reality was that if this deal didn't go through, and soon, Dave would be penniless. He could probably make the $20,000 he had left stretch a month. Two at the most. Beyond that, he was in real trouble.

"Ready for another?" the waiter asked.

"Not yet," Dave said, shaking his head.

"You here on business, or holiday?" the waiter asked.

"I live here, believe it or not."

"Well, there's a first," the waiter replied.

It's come to this, Dave thought. Drinking alone in one of the world's foremost, and cheesiest, tourist traps. He took a very small sip of his cocktail and surveyed the room. Out-of-towners, all. People in New York to visit Times Square and see *The Lion King* on Broadway. Loud, wide-bodied Americans, clusters of chatty Asians and a few scattered Europeans, suffering through. The Europeans, aghast at the portion sizes and the 37-floor trip to smoke a cigarette, no doubt. Standing out because of their clothing (higher-quality, fewer logos), lack of girth, and propensity to drink wine or beer instead of soda. What a fucking good-enough-will-do world. A world, he thought, snapping out of his daze, he might be forced to join if he didn't work things out with DuVal, and pronto.

Dave knew that if everything went to shit his only options would be to look for a job (the thought of which terrified him) or crawl back to Jodi to beg her forgiveness. A job search could take months, or even a year. The economy was soft, and having been at a single agency for his entire career he hadn't nurtured any significant contacts that could help him. He had no network to speak of. And like every other business, it was all who you knew. Moreover, other agencies would only be interested if he could bring a lucrative roster of clients in with him. And between Mitch Sanders' vendetta and DuVal's potential kiss-off, it was unlikely that he could do so. At Dave's age and with his history, it would be difficult to find work at any agency in New York. He could hang out a shingle and try to find some young talent, but that path would be expensive, and could take a few years to produce anything nearing a good income. He was in a desperate spot on the career side. The Jodi option, while completely unappealing, might be the more realistic of the two. Of course it had a significant downside: he would have to be with Jodi. Plus, he would have to go back to work for his father in-law, which would take some additional knee time. Perhaps a lifetime of it. And it was unrealistic to think that they would ever trust him again. He would be a walking target for his wife's invective and recriminations, and he would be reduced to the role of piss boy at work. It would be a like living in a gilded cage with a couple of rabid weasels. He had to make it work out with DuVal. It was his only shot. But there was nothing to be done at that moment. The time wasn't right to call DuVal. This type of situation required a cooling-off period. A day or two to let things settle.

On his way up to the bar Dave had rented a room in the Marriot with cash, paying for a week in advance. The rack rate was $299 a night, but he'd managed to get it down to $239. With tax it was close to another two grand out of pocket, altogether.

"Like the view?" the waiter, returning to his table, asked.

"Very nice," Dave replied.

"You here on business, or holiday?"

"Still live here."

"Well there's a first," the waiter replied.

"Or a second, depending on how you count."

"Ready for another?"

"Just a check," Dave answered.

He settled his bill, deciding that what he needed was to go to a liquor store and get a bottle. He felt like getting a load on, and it would be far cheaper to buy in bulk than drink out of the mini bar. Later, if he felt up to it, he might go over to ShowWorld to kill some time. Maybe look for a little companionship, who knew?

FORTY-SIX

"That was awkward," Roy said, as he and Diane descended from the station to the street, mercifully alone in the brushed-steel elevator car.

"I want to kill myself," Diane said, staring at the floor, unable, for the moment, to even look Roy in the eye. He placed a hand on her shoulder in what Diane took to be a non-committal way, offering neither an abundance of warmth nor a definitive degree of standoffishness.

"Well, don't do that," Roy said, "at least until we have a chance to talk."

"I'm mortified. I don't even know where to start."

"Okay then, I'll start. I'm a little freaked out—you should probably know that—but I'm not going to take off running when this elevator gets to the lobby. How's that?"

"Reassuring, I guess. But I may," Diane replied. Tears were welling in her eyes. "This is so fucked up."

They were largely silent during the cab ride downtown. Roy held Diane's hand in a firm grip, which she took as a good sign. Or, alternately, her mind wheeling through the various directions things could go, the gentlemanly thing to do before the blow off. At Diane's apartment they made an elaborate production out of ordering dinner, settling on Thai, neither especially eager to eat. Or to have the first truly difficult conversation of their fledgling relationship.

"DuVal and I had a thing," Diane finally said, "over several years. Casual. A marriage of convenience, in a manner of speaking," she began.

"Well, there's half the story," Roy deadpanned.

"Stop. Let me tell you the whole story—get it all out in one chunk—or I might start really crying," Diane said, raising both of her hands for emphasis.

"Fine."

"So DuVal and I have been sleeping together, on and off, for a couple of years."

"How many years?"

"Honestly? Three or four, maybe."

"Holy shit."

"On and off. It's always been very casual."

"So you said. But sincerely, how casual can it be if it's lasted several years?"

"I know, I know, but that's what it is. Was. Whatever," she said, staring again at the floor as, in the telling, the reality of the situation sank in.

"Look, I know it sounds lame, but I work really long hours. And have, for years. I've moved a lot. There's been no time—or opportunity—to date, really. I mean, I can count the number of sexual partners I've had on one hand, if that's what you're wondering about. Okay, one and a half."

"I think I met the half today."

"I'm serious."

"Me too."

Diane readjusted the way she was sitting. She was having trouble keeping still.

"DuVal was always there. He was safe. And there's never been anything improper about it. In a quid pro quo, boss/employee sense. It was really just two people having sex."

"You're speaking in the past tense."

"Well, clearly. Even if the two of us are finished after tonight, that's over forever. Especially after the abortion," she said, her back stiffening upon realizing that she'd opened yet another unsavory can of worms.

"Abortion?" What abortion?"

Diane started to sob. It came in huge heaves and shudders and, once it came, she was unable to stop it for several minutes. Roy put his arms around her and held her closely.

"I had a fucking abortion while you were out of town," Diane admitted, after she had finally managed to stop crying.

"I'm sorry to hear that. And DuVal wasn't supportive?"

"No. But I really didn't give him the chance to be."

"It was his?"

"I'm pretty sure."

"Pretty sure?"

"Dave and I always used condoms. Every time. But they're only 99% effective," she said, beginning to cry again, "or so it says on the box."

"Then it's probably a safe assumption," Roy said, trying to offer a little comfort.

"At this point, it doesn't matter anyway, does it?

"I suppose not," Roy said then asked, "You didn't have any desire to keep the baby?"

"Not for a minute. And strangely, I feel guilty about that," Diane said, "But it wasn't the right time, and it wasn't the right baby."

Telling Roy about DuVal—and especially the abortion—was cathartic. It also made Diane feel tremendously vulnerable. But if he was going to love her, she told herself, he had to know who she really was.

With that in mind, she addressed the topic of Dave. She told Roy how she thought it was purely sexual, initially, but that she had come to believe that she might have been acting out. That she may have been expressing some deeply-held resentment toward DuVal; or simply trying to break away from him for good. In any event, she summarized, both affairs were over. And if she had any doubts, meeting Roy—and experiencing what she felt at that moment, as she bared her soul and hoped he wouldn't judge her too harshly—put them to rest.

"Timing is one of the many things you really can't control," Diane said. "I didn't know I was going to meet you when I did, for instance, and I had no way of knowing I would love you the way I do."

With that, Diane leaned back on the couch and heaved a heavy sigh.

"I certainly can't begrudge you any former lovers," Roy began, "I mean, we're not twenty years old," he continued, moving closer to Diane on the couch and taking one of her hands in both of his.

"I've dated my share of women, sometimes thinking it might last, and other times just for sex, or companionship, or whatever."

"Really? I was hoping I was the first," Diane said, trying, for a moment, to lighten the mood.

"But the thing is—and this is something I really believe—if we're going to try being together we're going to have to be able to trust each other. Completely."

"I know, I know," Diane said, suddenly worried at Roy's tone and manner.

"I mean, there are lies, and there are, well, I won't call them lies of omission, but there are omissions. And I really, really wish you had told me about this stuff sooner."

"I can see how you might feel that way," Diane said, "but seriously, do you think you would've gotten involved with me if I told you I had just broken up with *two* men?"

"I'm not sure, to be honest," Roy answered.

"That's the thing. And that's not who I am. Or, at least, not who I think of my self as being."

Roy sat silently for a moment, considering what she had said.

"And if we're going to go forward after tonight, you're just going to have to believe that. And have faith in me," Diane added.

"What about the herpes? Can we talk about that for a minute?"

"Oh God, Roy," Diane said, "I had no idea Dave had herpes, I swear. And if he gave it to me, and I gave it to you, I'll never forgive myself."

"Very little shocks me, but I'm shocked that he didn't tell you."

"He's a scumbag. And that's what's so fucked up. I can't believe I was involved with the guy. That's just not me. I really want you to believe that."

Roy closed his eyes and covered his face with his hands, thinking. Is this what I want, he wondered? We have so much in common: she loves to read, she's funny, she's passionate about her work, we're sexually compatible, and I can talk to her. But is she crazy? Is that the trade-off? Roy was long past the stage of juggling women. It was a natural thing to do in your twenties, to his way of thinking: a confirmation of your virility, and a natural expression of curiosity and a healthy libido. But if you were still juggling multiple sexual partners by your mid-thirties, especially if you were a woman, did it start to border on pathology? A sign that you needed propping up? Constant affirmation? But was this case, this instance, an aberration for her?

Roy considered what Diane had said. He thought he might really love her. Or was starting to love her, in a way that seemed like it could be lasting. He didn't want to lose that. But he also didn't want to be with someone with too much baggage. Life is short, and there are too many people out there to choose from. Why invite trouble into your life?

"Diane," Roy said, uncovering his eyes and facing her, "I need to be alone for a while. Do a little thinking."

"What do you mean? Are you breaking up with me?" she asked, horrified that she sounded like a 16-year-old girl.

"I just think I should spend the night back at my place, that's all," Roy answered.

Locking the door behind Roy, Diane was overcome with the urge to throw up. She walked quickly to the bathroom and bent over the toilet, expelling what little of the Thai food she had managed to eat. When the convulsions had passed, she brushed her teeth and took a long, hot shower, wishing that water alone would somehow wash away the day's events, and more, the herpes virus that she imagined making an invisible invasion of her body. She examined herself for several minutes in the shower, even bringing a small mirror into the effort, but nothing looked out of the ordinary. She hoped she didn't have herpes. If she did have herpes, she knew that she could live with it. But she couldn't live with the notion that she may have given it to DuVal and Roy. And isn't that the way, she thought? Just when things seem to be going so right, your past comes and bites you on the ass. And she didn't even have that much of a past! It was just that the two really big mistakes she had ever made had come back to haunt her at once. On the very same day. In the worst way imaginable. And just when she had found, against incalculable odds, a perfect guy. Maybe even *the* guy.

Diane toweled herself dry and put on a pair of boxer shorts and a t-shirt. She wanted to call Roy. She wanted to tell him how sorry she was, and that it wasn't how it looked: she wasn't some crazy chick who slept with her boss and his agent and fell in love almost at first sight after meeting a stranger in a restaurant. But she knew she couldn't call. She needed to give him the time he asked for. Let it all sink in. So she went to the medicine cabinet and shook three Ambien tablets out of an amber plastic bottle, washing them down with a glass of wine. Then she lay in bed and tried to read, the task rendered impossible as the type on the pages of her book became blurred by a slow stream of tears and drowsiness came over her like an opaque veil.

FORTY-SEVEN

"1010 WINS, you give us twenty-two minutes, we'll give you the world."

Diane's clock radio made another attempt at waking her from a dreamless narcotic sleep. On the first she had thrown a leaden arm towards it, managing, against all odds, to hit the snooze button. Now that arm was hanging over the side of the bed like a thick, rusted anchor chain. She raised an eyelid and struggled to move the remainder of her body in the off-bed direction. When she had one foot on the floor she tested her weight against it and dragged the other down alongside, finally achieving—with some help from her arms bracing her against the bed—a mostly upright posture. She staggered toward the bathroom and splashed some cold autumn tap water onto her face.

Diane's habit was to leave the radio on for a few minutes in the morning to get a quick read on the major news stories and how they were being reported. She listened drowsily as she retrieved her around-the-house glasses from the medicine cabinet (where she placed them each evening before she performed her before-bed ritual of facial cleansing and moisturizing) and began the various elements of her morning routine. Depending on the ease or difficulty she was having with choosing an outfit, she would either leave the radio on or turn it off while she dressed. If she was having an especially hard time choosing something to wear she found that the radio distracted her from the task at hand, making a frustrating situation almost intolerable.

She finished brushing her teeth and turned the water off just in time to hear 1010 WINS coming out of a commercial break.

"In local news, conservative radio talk-show host Jack DuVal was assaulted in midtown Manhattan last night. In what police are describing as a

particularly vicious attack, the assailant, or assailants, apparently severed his
tongue. Sources within the department report that no witnesses to the attack
have yet been identified. NYPD officials are asking anyone with information
about the crime to come forward, or call 1-800-577-TIPS. That's 1-800-577-
TIPS. Mr. DuVal is said to be in serious but stable condition at Lennox Hill
Hospital. The severed portion of his tongue was apparently not recovered."

Diane gripped the sink. She felt as if someone had blown a hole
through her center. A fever-like heat rose quickly from her toes to her
head, and beads of sweat gathered at her temples. She splashed more water
on her face and dried it with a hand towel.

What was she going to do? She had to go to the hospital. Immediately.
She had to see DuVal. But she didn't know if she could face what she
might find. Or if she had the strength to look into his eyes. To see what
he must be feeling. Not alone anyway. She picked up the phone and dialed
Roy's number.

"Hello," Roy answered.

"Roy, it's Diane," Diane said, choking back a sob, "DuVal's been hurt."

"What happened?"

"He's was attacked. I heard it on the radio. They cut out his tongue,
and I really need you."

"I'll be right there," he replied, and hung up.

At the curb in front of Lennox Hill Hospital, Roy paid the cab driver
as Diane wriggled out of the car and rushed inside. She was told at the
information desk that visiting hours didn't begin until 11 A.M.

"But I have to see him now," Diane protested.

"I understand. But visiting hours are intended to ensure that patients
are able to get the rest they need," the woman before her explained.

"You don't understand. He doesn't have anyone else," Diane answered.

It was only then, as flashbulbs began to pop and piercing beacons
came alight atop video cameras, that Diane realized she had just become
a different kind of cog in the media machine. That the horror of DuVal's
attack, the abrupt end to his broadcasting career, and the personal tragedies

that this event would precipitate (from DuVal's own suffering to that of station employees, high and low, who would certainly lose their jobs after a decent—perhaps as lengthy as a month—period of grave concern by the Syndicate) were nothing more than fat in the fire. That the humanity of the event would be lost to all but those most closely affected; it would be stripped away, or compressed to fit into the allotted column inches, or between commercial breaks that promised whiter teeth, clearer reception, or better mileage. She had forgotten.

In her haste to get inside and ascertain DuVal's whereabouts, the presence—in front of the hospital—of several vans adorned with television station logos and equipped with pneumatically extensible satellite antennas, had gone unnoticed. Similarly, she had failed to register the cluster of reporters and crew members gathered in the lobby as she sprinted through. Now, however, as she pleaded her case to the largely unsympathetic person behind the desk, they made their presence known. They reminded her what this was really all about, what she herself was a part of, and how trivializing it had all become.

"Could you please speak with his doctor, or the supervising nurse on duty, and ask them to tell him Diane is here?

"Are you his girlfriend?" asked Kristen Shaughnessy, a reporter for the all-New York news cable station, NY1.

Diane turned in the direction of the voice that had asked the question and, possessed with the familiarity that comes with having seen someone on television so often for several years, blurted, "Hi Kristen."

Roy pushed through the crowd to Diane's side, and put his arm around her for support. After a moment of feeling stupid and disoriented, Diane regrouped. For all the other reporters knew, she and Kristen were friends. She also knew that she hadn't yet given them a usable sound bite, and that realization made her feel better. For the moment, at least, she was in control. As a producer, Diane knew all too well that the media abhors a vacuum. In absence of something substantial to report, or at a minimum, something insubstantial to fill airtime, they would speculate wildly. There was no upside to that for DuVal. And, perhaps, at this point, little downside. But Diane realized she needed to give them something—some fluff, even—if only to keep them from trying to storm the gates. She took a deep breath and faced the group.

"As some of you know," she started, trying to cover her earlier gaffe, "I'm Diane Healy, Jack DuVal's producer. At this point I have no new information about his assault or current condition. My understanding is that Jack DuVal has been injured, and that his condition is stable. My hope is that he makes a rapid and full recovery. Thank you."

The woman behind the information desk was returning the phone receiver to its cradle as Diane turned away from the cameras. Quietly, she spoke.

"He's been asking for you. You can go up."

Reporters nearby scribbled in their notebooks.

"He's speaking?" Diane asked.

"Don't know," the woman answered.

Again, the scribbling began, along with hasty arrangements by the television reporters to do live updates.

Diane and Roy slipped away toward the elevators. Roy gripped Diane's hand.

"Are you okay?" Roy asked, when they were alone in the elevator car, traveling upward, out of earshot of the reporters.

"No, I'm not," Diane answered, her body rigid, "this is unbelievable. I cannot accept that this has happened."

They exited the elevator on DuVal's floor. DuVal had been stabilized in the ICU overnight, then moved into a room of his own that morning. Roy and Diane scanned the printed name tags mounted at the side of each doorframe as they walked the length the hallway. Some rooms had two patients, some one. In the room next to DuVal's they could see a patient lying in bed connected to a laboratory-worthy arrangement of monitoring devices. A floor-to-ceiling curtain was drawn, presumably separating his bed from the other one in the room. Diane and Roy looked at the nameplate: Levine, Lawrence/Jones, Curtis. The sight of the man tethered to the machines made Diane's eyes well with tears. In preparation for entering DuVal's room she took a moment to wipe them away.

"Do you want me to come in, or wait out here?" Roy asked.

"I'd like to go in alone first, if that's okay," Diane replied. Roy kissed her on the cheek and gave her hand a final squeeze.

DuVal was lying prone in his bed, a tube extending from the crook of his arm to an IV bag full of clear liquid. His head was turned to the side. He was staring out the window, or perhaps, Diane thought, sleeping. Not wanting to startle him, Diane took measured steps and approached cautiously. As she advanced toward the bed, her gentle footfalls, quiet as they were, seemed to catch DuVal's attention. He slowly turned his head in her direction. His face was puffy and swollen, with dark purple bruising around his jawline and lips. A white nub of bandage was visible through his open mouth. Diane stopped. DuVal's eyes, sunken in their sockets and underscored with dark circles, were filled with what Diane would later realize—each time she would revisit that moment in the remaining years of her life—was a haunting mixture of fear, dread and regret. A single tear rolled down DuVal's cheek, and fell silently into the white folds of his bedding.

"Oh, Jack," Diane said.

FORTY-EIGHT

Dave's first breath as he woke was filled with the intermingled odors of stale cigarette smoke, vinegary sweat and too-sweet perfume. His mouth was dry, and a dull pain inhabited the regions between the top of his eyeballs and the rear of his skull. He had a hangover; but moreover, he had hangover fatigue—he was down in a trough, having been fairly-to-extremely drunk for several nights running. His desire to wake up feeling better had been trumped by the desire to forget; soundly, and repeatedly. He took a sip from a glass of water that sat on the bedside table, then felt a stirring in the bed beside him. He looked over his shoulder. A whore. Why was she still here? Dave tried to marshal his intellectual forces. Restore some order. He did a quick once over of the woman, then scanned his surroundings. The Marriott Marquis. He had taken a room early the previous evening. This was his home. Or at least, he remembered, it was for the next week. There had been cocktails alone at the bar upstairs and then he'd decided to go down to the street to get a bottle. Had he found her out there? He plumbed the depths of his memory. No. He had come back to the room and started looking at porn on the Internet. That's what had happened. And that, in turn, had inspired him to consult the "erotic services" section of Craigslist. He had e-mailed her. She was, in effect, a mail order bride-for-a-night. Mystery solved. Or partially solved, he thought. He came back to his original question: what the hell was she still doing here?

"You owe me a thousand dollars," the woman said, her waking words making Dave wonder if he had been thinking aloud.

"What?" Dave replied.

"You owe me a thousand dollars," she repeated, more emphatically this time. "You said you were lonely and would pay me an extra grand to spend the night."

"Look..." Dave struggled to remember her name.

"Brittany," she offered, with a detached, sleepy/bored look on her face.

"Look, Brittany," Dave said, "I don't remember saying that."

Brittany's look of boredom was quickly replaced by one of rage. "Motherfucker!" she exclaimed, rising to a surprisingly threatening sitting position in less time than it took to get her words out.

"But of course, I believe you," Dave said, seeking to ward off any unpleasantness or violence that might complicate his living arrangements or his hangover. "Let me just get my bearings here, and we'll go downstairs and find an ATM."

"I take credit cards," she replied smartly.

"That's convenient." Dave said, "but I don't have a credit card."

"What the fuck?"

"My sentiments as well," Dave replied, as he reached for the remote to turn on NY1. As the image on the screen grew from a dot in the center outward, the sonorous tones of Pat Kiernan's voice greeted Dave like an old friend. Watching NY1 in the morning had been a habit of Dave's for the better part of a decade, and just hearing the sound of the anchor's voice made him wish he were home. Did he even have a home? On the face of it, Dave thought, the answer was no. He felt utterly lost. He was in a room that had been designed to be impersonal—the lodging equivalent of a cube farm—and he was with a trapped in that room with an angry, somewhat-unattractive stranger who wanted a thousand dollars from him. But things could change. Dave was a glass half-full type of guy. Optimism would be key. He could get used to this kind of lifestyle. It wasn't that bad. Adaptability was hardwired into human beings. And for good reason. Life is, above all, random. One minute you could be sitting at your desk looking out the window, and the next a hijacked airliner could come howling into view and be flown, full-throttle and with the worst intentions, into the skyscraper across the street. You just never knew. Shit happens, you move on. Once, for instance, he had depended on Brad Holbrook to give him his morning news. Funny Brad Holbrook, with his meaty fingers and wry, insinuating tone. And poof! He was gone. Off to who knows where. But then Pat Kiernan came along. Sure, it took a little getting used to, but Pat Kiernan brought an entirely new level of bemusement into the equation. And a Canadian accent, which made his broadcasts all the more interesting. *Abooot* this, *abooot* that. Plus, he had a weather background, which gave new weight to the "Weather On The Ones" segment. All in all, the change had been good. Dave could honestly say that he didn't miss Brad Holbrook anymore. Perhaps the same thing would happen with his attachment to his home, his wife, his job and his money.

"Hey, are you going in to the bathroom? I need to take a dump."

Dave looked at his guest. "Why don't I go first," he said, "I'll try to be quick."

No sooner had the skin of Dave's ass touched the cool surface of the toilet seat did a riotous cacophony of *blaaats*, sputters and splurts begin. The drinking was playing havoc with his bowels. For a brief moment he worried that his guest might hear the commotion through the door. But Dave quickly comforted himself with the thought that even if she did hear the sounds of this loud, loose, and messy shit, he didn't care. Her opinion of him was meaningless. On balance, he was lucky he had even made it to the toilet in light of what had happened at DuVal's apartment the previous morning.

It hadn't been his intention to do so, but after flushing Dave felt obliged to take a quick shower. It had been a tricky clean up, and he had little confidence in the quality of his work. The water did him good. It helped to smooth the rough edges of his hangover. After a few minutes of this hydrotherapy he closed the valves, toweled dry, and wrapped himself in the terrycloth robe that had been provided by the hotel. He felt refreshed, if not invigorated. Opening the bathroom door, the quality of Dave's day changed. Gone was the prostitute, and along with her, his laptop.

"FUUUCCCKKKKKK!"

Dave was at a loss for what to do. He couldn't very well report the theft to the hotel management. Or to the police for that matter. He could go look for her, but it was unlikely he would have any success tracking her down. And even if he did, the chances were very good that the laptop would no longer be in her possession.

Dave could get over the financial setback. If need be he could buy a new laptop. But he was extremely concerned about the loss of all his files and contact information. He had almost everything backed up on the server at the agency, but the odds were that they had already stripped out his user name and password.

There were a few pawnshops over on Eighth Avenue in the 40s. If he was lucky, she had done the lazy thing and just gone a block over and turned the laptop around for a quick buck. He would get dressed and go have a look.

Suddenly, DuVal's name was being spoken on the television. Pat Kiernan was talking about a violent attack that had taken place and saying that DuVal was in serious condition at Lennox Hill hospital. Dave hadn't been listening at the top of the piece, and couldn't sort out what had happened. Then the station cut to an on-scene report filed by Kristen Shaughnessy. Dave watched, mesmerized, as Diane Healy made a vague statement to the effect that DuVal had been injured and she was praying for his recovery. But what sort of injury? Dave wondered. Kristen Shaughnessy came back on the screen, responding to an invitation from Pat Kiernan.

"Yes Pat," she said.

"If Mr. DuVal's condition has been upgraded from critical to serious-but-stable, what exactly does that mean?" He asked.

"Well Pat, it means, among other things, that his injuries are not life-threatening at this point."

"Have they given any indication about his prognosis for recovery? Is it expected, for instance, that he will able to speak again?"

Dave clenched his teeth together, and gripped both sides of his head with his hands. He felt as if he might need to head back to the toilet.

"Well, the staff here is being very cautious about that. They're not saying one way or the other. I did speak with a resident earlier who told me—off the record—that it would be very unlikely for a person who had lost as much of his tongue as Mr. DuVal apparently has to ever speak normally again."

"Thank you Kristen. We'll check back with you later in the hour. Until then, I guess we'll just have to hope for the best."

Dave sat on the bed. DuVal had lost his tongue? Somebody had attacked him and ripped—or cut—his tongue out? He couldn't believe what he had heard. It was the worst possible thing that could have happened. Poor DuVal. And poor me, thought Dave; I'm completely fucked. He needed to get over to the hospital. He needed to see DuVal and talk to his doctors. He needed to know exactly what had happened, and what would happen.

On the street in front of the hotel, Dave decided to take a brief detour and do a drive-by of the pawnshops on Eighth Avenue. Just on the off chance that his laptop might turn up. DuVal wasn't going anywhere, and it would save him a world of headaches if the laptop did manage to appear. He walked west from Broadway to Eighth on 44th Street, past the Shubert Theatre and the St. James, where he and Jodi had gone to *The Producers* the year before. They were happy to have seen the production with the original cast of Matthew Broderick and Nathan Lane, even though Dave thought Nathan Lane was a terrible over-actor and the sight of his inwardly/upwardly-arched eyebrows made his butthole pucker. He thought back to that night. It had been a very pleasant night out, and Jodi had seemed happy. Dave wiped a miserly little tear from the corner of his eye.

In the front window of the second of two pawnshops Dave encountered he saw a wide variety of old cameras, electric and acoustic guitars, VCRs, and DVD players. No laptops, but Dave figured they might be kept inside. As the proprietor—a caricature of a figure in his early 60s with a comb-over, a belly like a 40-pound medicine ball, and an inch of unlit cigar protruding from his mouth—helped another customer, Dave looked at the sad collection of jewelry and watches contained under the smudged glass of a diner counter-length display case.

There, amongst plated Seiko timepieces and badly-cut, poorly-set diamond rings, lay DuVal's cherished gold lighter. Dave craned his neck to the side to read the inscription: *A voice is a nice thing Jack, but you'll never earn your living with it.*

FORTY-NINE

Jodi Miller climbed the internal stairway of the tenement building, her Manolo Blahniks falling noisily in the deep grooves worn into the center of the smooth marble steps by eighty years of human traffic. The walls of the stairwell would be due for painting in another year, the depressing beige-over-brown scheme having faded in places where the superintendent had scrubbed away graffiti. Jodi believed in the broken window theory, and as such, wouldn't stand for graffiti in or on her buildings. It was an invitation to these people. An offer to achieve the only kind of immortality or recognition any of them could ever hope for: an indecipherable scribble of paint or magic marker on a mottled wall in a shithole neighborhood.

She had decided to pop over to look in on a few of her buildings after a second look at a loft on which she was considering making an offer. The loft was a bright and airy 2600 sq. foot co-op at Hudson and Franklin. At $2.8 million it was within Jodi's range, but the maintenance seemed high ($5200/month) and the broker seemed a little unsure about the board. She'd been full of gossip and a shameless name dropper, pointing to this building and that with "John John Kennedy lived there," or simply "Harvey Kietel."

In the course of this forced-yet-meant-to-sound-casual barrage of self-important blather, she'd said, "Did you hear about Jack DuVal? He lives up there," pointing to yet another building, "Terrible. Just terrible. And after what this neighborhood suffered on 9-1-1."

"I heard it on 1010 WINS on the way into town," Jodi had answered.

She'd never much cared for DuVal, but she certainly didn't wish him any harm. The poor bastard, she thought—he'd be better off if they'd taken his cock.

The mention of DuVal's name, and the story, had set Jodi to wondering about Dave. She had no idea where he was staying, or what he was up to. Her herpes outbreak was beginning to show signs of clearing up, but she was still furious with him. And humiliated. How many other women had he slept with? Had he not thought of her at all? Her feelings? Her health? He was probably off with some girlfriend somewhere, having the time of his life. She wondered what effect this latest DuVal development would have on his finances. Surely DuVal's radio career was over if he couldn't speak. But perhaps they had already signed the deal Dave had been working on. In that case, she supposed, some insurance company was out of luck. She figured she probably wouldn't know the details until their divorce moved a little further along. And even then, depending on who Dave had hired to represent him. Fucking lawyers, she thought, shady.

On the landing of the third floor Jodi sorted through the numbered keys on the key ring in her hand. She had keys for all the locks that were originally installed in the doors of her buildings, including those for the individual apartments. If the tenants were too careless or cheap to change the locks she felt it was well within her rights to look in on what they were doing to her property every now and then.

She knocked on the door of apartment 3A, and after a moment of hearing no response, let herself in. What a mess, she thought. Children's toys were strewn around the floor, articles of clothing were draped over the backs of chairs and hung from doorknobs, and a half-eaten sandwich sat on the piece of plywood that—stretched between two purloined milk crates—served as a coffee table. It was disgusting. Who lives like this, she wondered? With so many tenants, it was hard to remember who lived in which apartment in what building. Jodi scanned the room for evidence. On a shelf above the television set she spotted the spine of a photo album. She pulled the book down and began perusing its pages. She stopped at a page that held a family portrait. The photograph looked as if it had been done in a local photo studio. A young Asian family posed against a background of a garish cherry blossom tree. A man in glasses wearing an ill-fitting suit, his tie knotted loosely around his neck. His smiling wife seated at his side, her arm around the waist of a happy looking child who was perhaps three years old. As Jodi stared at the picture a feeling of sadness began to well up inside her. The feeling was quickly dispelled, however, by the sound of a key turning in the front door. Suddenly, Jodi was face to face with the family in the photo. They had aged. The girl was now perhaps five or six years old and no longer clinging to her mother. She ran toward Jodi, stopping perhaps eighteen inches away.

"Who are you?" she asked.

"I'm your landlady," Jodi answered.

"What are you doing in our house?" the girl demanded.

"It's okay," her mother interjected, seeming afraid to offend Jodi.

Probably illegals, Jodi thought, setting the photo album back on the shelf where she had found it. "I thought I smelled fire," she said, lying. "But everything's fine. I'll be going now."

She stepped past the man who was still standing in the doorway. As she passed, the white fur of her coat brushed his hand, startling him.

"Goo-bye," he said, in heavily accented English.

As the door closed behind her, Jodi turned her attention to the floor of the landing. Dust had piled in the corners and there were scuff marks beneath the stairs that led to the floors above. Sloppy. She would have a word with the super.

Across the way, on a welcome mat in front the door to apartment 3C, sat a fortune cookie. That's odd, Jodi thought. Well, maybe not, she reconsidered—this is Chinatown. She stepped across the way and bent to pick it up. Curious, she broke the cookie in half and pulled the slip of paper from the gulf between the sections. WHAT GOES AROUND COMES AROUND, it read.

"Un-huh," she said aloud, her voice echoing against the hard surfaces of the empty landing. A sharp autumn breeze came through the hallway, and Jodi closed the front of her coat against the chill.

FIFTY

"I got you an iced coffee with milk. Large."

"Sugar?"

"Two," Roy said, placing the plastic cup in front of Diane.

He sat down next to her in a weather worn metal lawn chair facing the South Congress Avenue morning traffic. Though they were under the awning, the 90-degree heat had sweat gathering at Roy's temple. He took a sip of his iced tea.

"I was going to say that I won't miss this heat, but I saw that it's going to hit 90 in New York today too."

"Yeah, but if we were staying here we could swim."

"True."

"I think I'm ready to go home, though."

"Me too."

Jo's was crowded. As the anti-Starbucks of South Austin, it did a brisk business in high-priced coffee. And attached, as it was, to the Hotel San Jose—the boutique hotel of the moment—it also benefited from the tourist trade. A pair of tattooed hipsters next to them gathered their yoga mats and American Spirit cigarettes and left, making way for another pair who looked remarkably like them standing at the wait.

After finishing their drinks, Roy and Diane headed back to their room, packed, and checked out of the hotel—their home away from home for the previous six weeks.

When it was clear that her work with DuVal had come to an end Roy had asked Diane if she would like to take a shot at working on a documentary; at a greatly reduced salary, he was quick to add. She had jumped at the opportunity. She was ready for a change, and couldn't stand the thought of being apart from Roy for the month or more it would take to shoot the piece. So after a few months of pre-production the two of them and a small crew had headed south to Austin to spend six days and nights a week filming local bingo games, following the stories of the participants, and soaking up life in the Texas hill country.

Diane had enjoyed her time in Austin. They'd eaten a great deal of Tex-Mex and barbecue and seen a lot of good music. She and Roy had been out late the night before, watching Junior Brown at the Continental Club. The bar was conveniently located just across the street from the hotel, and they had taken the opportunity to drink a few too many Shiner beers. As they watched the band play deep into the warm night, Diane had fantasized about a long life of working together with Roy. They'd been spending the better part of twenty-four hours a day together for months, and there was remarkably little friction. Diane loved him like she had never loved another man, and the difficult patch they had gone through the previous fall was now little more than a memory. It turned out that neither of them had contracted herpes, and the process of working through that period had, in the end, brought them closer.

At Bergstrom airport they sat, bags piled around their legs, savoring a last meal of smoked meats from the Salt Lick. One of the enduring charms of Austin was that the airport featured real food from real local restaurants, instead of the McDonalds/Burger King/Pizza Hut juggernaut found in most of the nation's flying centers. As Diane struggled with an overly ambitious bite of her brisket sandwich, an attractive blonde woman with low-cut jeans approached their table.

"Roy!" she said.

"Hello," Roy answered, looking uncomfortable.

"You don't remember me, do you?"

"Uhhh…"

"Sandy," she said, "we met on the plane to New York about six months ago."

"Oh yes, now I remember," he said, looking toward Diane, who had a jealous glint in her eye.

"I'd just been dumped by my boyfriend," she reminded him.

"Okay," Roy said, placing his hand on Diane's knee, "by the way, this is my girlfriend Diane."

Diane swallowed, then stood to shake the blonde's hand.

"Sandy," Sandy said.

Diane opened her mouth to speak, but nothing came out. She reached for her throat, then tried to speak again. Nothing. Her eyes widened, and she tried to cough. Realizing she couldn't speak, she put both hands to her throat. She was choking. Roy stood, looking alarmed.

"Can you breathe?" he asked.

Diane shook her head from side to side quickly.

"Oh my God," Sandy said.

Roy moved behind Diane and reached his arms around her midsection. He gripped his right wrist in his left hand, located the bottom of her rib cage, and with a sharp jerk, squeezed back. A large ball of partially chewed meat and bread shot from Diane's mouth onto the table in front of her. She coughed loudly, and a foot-long string of debris-laden saliva descended from her lower lip. She reached for a napkin.

"Why did he do that?" a little girl at the next table asked her mother.

"She was choking," her mother said, "so he gave her the Heimlich Maneuver to get the food out."

"Oh."

"That's why you should always chew your food good," the mother added.

"I'm so embarrassed," Diane said, wiping her mouth with the napkin.

"Don't be," Sandy said, "are you okay?"

"I think so."

"Do you still have my number?" Sandy asked Roy.

"I think so," Roy answered, eliciting a glare from Diane.

"Call me some time. I'm in New York once in a while."

"Okay."

"I met a guy up there. You know, nothing serious."

"Good."

"He's an agent."

"Watch out for those types."

Sandy laughed.

Diane began gathering their bags.

"I guess you guys have a flight to catch."

"Yeah," Roy said, shaking Sandy's hand, "see you around."

"Maybe in New York!"

"Maybe," Diane said.

With that, Sandy walked toward the baggage claim and Diane and Roy walked toward the gate. As they reached the line for the metal detector, Roy turned to Diane.

"That was weird."

"You have her number?" Diane asked incredulously.

"I'd have to look," he said, "there are so many."

Diane punched him in the arm.

FIFTY-ONE

DuVal reached forward and to the side with the blunt end of his tongue, stretching to touch his lower left wisdom tooth. It was an unconscious tic; one he caught himself doing countless times through the day as he wrote.

He looked up from the screen of his laptop and stared out over lower Manhattan. It was warm on the terrace, even in the shade of the umbrella. But he was comfortable, and strangely content.

He was working on a book. An autobiography. He'd signed a seven-figure deal with Judith Regan less than a month after the attack, and was struggling against a tight deadline. Time was of the essence. The publisher wanted the book in the stores while the memory of the incident was fresh, and the war on terror still raged. Knowing what he did about the attention span of the public, DuVal thought she had reason to be concerned about the former. He was, however, confident that the war on terror had legs.

He decided to take a short break, and opened a browser to address an email to Diane.

Hey-
Are you back? How does the footage look? Do you miss Austin? Give my best to Roy.
-Jack
P.S. Dinner? When are you guys free?

He pushed "Send" and checked for new mail. His speech therapist Lorraine had pinged him from her Blackberry to tell him she would be late for their appointment that afternoon. The Blackberry was a gift from him, given (along with a set of keys to the apartment) a few months before when their relationship had taken on a new dimension. DuVal was confident he would never speak again, but was obliged to engage a speech therapist to satisfy the conditions of his disability policy. It was a small price to pay for a multi-million dollar payout. That he had gotten a girlfriend out of the deal was a nice bonus. It was nice to have a girlfriend. And for DuVal, it was nice to think it was nice to have a girlfriend.

His Junk Mail folder indicated there were 11 new items within. He opened the folder to see what had accumulated. There were nine emails offering low cost Viagra and two missives from Dave Miller. He checked the boxes beside all 11 items and pushed "Delete".

FIFTY-TWO

Dave sat in his office screening calls. A half-eaten tuna sandwich lay in a plastic container beside his laptop. He looked at the walls around him. After he had gone crawling back to Jodi (and at her request), Mitch Sanders had let him back in. Barely. Of course, Sanders wouldn't talk to him directly, and he was now seated on a floor with juniors who were a couple of years out of school. Without DuVal, his client roster was slim, and negligible in terms of revenue for the agency. As such, he was relegated to assisting other agents in the day-to-day management of their rosters. It was a lot of bullshit phone calls, and it was humiliating.

Dave was planning his comeback. On one front, he was scouting new talent by listening to the radio more and going out to comedy clubs. It was hard and thankless, and other than the chance to spend some time away from his wife, he dreaded every minute of it. On another front, he was trying to rehabilitate his reputation. Reaching out to whomever he could whenever he could. He had sent DuVal several e-mails, but had yet to receive a response. He knew it would take time.

Jodi had him on a short leash at home. A limited allowance, multiple check-in calls per day, close examination of his cellphone records, and so on. His entire life was under a microscope, and to operate required serious work-arounds. On a happy note, he had met a girl at a comedy club a couple of months before. She was an out-of-towner, which was perfect. Casual. But seeing her was problematic. His time was not his own, and his privacy was seriously compromised. Which was why he was delighted to have discovered the calling card. Purchased at a deli or a newsstand for $10 a pop, a calling card enabled him to place long distance calls without scrutiny. It was a work-around that allowed him a little bit of freedom. Freedom that he desperately needed. Now. To that end, Dave took the wallet from his hip pocket and removed his calling card, using the digits on the front and a number he had committed to memory to call his new friend. After several rings, she picked up.

"Hello?" she said.

"Sandy?" Dave responded.

ACKNOWLEDGEMENTS

I would not have developed my love of words, books, and stories were it not for my late parents, H. James and Jane T. Henderson, who were deeply devoted to those things, each other, and their children.

I would not have pursued writing as a career were it not for the encouragement of William Hauptman, a great writer, friend, mentor, and influence.

I would not have published my first book without the help and guidance of Christopher Schelling, who also provided key editorial direction on this book in its early iterations.

I would not have been able to recognize this book as finished without the line editing and suggestions of Dr. Fred Reynolds, who is a good friend, a great teacher, and a fine writer in his own right.

Finally, I could not have written this at all without the encouragement and support of Meghan Henderson, who has read this book more times than anyone else except me. I value her opinion as a reader, I count on her candor as a companion, and I live for her love as my wife.